D1422091

By Seraphina Nova Glass

SOMEONE'S LISTENING

SERAPHINA
NOVA GLASS

SUCH A GOOD WIFE

TITAN BOOKS

Such a Good Wife
Print edition ISBN: 9781789099072
E-book edition ISBN: 9781789099317

Published by Titan Books
A division of Titan Publishing Group Ltd.
144 Southwark Street, London SE1 0UP
www.titanbooks.com

First Titan edition: January 2022
10 9 8 7 6 5 4 3 2 1

A CIP catalogue record for this title is available from the British Library.

Printed and bound in the UK by CPI Group Ltd. CR0 4YY.

For my sister, Tamarind Knutson

PROLOGUE

The door was open when I arrived. I didn't think it was strange. I thought maybe he'd left it that way to let in the breezy night air. Perhaps he was enjoying a glass of wine on the porch and had run in for a refill. I didn't know what it would mean that the door was ajar, and I shouldn't have shut it. I shouldn't have touched anything. I called his name, setting my purse on the counter and cocking my head to listen for maybe a shower running or footsteps upstairs. No answer. No sounds. That's when I noticed his phone on the floor of the kitchen. The glass screen was smashed, but it worked. That gave me pause. Why would he leave it there like that if he'd dropped it? When I looked through into the living room, I saw the couch cushions tossed on the ground. It was so quiet. What the hell was going on?

I called his name again; my heart sped up as I yelled for him and threw open doors to find him. Had there been a robbery? I raced up the stairs and started to panic a bit. He should be home. The television in the upstairs family room was on, but no one was watching it. When I turned it off, the silence rang in my ears. I saw that the French doors to the balcony off of the bedroom, which overlooked the pool, were open. When I walked out onto the balcony, I felt a tremor of unease even before I saw it.

The backyard was canopied with Spanish moss dripping from the trees and it hummed with the sound of cicadas, invisible in the branches. The humidity was palpable in the thick night air. I thought of calling him, but remembered I'd just seen his phone downstairs. All of a sudden, I wished, desperately, that I could take back every decision I had made over the last couple months that landed me here, witnessing what I could never unsee.

He was there. I saw him in the shadowy blue light that the swimming pool cast across the patio. He was lying on the concrete slab next to the pool with ribbons of blood making a river from the back of his head down to the pool-deck drain. I could tell from the eerie, lifeless stare and gloss over his eyes that he was dead.

1

BEFORE

The August heat hangs heavy in the wet air. I try to keep
Bennett occupied in a way that doesn't involve a screen, so
we sit barefoot on the back steps behind the deck, peeling
muddy red potatoes and snipping green bean ends, discarding
them into the rusty buckets we hold between our knees. He
loves this. The ritual of plucking off each knotted end soothes
him. Inside, I see Rachel and her friend from school eating
strawberries over the sink, throwing the green tops into a soggy
pile in the drain; she rolls her eyes when I call in to tell her to
run the disposal and pull the chicken out to defrost. It's only a
few weeks until school starts back up, and I'm using the advent
calendar leftover from Christmas to count down the days.
Bennett helped me tape cutout images of book bags and rulers
over the old Santas and stuffed stockings.

He starts a new school in September, one he's been on a
waiting list to attend because his doctor says it's the best for
kids on the spectrum. He should have started in kindergarten,
and now, as he goes into the second grade, I try to curb my

resentment at the bougie place for keeping us waiting that long, even after a hefty donation we made two years ago. But I'm hopeful the new school might be a better fit for him because it specifically caters to neurodivergent kids. He can be rigid and set in his ways. He can also be easily agitated and this school is the best in the area. I've read every book, I've gone to every specialist, and still feel like I'm failing him when I struggle to understand what he's feeling.

Ben gets the little chocolate Santa out of the pocket taped over with a cutout of colored pencils, and we cheer in anticipation of the exciting first big day (only eighteen days left), and I get a secret reward of my own. I'm a day closer to a few minutes of peace and quiet. I swell with love for him as he opens the foil around the chocolate with the care and precision of a surgeon. He is my joy, but I'm so very tired these last weeks.

The heat is getting to him—making him irritable. I can tell because he loses interest in counting each green bean end, and stares off.

"There's a firefly!" He begins chasing it along the bushes near the fence. "Did you know they're bioluminescent?"

"Pretty cool," I say.

"And they eat each other. Does that make them cannonballs?"

"Cannibals," I correct him.

"What's the difference?" He has come back over to the deck after losing the insect, now genuinely interested in the answer.

"Well, a cannonball is when you jump in the pool and splash everyone, and cannibal is the thing you said." I decide on this explanation rather than going into descriptions of weaponry.

"They eat each other!"

"Yes."

"Cool, can I see if they like ice cream? I can leave some out for them."

"Mom!" Rachel yells from inside the sliding glass door she's cracked open, "I don't see any chicken!" All I have to do is give her a warning look and she shuts the door and goes back inside, muttering "whatever" under her breath. She knows yelling will almost always set Ben into a panic. As recent as last year, she'd be immediately remorseful if she did anything to upset him, but now that she's headed into junior high, the arm crossing and annoyed sighing is a constant. The unkindness of puberty has changed her. Now, when we drive past the Davises' house down the street, and their boys are out front playing in the drive (or "hanging" in the drive because, as she points out, kids don't "play" anymore), one of them will shoot a basket or tackle another boy at that very moment—like birds of paradise, putting on a show—a primitive mating ritual. Rachel always giggles and avoids eye contact with me. It's maddening. She's just thirteen.

"Bennett," I say, smiling, "I think there's some mint chip I hid in the back of the freezer." I pat his back gently and his eyes light up. He bolts inside before I can change my mind.

I pile the buckets of beans and potatoes on the patio table and step my feet into the pool. I sit on the edge and close my eyes, letting the cool water caress my feet and whisper around my ankles. It's momentarily quiet, so I allow myself to think of him for just a few minutes—just a small indulgence before bringing Claire her medication and starting to make dinner.

He's practically a stranger. It's so shameful. I think about the way we tumbled in his door and didn't even make it to the couch. He pushed me, gently, against the entryway wall and pulled my shirt over my head. The flutter in my stomach is quickly extinguished by the crushing guilt I feel, and I try to push away the thoughts.

"Mom!" Rachel calls from the kitchen.

"Dad's on the phone!" She walks out holding her phone, and hands it to me with an annoyed sigh. My hands tremble a little. It feels as if he overheard my thoughts and interrupted them on purpose. Rachel notices my hands.

"What's up with you?" she asks, standing with a hand on a hip, waiting for her phone back.

"You just startled me. I'm fine. And stop yelling."

"He's in the living room," she says defensively, glancing in the screen door to make sure Ben is truly out of earshot. She sits in the patio chair and twirls while I talk to Collin. "Hi, honey. Honey? Hello? Collin?" There is no response. My eyes prick with tears. It's totally irrational, but suddenly, I imagine he knows what I've done and he's too angry to speak. Someone's seen us and told him. I sit, weak-kneed, and strain to hear. "Collin?"

"Sorry, hon. I was in an elevator for a sec," he says, upbeat. The ding of an elevator and muffled voices can be heard in the background.

"Oh. Why are you calling on Rachel's phone?" I ask.

"I tried you a few times. I wanted to see if you needed me to pick up dinner. I'm on my way home."

"Oh, I must have left mine inside. I was in the yard with Ben. Um…no that's okay, I've already got things prepped, but thanks." I wonder if my voice sounds guilty or different somehow. I never leave my phone, not with Bennett's condition and Collin's ill mother living with us. So, that seems out of character. He's too kind to say anything, but I'm sure it struck him as odd. It's a pact between us as we juggle all the health issues and crisis calls from school. Both of us will stay available. As a high-profile real estate agent, it doesn't bode well for Collin to have his phone ping during a showing or a big meeting, but he won't let me carry all the weight of this myself. It's his gesture of solidarity, I suppose. The same way he stopped drinking beer when I was pregnant, both times. If I couldn't have my wine, he would suffer with me. That's just the way he is.

My face is flushed with shame. I can feel it. I turn away from Rachel slightly.

"Roast chicken and potatoes. Ben helped," I say with a forced smile in my voice.

"Sounds great. See you in a bit, then."

When we hang up, Rachel snatches her phone back. She crosses her long legs and hooks a foot inside the opposite ankle. It looks like they could wrap around each other endlessly. She's always been thin. Her kneecaps practically bulge compared to the rest of her threadlike legs, which seem to dangle loosely inside her too-short shorts. I don't say anything about them, choosing my battles today.

On my way inside, I stop to smooth her hair and kiss the top of her head. As if each good, motherly thing I do is a tiny bit of atonement for my sins. She smells like sickly sweet Taylor Swift body spray, and doesn't look up at me, just scrolls on her phone.

Dinner is quiet, but when Collin tells Rachel "no phones at the table," she fires back.

"You haven't looked up from yours since we sat down."

"That's different. It's work and it's urgent." He gives her a twirly gesture with his hand to put her phone away. It's true, Collin almost never uses his phone during dinner, but I know he's working on a huge commercial sale and lately all he can talk about is how a train track is too close to a hospital they invested in and it's causing the building to vibrate. I pour a little more wine into my glass than I usually would, but take advantage of his distraction. He wouldn't say anything if I drank the whole bottle, but sometimes that's worse— wondering if someone harbors quiet disappointment in you, but is too kind to ever point it out.

"How's Mom?" he asks.

Jesus Christ. I can't believe I forgot Claire.

"I poked my head in before dinner, but she was asleep. Should I bring her a plate?" he asks.

I never brought her her 4 p.m. medicine. Shit. I'm so distracted. I leave my phone, I forget important medication. I try to cover quickly.

"I told her I'd bring her something later. She wanted to sleep awhile," I lie.

"You're a saint." He smiles and kisses me.

"Barf. Can I go now?" Rachel doesn't wait for an answer; she gets up, scrapes her plate in the sink, and leaves, too much homework being her staple excuse for getting out of dish duty, which is fine. I usually revel in the quiet kitchen after Collin is parked in front of the TV, and the kids are in homework mode.

"Why don't you let me get this?" Collin playfully hip-checks me and takes the plates from my hands.

Recently, he feels like he's burdened me beyond reason by asking to have his ailing mother come to live in the guest room last month. Of course I said yes to her staying. Not just because of how much I love and would do anything for Collin, but because I cannot imagine myself in her position. She's suffered years with atrial fibrillation, and now lung cancer and dementia. Isn't that what we should do, take her in? Isn't that what makes us shudder—the thought of being old, sitting alone at a care facility that smells of stale urine and casserole. Spending your days staring out at an Arby's parking lot outside the small window of an institutional room, or sitting in a floral housecoat in the common area, watching reruns of *The Price Is Right* while putting together a jigsaw puzzle of the Eiffel Tower.

Maybe it's human nature to care because it's a reflection of ourselves—what we can't let happen to someone else for fear of it happening to us someday—or maybe it's compassion, but I could never let Claire be cast off and feel alone in a place like that. Even though having her dying in the back bedroom is breath stealing and unsettling, and very hard to explain to your children.

15

I let Collin take the dishes so I can bring Claire a plate and her pills. I pad down the long hall to her room, carrying a drab-looking tray with chicken cut up so fine it looks like baby food. I tap lightly on her door even though I know she won't answer. When I enter, I resist the urge to cover my nose so I don't hurt her feelings, but the air is stagnant and the odor is hard to describe. It's vinegary and acrid, like soured milk and decay.

"Evening, darlin', I have some dinner for you."

The light is dim, but I don't switch on the overhead because she complains of the headaches it gives her. My heart speeds up when I don't see her shape under the blankets.

"Claire?" The room is hot and a box fan hums at the end of her bed, propped on a chair. The smell and humidity make me lose my breath a moment, and I notice she's opened a window. No wonder it's so unbearably hot. August in Louisiana and she opens a window. Shit. I should have checked on her at four. I close the window and cover my nose with my arm. When I turn back around, I can see Rachel down the hall, and her expression is enough to betray Claire's whereabouts. Rachel stares, frozen with tears in her eyes, looking at Grandma Claire standing, exposed, in an unbuttoned robe without her wig. She's been sick on the bathroom floor, and stands in the hallway, hairless and breasts bared, disoriented, looking for her room.

"Honey," I try to say to Rachel before I help Claire back to her bed, she's run off, crying, traumatized by what she saw. I should have fucking checked on Claire at four.

What I've done—my distraction—now it's hurting my kids and poor Claire. I need to pull it together.

I help Claire to bed and switch on a rerun of *Frasier*, her favorite. I leave her a tray and give her her pills, then I clean up the vomit on the bathroom floor without telling Collin about what's happened. He'd worry and he'd want to help, but this is my negligence, so I'm glad he has a work disaster of some sort and is drinking a beer out on the patio, making calls.

Rachel has her door closed when I finish, and I hear an angsty, acoustic, festival-sounding song turned up loudly in the background, so decide to leave it until tomorrow.

In the living room, Bennett is sitting at the coffee table, coloring. My sweet baby. I wish so desperately that I could wrap him up in my arms and kiss and hug him, tickle him, and joke with him, but he's the most sensitive soul I've ever known, so I pour myself a little more wine and sit by his side, hoping he lets me have a moment with him. He doesn't say anything for a minute and then…

"You wanna color the Big Bird? You can't have the Transformers page 'cause it's mine, but you can have this one." He pushes a ripped-out page across the table. It's Big Bird with one yellow leg colored in. "It's for babies, so you might not want to," he continues.

"I still like Big Bird. I guess that makes me kinda babyish, huh?"

"He's not real, he's just a guy in a suit."

"Right." I smile, taking the page and finding a crayon to use.

"Adults can still like that stuff though. Mr. Mancini at school calls it nostalgia," he says. I stifle a laugh.

"That's very true."

"Is Mr. Mancini in the Mafia?" he asks, without taking focus off his Transformer. I don't let my expression show my confused amusement.

"Pretty sure he's not. Why?" I say, matter-of-factly.

"'Cause his name is Mancini, like Vincent Mancini."

"Vincent Mancini?"

"You know. *The Godfather*."

"You watched *The Godfather*?" I ask, wondering when he would have seen it.

"It's only the best movie ever written."

"Says who?" I laugh.

"Uh. The internet." He looks at me, hoping that I agree.

"Oh, well, that's a good point. But I don't think he's any relation."

"That's good," he says, the topic apparently resolved.

"Yeah," I agree, coloring the rest of Big Bird. I'm so incredibly in love with my son in this moment. The times I see the true Ben come out, and he's totally himself, are breathtaking.

When the kids are asleep, I take my time before getting into bed. I gaze past myself in the mirror, removing eyeliner with a makeup wipe and closing my eyes against the intrusive heat I feel between my legs at the thought of him. I push the thought away and undress, pulling on a T-shirt and clean underwear. In bed, Collin is on his laptop, but he closes it when I sit down.

"Hey, beautiful."

"Hey. Everything okay with work?" I ask, knowing the answer.

"Eh. It will be. Sorry I got busy there." He puts his readers away and shakes his head.

"The hospital project?" I feel obliged to ask.

"Can you imagine having a spinal fusion and a goddamn train full of Amazon Prime packages paralyzes you? It's unfathomable." He says this like I'm hearing this for the first time. I smile at him.

"Sorry," he says, holding his hands up in surrender. "No work talk in the bedroom. I promised."

"It's okay." I pull the down comforter over my legs and rub lotion into my hands and up my arms.

"No. It's a sanctuary. Who said that? Someone wise, I think." He always pokes fun at me and my insistence that no TV, work or arguing belong in the bedroom. He pulls me over to him and kisses me. So comfortable, so innocent. I breathe into that familiar, faded scent of Dolce & Gabbana left on his neck, the feel of his sharp whiskers, grown out from this morning's shave, sandy against my skin, and I want to cry.

All I see are threads of memory strung together from the other night. The ride home I should have refused, a benign acquaintance turned more, his mouth on mine, the keys unlocking his door, every time I said yes, never trying to stop it. I can't bear it. As tears run down the sides of my face, I push them away quickly before they fall on Collin's bare skin. Sweet Collin, kissing down my neck, his discarded reading glasses about to tip off the side of the nightstand in front of a photo of Ben and Rachel.

What have I done to us?

2

I can pinpoint the day that set everything in motion. Gillian Baker, one block over, holds a book club at her house once a week. Reluctantly, and at her insistence, I finally decided to join. I squeezed a cylinder of cookie dough out of its plastic tube, cut it into disks and put a tray of the artificial-tasting dough in the oven so I had something to bring and pass off as my own. Collin thought the book club idea was great and might inspire me. I told him it's just a kid-free night for the neighborhood wives so they can drink wine and make vapid, uninformed comments on great literature, but he still thought I would be in my element and should give it a try.

I was going to be a scholar once upon a time, but I dropped out of my master's program when we learned about Bennett's condition. I wasn't forced to stay home, but we decided it made sense. It was for the best, and even better than a degree, because I could write books from home and still pursue that dream. What a gift! All the time in the world to write the great American novel. Except I haven't written any books, have I?

What the hell do I really have to say anyway? Life has gone out of its way to ignore me in many regards. Shelby Fitch two doors down was in the peace corps in freaking Guatemala for two years before she married into this neighborhood. She should write the book.

What will my topics be? "Mom cleans up kid's barf during car pool."

"Mom waits half a day for dishwasher repair guy, and guess what? He never shows."

"Mom tries a Peppa Pig cake recipe from Pinterest, but it looks like deranged farm swine with a phallic nose and makes son cry." I have nothing to say. The other day I thought I'd get serious again and try to really sit and brainstorm some ideas. I ended up watching videos of people getting hurt on backyard trampolines and a solid hour of baby goats jumping around in onesies. So, I guess maybe at least getting my mind back into the literary world can't hurt.

At my dressing table, I pulled my hair back and slipped on some dangly earrings. It was my first time out of yoga pants that week, and it felt nice. I applied lip gloss and pressed my lips together; I could hear the chaos begin in the background. The oven was beeping nonstop, beckoning Collin to take out the premade dinner he'd been heating up for the kids, but he was arguing with Ben about a video game he refused to turn off. He still had to make a plate for Claire and help the kids with homework after dinner, and Ralph, our elderly basset hound, was barking excessively at something outside, raising the tension in the room. I felt guilty leaving, but when

I appeared in the front hall in a sundress, Collin lit up and gave me a kiss, telling me he had it under control. I knew he ultimately did. It's not rocket science, it's just exhausting and emotionally bloodsucking, and he'd already had a twelve-hour day of anxiety at work.

I kissed the top of Ben's head and said goodbye to Rachel, who was paying no attention, and then I walked out the front door. I carried the plate of cookies and a copy of *The Catcher in the Rye* as I walked across the street. They were trying too hard, trying to be literary. Why not just choose *Fifty Shades* or a cozy mystery? When Rachel had to read this book for English, she called it a turd with covers. I, on the other hand, spent hours making meticulous notes so I could be sure to make comments that were sharp and poignant. I rehearse them in my head as I walk.

I was the last to arrive; there were a few other moms from the block already there. We all did the obligatory cheek kisses. Gillian's living room looked like she was hosting a dinner party rather than a book club. Chardonnay was chilling in ice on the kitchen island next to a spread of food that could have come from a Vegas buffet. I wished I could hide my pathetic tube cookies.

"Wow, Gill. Did you do all this?" I asked, impressed.

"Oh, hell no. Are you kidding? It's catered, silly."

I can't believe she's had her book club catered. Everyone has wine and something fancy on a toothpick in their hands. She put my sad cookies next to the beautiful chiffon cake on the island, and I was mortified. There was cling wrap over them for God's sake—on a Spider-Man paper plate left over from Ben's last birthday. Kill me.

She poured me a glass, pretending not to think anything of my trashy offering, and I walked carefully over her white rug as we made our way into the sitting room. Of course she has a "sitting room." It's a bright space in the front of the house with vaulted ceilings and a blingy chandelier. We all perched on the edges of pale furniture. I never did quite know how to feel about these women. They've welcomed me so warmly, but they sometimes seem like a foreign species to me. Yes, I live in this neighborhood too, but it's because of Collin's success, not anything I've done. I guess they can probably say the same. I still feel sort of like an imposter. I don't lean into it the way they seem to.

I didn't intend to stay home, of course, but I still feel like I was destined for a career, never dependent on anyone else. It's not that I feel *dependent* on Collin. That's not the right word. What we have is ours. The way I contribute is something he could never handle, but I guess I don't take it for granted the way they seem to. Gillian was constantly remodeling her house and upgrading things that you'd think it impossible to upgrade. She had a stunning outdoor kitchen next to a pool that appears damn near Olympic-sized. It was even highlighted in the local home tour magazine. One day she gutted the whole thing because she wanted the pool to be teardrop-shaped instead. And here I am using Groupons for my facials.

Even that sounds indulgent. Facials. I grew up in a double-wide trailer in Lafayette with a mother who worked the night shift at the hospital and an alcoholic father who spent his days quiet and glassy-eyed on the front porch, staring at some invisible thing, lost in another time. It will never feel right to buy five-hundred-dollar shoes or drive a luxury car, although I'd never want to lose the safety of it and I'm grateful my children will never have to struggle the way I did. This comfort is for them. This safety is for them. That's the bottom line, so I brushed away the negative thoughts.

Tammy commented on Gillian's bracelet. She held Gillian's wrist, examining it. Everyone oohed and aahed as Gillian explained that it was an early birthday gift from Robert and she had to get it insured. I have never understood charm bracelets. An ugly soccer ball hangs off of her silver chain, but I made my face look delighted along with the others. After we settled in, I assumed the small talk was over and we'd dig into a great piece of literature. Kid-free, wine-lubricated, I was ready.

"Oh my God, you guys, did you see Bethany Burena at Leah's wedding?" Karen asked. There was mocking laughter. I'd been at that wedding, but I didn't know what they were referring to, so I stayed quiet. Liz chimed in.

"God, it looked like someone stuffed a couple honey-baked hams into the back of her dress."

"And the worst part is she did that on purpose," Tammy said, placing her glass of wine on an end table so she could use her hands to talk. "That ain't too much buttercream, y'all!" Then she held her hands to her mouth and pretended to whisper sideways. "Although did you see her shoveling it in at the cake table?"

"She had those babies implanted," Karen agreed.

"No!" Gillian gasped.

"Yep. Ass implants. Ass-plants." Everyone roared with laughter. I forced a chuckle so I didn't stand out. I hated these people, I realized right in that moment. I longed to leave. I could fake a headache, or check in at home and say there's a problem with Ben, I thought. Why didn't I? Why do I need their approval? Karen kept the gossip going. "That's not as bad as Alice. She brought the guy who cleans her pool to the wedding!"

"What do you mean?" Liz asked.

"As a date."

"No!"

"Scandal much?" Tammy was delighted she had everyone in hysterics.

"Alice Berg?" I asked, not understanding the social sin she'd committed. "Isn't she single—like, divorced, I thought."

"Yeah, but she brought The. Pool. Guy. Sad."

"So sad," Karen echoed.

"Desperate," Liz added. She noticed the book in my hands. "What's that?"

"What do you mean? It's *the book*," I said with a light-hearted scoff.

"Oh, Mel. I'm so sorry I didn't mention it. I guess I thought everyone just sort of got it—especially since the book was something so random," Gillian said.

"Got what?"

"We don't, like, read it. We just need an excuse to get rid of the kids and hubbies for one night. I think we deserve at least that?" she said, glancing around for allies.

"Damn right we do." Liz held her wine up and gulped it down, a sort of toast to herself. "You didn't read it, did you?" I didn't answer. I felt like an idiot. I was joking when I said it was an excuse to drink and have a night away. I was at least half joking. I thought that I may have found a few kindred spirits, perhaps—that they were at least making a half-assed attempt at self-betterment.

"I just skimmed it," I said.

I was probably visibly blushing, so I picked a strawberry carved into a rose shape from the table and picked at it.

"Mel has a master's in literature. Did y'all know that?" Gillian said, maybe in an attempt to redeem herself from indirectly embarrassing me.

"Oh my gosh, smarty-smart pants. Look at you." Karen swatted my leg and smiled, supportively. I wanted the attention off me as soon as possible, so I didn't correct her and say that it was creative writing…and that I never finished the degree.

"You should give me the name of your caterer," I said, picking up a skewer of chicken and taking a bite. "I was gonna do a thing for Collin's birthday. Maybe a trip, but if we stay in town we'll have people to the house." The subject was officially changed. Her eyes lit up.

"Oh my gosh, I have their card. I told them they should pay me for how many referrals I'm getting for them. Their almond torte is totally to die for. Seriously. If you don't do a cake, maybe mini tortes."

"Oh, cute!" Liz said.

We talked about mini tortes, whose phone carrier is the worst, Karen's daughter's (nonexistent) modeling career and Botox for the next two hours until I walked home unsteadily with my plate of cookies that Gillian gracefully sent home with me. I had to laugh a little at the idea that they met weekly, like they'd read that much. Made sense now. I tossed *The Catcher in the Rye* in Brianna Cunningham's garbage can, which she'd failed to pull back into the garage (Tammy actually made mention of that particular oversight earlier in the evening), and I didn't know if the crushing disappointment of the evening was worse than going back home to Claire's bedpan and the mounting stress of teen angst and Ben's moods. I wished I could just sit in the Cunninghams' yard, drunk for a little while, but someone would see, and it would be discussed at some other neighbor's book club.

The temperate dusk air was dense with mosquitoes and the chatter of crickets. I took my time walking back. When I approached our house, I saw Collin in an orange rectangle of warm kitchen light. He was washing dishes, sort of, but mostly looking past the kitchen island at the TV in the living room. I concentrated on appearing more sober than I was as I entered the kitchen. I sat at the table, pulling off my shoes, and he offered me a glass of wine.

"No, thanks." I got up and filled a plastic Bob the Builder cup under the tap, then sat on a counter stool. He pulled one up next to me.

"Was it fun?" he asked, hopefully, wanting me to find an outlet—some joy in my life while things are so tough. I didn't know if I should tell him the truth or make him happy, so I went down the middle.

"It was okay."

"Just okay?"

"Eh. Not exactly the literary minds I was hoping to connect with."

"I'm sorry." He squeezed my hand. "I took Ben to pick out a new chapter book at Classics tonight."

"Oh fun. What did he pick out?" I asked, thinking Collin was changing the subject.

He handed me a little postcard advert. "There's a writers' group starting next week."

I looked over the glossy square and it had details welcoming any local writers to join the weekly Thursday group to workshop their writing. Before I could dismiss the assertion that I'm a "writer," he pointed to the bullet point that stated "all levels welcome." It was so incredibly sweet that he brought this for me, not only to encourage me in pursuing something I care about, but was also willing to hold down the fort every Thursday. I kissed him.

"That's very thoughtful of you."

"But?" he asked, anticipating a "no," but I didn't have a reason to say no. I mean, except that I had no writing to present to the group. I could write a critical essay on *The Catcher in the Rye*. That was about it. It sounded thrilling though. Maybe some accountability and pressure would be just what I needed. I glanced past Collin into the living room and saw Bennett asleep in front of *WWE SmackDown!* on the TV. I gave Collin a look.

"Well, he's asleep, isn't he?" he defended himself. I smiled and shook my head, pressing my thumb into the crumbs on his plate and tasting the remnants of the cookies I left behind for the kids to eat.

"I guess I can try it," I said, standing and rinsing the plate. Words I'd give anything to take back.

3

I arrive at the café inside the bookstore, feeling completely out of my depth. It's my first writers' meeting, and there are seven of us, plus the group leader, Jonathan—a scruffy-haired man in his fifties who looks like someone who would go by Jonathan rather than simply John, or maybe Johnny, the sexy, bad-boy version of the name. I guess I think of it that way because I had a high school crush named Johnny who rode a motorcycle. I guess I'm thinking of high school because that's exactly where I feel like I am. Over the last few days, I've sat out on the patio after the house was dark and tried writing. I ended up with a few pages of scribbles, what can only be described as adolescent "poetry" inside my spiral notebook, which I now clutch to my chest as I walk to the writers' table. I know I won't share it with anyone, but I'm still embarrassed when I sit down.

Everyone else has laptops or tablets, and one guy is handing out bound copies of something that looks gigantic—a whole novel it appears. They're all very serious. A couple of them introduce themselves. Vanessa, a young hipster-looking woman with dirty fingernails, asks me what genre I am. Before I have to decide on how to answer her, another man introduces himself as CJ and welcomes me, announcing to the group that "we have new blood." Apparently they have all been in groups together before and I'm the only newbie. CJ is a tubby guy with a checkered, short-sleeved shirt buttoned up too high. Chest hair and neck fat protrude above his tight collar line. He shoves an open hand at me, and I shake it; he introduces me as if he's the one who brought me into the group.

I thought it would be more like a classroom setting in school, but it's just a few of us at a café table. Coffee beans grinding and milk steamers hissing interrupt Jonathan's opening statements; he's easily annoyed. He rolls his eyes a lot at the patrons who talk too loudly, and he makes a lot of literary references I don't get. Some I do. When he refers to his own new short story he hands out as "Kerouacian," I glance around to see if anyone else found his remark to be a bit self-congratulatory, but no one seems to notice, so I just nod, taking a copy: "The Toughest Journey" by Jonathan Wilderman. I skim the first page. "What is Art?" it begins. Jesus. I have a feeling the toughest journey is going to be sitting through a reading of this existential mind-number.

I was hoping for some, I don't know, relatable, gritty fiction, maybe a little sex or murder. I do not care "how we measure life" or "why we exist" right now. People take down careful notes as he reads his story out loud. I try really hard to think of something to say about it. The less friendly members of the group, Mia and Steve, speak first. Mia says it could use more conflict. Jonathan argues that it was intentional to leave the conflict to the mind of the reader. Steve seems to have developed a more subtle way to critique Jonathan, saying something about how naming his character Jean-Paul Sartre is being a little heavy-handed. I don't really listen. I've zoned out a bit because I notice that, across the store on the other side of the café, people are gathering. There are refreshments out and folding chairs set up. I squint to see what sort of event it is.

When they finish discussing the next couple of stories and get to me, I say I'm still working on mine. I expect them to coax me into reading, and my confidence is actually up a little after hearing Jonathan's story, but they tell me it's not required to share if I don't want. They're very gracious, and I'm grateful for it.

People begin to filter in and sit in the chairs across the bookstore. A few people are standing in the back. A man walks out to the small music stand and sets an open book on it, greeting everyone using the fuzzy mic. Jonathan slams his pages into an old-timey leather briefcase.

"That's it, I guess." He shakes his head.

"We haven't heard Steve's work yet," CJ says.

Steve says he's happy to go next week, and I look to Vanessa, wondering about the sudden mood change in the group.

"That's Luke Ellison doing a reading over there. Jonathan hates him," she whispers loudly.

"Thank you, Vanessa, for sharing that with our new recruit. For the record, I do not hate Mr. Ellison…"

"Sorry," she starts to say, but he just speaks over her, louder.

"EVEN THOUGH he stole my book idea and made it his own. I am adjourning because it will soon be too loud to focus on our own very important work over the sound of Luke Ellison making money off of stolen intellectual property. Thank you and good night." Jonathan closes his briefcase and walks pointedly toward the front door in large, awkward steps.

"Wow," I say, as everyone gathers their things. Vanessa just shakes her head no, and makes a little gesture indicating drinking, like Jonathan's accusations are because he's drunk or not right in the head. I smirk, understanding what she's saying.

"He's jealous of anyone published. Luke's not a bad egg. He writes steamy romance stuff which, shocker, has a bigger market than philosophical stories with no conflict."

"Did Jonathan write romance? I can't see that?"

"God no, I think Luke's character had the same name as one of his or something ridiculous. Don't name one of your characters Bob. Jonathan will sue you." She laughs and pulls her purse over her shoulder. "Anyhoo. See ya next week."

"Yeah, great," I say. When everyone in the group is gone, I pick up a plastic cup of wine at the folding table next to the small audience gathered in front of the romance writer, Luke Ellison. *A real published writer*, I think. Someone whom our writing group leader is jealous of. It's exciting. It seems impossible and out of reach to ever imagine myself reading from a whole book I've written. He's in the middle of an excerpt when I pick up a copy of his book from a stack next to the wine cups and settle in to listen.

"He parted her lips with his tongue, and slipped his hands down

her trembling thighs, tearing at her clothes, pushing her to the bed." My eyes are bulging out of my head and I'm sure my mouth is hanging open. What is he reading? I feel a strong instinct to cover the ears of nearby children. I look around in horror to make sure no kids heard that, since we're only a few feet from the children's reading area. Then I notice an "18 and Older/ Adult Content" sign with a little velvet rope sectioning off the area. Okay. I relax a moment and close my mouth. God, this guy gets a velvet rope. Fancy. I flip his filthy book over and look at the book jacket. Who *is* this guy?

I read that this is his third novel. His last book, *Dark Pleasures*, was a *New York Times* bestseller. My, my. He's originally from the Boston area, but has lived in Louisiana for a few years to be near family. His photo, next to his bio, looks like a wedding photo he cut someone out of. Not his own wedding, he's not in a tux, but definitely not a professional photo. Maybe it's the only one he could find with him in a suit so he photoshopped it. Not a bad picture, all in all. I'm probably the only one who would notice something like that anyway. I wonder why in the world he's reading at this Podunk place if he's so successful.

I feel the red blotches forming on my chest as he continues detailing the cunnilingus Dahlia and Xavier are engaging in. I keep my focus down on the book and sip my wine so no one sees how flushed I am. After he finishes reading he opens the floor for some questions. The front row of middle-aged women fall all over themselves trying to ask him smart questions about his "process" and "where he gets his ideas from." He offers generic, tasteful answers; not what they were looking for, I think. They want something sordid, revealing, but he offers only just enough to satisfy them.

After the question period finishes up, he's signing copies at the refreshment table. I want to go and get a signature. Even though it's not the sort of stuff I read, I've never met a bestselling author before. I don't want to put myself in the same company with these ridiculous women mauling him, so I move over to the café counter and buy a real glass of wine while I start to read the first chapter of *Summer Heat* by Luke Ellison.

Before I can get to the end of chapter one and learn why Xavier showed up to Dahlia's house, shirtless, to fix the broken air conditioner, I'm startled by the sharp squeak of the stool next to me moving. When I instinctively jerk my head up with a start, I see Luke sitting down and ordering a glass of wine himself. He is sitting right next to me. I close his book, and look the other direction. I didn't pay for it. Oh my God, I just wandered off with it, and now they've closed the display table. I probably look like I stole this friggin' book. He looks down and notices it.

"Oh, you're reading it?"

"No, I'm not," I blurt, and push it away. Oh my God, I'm a total moron.

"I saw you in the back, but I didn't see you at the signing after, so I didn't imagine you would be reading it—my book— is all I meant."

"I'll pay for it! I mean, I planned to pay for it. Of course. I know it looks like I'm some person who steals books, but that's—I mean it's not a library, right? I know that. I was waiting for the—you know—the mob to thin out. I'm sorry."

I cannot shut up. But he doesn't react to my deranged monologue, he just smiles and holds his hand out for me to… give him the book? I guess?

"Please. I'd love for you to have it," he says, signing the inside cover. "On me."

"Oh, no…I…"

"I insist." He hands it back and I take it, looking down at his signature.

"Well…thank you," I stutter, and he holds his wine up for a toast.

"My pleasure. You're in the writing group?" He nods his head toward the table the group had met at earlier.

"Oh. Me? No. Well, yes, technically." Why am I talking like this? I can't form a sentence. "Just started it, so… we'll see."

"You're a writer, then."

"God, I wouldn't go that far. I'm just…an imposter, I think."

"Well, I think I'm pretty good at reading people and I have a sneaking suspicion you're underestimating yourself."

"Ooooh," I say in a weird singsong way, "I don't know."

"Look, take my card if you ever wanna send me any of your stuff. I'll read it, maybe pass it on."

I think my mouth is hanging open again. Pass it on?

Like to an agent or something? What the hell?

"Why?" I ask, with genuine confusion. "You don't even know me."

"I know Jonathan and he's kind of an asshat," he says, and I pull my glass away from my lips so wine doesn't come out my nose as I laugh at this. "Just in case you're looking for additional feedback. Besides, well, Jonathan. No pressure."

I take his card and slip it into my purse.

"Okay," I say, feeling suddenly shy and ridiculous. I have half a glass of wine left, it would be strange to leave, even though I'm incapable of masking my chest, which is sporting red, embarrassed blotches again. I probably look like a leper. Also, I find that I don't want to leave. He's probably the most fascinating person I'll ever have the opportunity to meet, so I use the back of his book to make conversation and pull the focus far away from my own "writing."

"It says here you're from Boston. Pretty big switch—big city to this. How do you like our little town?"

"Well, yes. I love it. It's quaint. I like how quiet it is. I actually spend most of my time at my place in New Orleans, but holidays and summer here."

"Really, why's that?" I ask, then stop and laugh. "That's absolutely none of my business."

"No, doesn't bother me. My brother met a Louisiana girl on a business trip and they settled here near her family. So, naturally my parents moved here to be near the grandkids when they retired."

"You were all alone in Boston?" I ask. Did that sound like I was asking about his relationship status? Oh, that was like bad exposition. What am I doing?

"Yep. So the deal was I'd move down, but I need the city, so New Orleans is close enough for visits, and I rent a summer home here to get away and write from July to September, so it works."

"I don't blame you for not being able to live here full-time."

I think I make a disgusted sound, though I don't mean it to come off the way it does.

"Not a fan?" he asks.

"Oh. No. Yeah. No, I just, it's fine. It's no Boston or New Orleans. I've never been to Boston actually, but I just mean, when you've lived in exciting places, it would be tough to have a karaoke bar with a mechanical bull as the most interesting form of 'culture' within a sixty-mile radius." I laugh, but it's sort of sad sounding. I don't know what else to say so I focus my attention on the barista girl, and pull out my card to pay. He places his hand over mine.

"I'll get this," he says.

"Oh my gosh. No way, you gave me a book, I should be getting yours." But he's already handed the girl cash.

"It's not every day I get a chance to have a nice chat with an attractive and very funny writer."

He thinks I'm funny? I'm a Neanderthal. I can't even string a sentence together.

"Thank you. You didn't have to…" I start to say. He stops me.

"I'm here the next couple Thursdays, giving readings. Maybe I'll run into you again."

"Oh, for the summer romance series thing. You're the big surprise author. I see."

"Surprise!" he jokes, making jazz hands, and I laugh. "Your name? Sorry, I didn't ask your name."

"Mel. Melanie." I hold my hand out to shake, or rather, sort of charge at him with it. I'm sure it's more awkward than charming.

"Beautiful name. Nice to meet you, Mel."

I blush and stand to leave just as a leftover fan taps him on the shoulder.

I walk out, or maybe I float out, through the rows of stacked books and past the rows of elderberry bushes in front of the building to my car.

I hear a voice behind me and turn. Luke stands there in the glow of a streetlamp, and he's holding my credit card.

"You left this," he says, smiling. I never picked it back up off the counter I guess.

"Oh gosh. Thank you."

"My pleasure, Ms. Hale." I look down at my card, my full name in raised letters across it. I smile back at him. He reaches his hand toward my face, gently, and I have no idea why, but instead of backing away, I close my eyes. Then, he plucks my dangly earring from where it must have fallen out of my ear and is twisted in my hair. When I realize that all he is doing is saving my earring, I feel a flush of embarrassment for thinking he was going to do something else. Kiss me? That would be absurd. But then he lingers a few moments and looks me in the eye. I think he might kiss me then, so I pull away, abruptly.

"Thank you. Thanks. I…appreciate it." I get into my car and he waves as I drive away.

I look at my shaky hands on the steering wheel and notice I don't have my wedding ring on. That whole time, he never saw a ring. Not that Luke Ellison was flirting with me. I am 100 percent positive that the stress has made me delusional, and he was just being friendly the way he would with anyone he found sitting, reading his book. He wasn't making a pass. No.

I look at my naked ring finger. I didn't leave it off intentionally. I was making turkey meatballs with Ben, and I was wrist-deep in raw meat. Last time we made them, bits got stuck in the grooves of my ring, and it took me half a day to figure out why a tinny, bloody smell was following me around. It's sitting in the windowsill above the sink right now. But it doesn't matter. He wasn't coming on to me. I didn't do anything wrong. Except that I was going to let him.

I drive home thinking of Luke Ellison with his typewriter (I don't know why he would use a typewriter, of course that's stupid, but I still imagine him with it), and a cigar hanging from his lips. He sits in a rented room above a bar in the French Quarter and writes to the sound of jazz music and bits of chatter from the crowded streets beneath him. What that life must be like.

Before I go inside, I hide his book in my purse. I stuff it down deep and pile a couple things on top of it—my wallet and sunglasses. Collin would never know any author I'm reading from another. He wouldn't care. But I still do it. I hide it as I walk into the house. I'm not really certain why.

4

I feel like they're looking at me, like they know something. I find a place away from where most of the moms sit and I spread a blanket out on the matted grass behind right field, laying out snacks. Ben forgot his cleats. He gives me a wave from the dugout to tell me he's borrowing a pair. He points to his feet, smiling. He loves baseball practice. Maybe only because he gets to use allowance money to stop at Dairy Queen on the way home for a frosted fudge Blizzard. Whatever the reason, I'm grateful he's found an activity I don't have to drag him to, howling. All the other kids are special needs too, so there are a lot of social rules put in place by the coaches that are much better for Ben than the free-for-all that basketball was.

I see Marcy Tritto and Carrie Rivard sitting in camping chairs on the other side of the dugout. Marcy waves. Her son, Trevor, has Down's and always tries to hug Ben, which doesn't go over well. Carrie fans herself with a coloring book and tries to look interested in the kids as they find their spots on the field. She gives a little clap and thumbs-up to her kid. I can never remember his name, but he bites. I feel a prickle of heat climb my spine. Of course they don't know anything. It's strange how intensely it feels as though they are looking at me differently. I'm the one who set my chair away from them, but they didn't wave me over either. I'm being ridiculous. Everything is okay. When did I turn into such a prude, nothing happened. But what if someone I know had driven past in that moment— when my lips were inches from Luke Ellison's?

I wait a little while until everyone seems to settle in and I can be sure that no one is going to sit near me. Then I pull out his book and hold it in my hands. *His book. He wrote it.* It's a juicy romance, and on the cover there is an image of two lovers on a beach at sunset. I'd usually scoff at this sort of drivel, but it's different when you know the person who wrote it. It's so…impressive. I have the cover masked with a different book jacket—a respectable Jonathan Franzen cover. He's too smart for most people to get, so I feel safe that no one in this crowd will ask about it because they won't know what it is.

I turn each delicious page with shaky fingers, stopping after every paragraph or two to peer over the book and make sure no one's hanging out behind me. Linda Singer likes to creep over with her purse-wine and try to hand it out to all the moms. She could be lurking along the fence, trying to be subtle. I feel totally paranoid. It's hard to look away from these filthy pages. Each one lustier than the last—inner thigh caresses and nipple sucking.

I hear Ben in the distance, so I hold my hand over my eyes and squint against the sun to see him. Oh no. A kid pushed him and now he's crying. Shit. Practice is from five to seven and it's barely five twenty. I have been looking forward to these two hours of reading time all day. Sometimes, if Coach Joe can get everyone to quiet down, the crisis will pass. Nope. Not this time. Ben's lying next to third base, kicking his heels into the orange clay; he's got Gavin McCullen and the biter kid crying now too, all feeding off of one another's howls. That's it. Joe looks my way, and I nod, stuffing my portable chair into its vinyl carrying case and crossing to third base.

I kneel and go through my steps to calm him. A soft voice and praise.

"You're doing a great job, bud," I say, lightly touching his shoulder. I hand him his Dumbledore action figure. He takes it and twists its head, but it's not going to be enough today. I tell him that we can go if he wants and he charges across the field, a small, marching silhouette, headed toward the car. I see him sit on the curb and make Dumbledore walk across the bumper while Joe talks to me.

"Maybe he'll want to come back after a little time," Joe says, but I know my son, and I can tell when there will be a quick recovery and when he's done. His eyes change when he's about to vehemently refuse to do something. Forcing him is not how to handle it. Joe blows his whistle abruptly, causing me to yelp.

"No spitting, Jason!" His attention is across the field, pointing at, presumably, Jason, who shrugs and looks around to pass the blame.

"Sorry," Joe says. He's realized he's blown my eardrums out with his aggressive whistling.

"It's fine." I dismiss it and dig for my keys.

"New haircut?" he asks. Even Collin didn't notice the layers I added. I think I blush a little.

"Oh, sort of."

"Looks nice," he says, smiling. Joe Brooks has one of those personalities. He always asks people about themselves. Maybe it's a police tactic to draw people out, because who doesn't love to talk about themselves? It makes people feel good and open up. I thought he was an asshole in high school. He was popular, always had something to prove, and girls threw themselves his way. He asked me out a couple times junior and senior year, but I rejected any interest he showed out of principle. I was not going to be another girlfriend of Homecoming King Joe Brooks. I guess that was just a part of being young, his obnoxious arrogance, because here he is now: local cop, volunteer coach for special needs kids, of all things. One of the moms, Julie, says he does it because it attracts women more than if he'd gotten a puppy. He does play a large part in the moms' fantasy lives, but he smashed all of these rumors by actually just being a stand-up guy over the years.

"Thanks, Joe," I say, involuntarily smoothing my hair with my fingers.

"I can try getting Ben back in the game if you want me to take five and go and talk with him."

Not many people would go out of their way to deal with Ben. It's so kind. I feel bad about all the bias I've held against Joe over the years without any real justification.

I might have said yes, but I already know it's not happening, and maybe if I get Ben to the promised DQ and then home early, I can sneak in a chapter or two before Collin and Rachel get home.

"Thanks, but I think we'll just try again next week," I say and he puts his hand up for a high five like I'm part of the team. I reluctantly slap his hand, feeling a bit condescended to, but it's just his way, I suppose. His hand lingers on mine a moment longer than it should.

"All right," he says, and hollers over to Ben, "Good job, champ!"

Ben doesn't look up from his fantasy world. I get him in the car with the promise of ice cream and leave, wondering if I've just been flirted with or if the guilt I'm wrestling with is causing delusions.

Collin calls after picking Rachel up from cross-country practice and they decide to meet us for a burger and ice cream. It's a rare occasion that we veer from our local, organic dietary guidelines. Collin and I both cook and share a love of the farmers market. We bonded over the belief that a child's palate is largely developed depending on what they're exposed to early in life, so we have been strict about leans and greens at every meal, but lately, I've been a little lax. The news of now ice cream *and* burgers has Ben in the backseat whooping and singing a song about waffle fries that he's composed, impromptu. He sees a woman hollering at her kid, blocking the only parking spot as we pull in.

"Fat ass, fat ass, fat ass," Ben starts to repeat. "Waffle fries. Fat ass thighs!"

"Ben! That's not very nice to say, is it?" And he is quiet,

afraid burgers may be taken from him if he continues.

"Ricky!" the woman calls. She's carrying a full tray of large Cokes in one hand and three greasy DQ bags in the other. I silently calculate the grams of sugar in a soda that size while I wait for them to clear the way.

"Ricky Jr., you get your skinny, little butt right out of the way, right now."

The child pays no attention. He just continues mimicking *Karate Kid* moves, kicking high and creating his own sound effects.

"Whaaa. Kwaaah."

The woman is stuffed into blue sweatpants and a long, stretched-out, stained T-shirt with Got Milk? scrolled across the front. She's helpless to catch him. She waddles off the curb and moves closer to her son, giving us an anxious wave of apology.

"Now, Ricky Jr., I mean right this very second, or you will not have this Blizzard. I'll give it right to your sister, and don't you think I won't!" Ricky still doesn't seem convinced. "And no fries. You'll eat a salad!" Ricky scurries to his mother's side and quickly shifts his attention from karate moves to jumping up on her, trying to snatch a Coke from her tray.

After negotiating a spot in the packed parking lot for some time, I stand in line at the walk-up window. There are four red plastic tables with attached benches where Ben sits, on his best behavior, watching the busy patio with delight. There are families—moms and dads bent over dripping cones, children running around them in circles or calling emphatically for them to "watch me, watch me" while they perform some unimpressive activity like jumping off the six-inch curb or dabbing a dot of ice cream on their nose and laughing as if it were a great accomplishment.

A Celine Dion song pipes through the speakers and I feel inexplicably depressed. I treasure family nights like this, unexpected and serendipitous, but I want to be anywhere else right now. I want to be by myself. Just for a little while. I shouldn't have suggested this.

When we are all finally finishing up and Ben is delighting in crumpling up the oily burger wrappers and making multiple trips to the trash with each of our plastic trays, Rachel is weighing the pros and cons of trying out for cheerleading when school starts. The paper tray liner has two columns she's written in crayons pilfered from the Kid's Corner. She's treating it like the most important decision she'll make in her life. Collin is ever attentive and indulgent.

"I'll look like the biggest loser though. I can't even do the splits. I'd be like the only one on the team who can't do the splits." She looks at me sideways for a moment as she goes off on her diatribe, harboring anger that I didn't put her in dance when she was young. All the other girls started at five years old and she didn't show interest until twelve, so it's my fault she "totally sucks."

"You're tall," Collin tells her. "It's much harder to do the splits when you're tall. Girls would kill for your height." He always says the right thing. She softens.

"Really?" she asks, self-consciously.

"You'll get the splits down. It just takes longer for tall people," I add. Her dance teacher is Linda Waters who, I happen to know, is looking for extra cash and offering private lessons; it came up

47

at a brunch with Gillian and the girls recently. Linda happens to have the misfortune of being young and very pretty, so naturally, all the women hate her. *Why doesn't she just work the pole at Bottoms Up Gentlemen's Club across town,* Liz had joked.

"Why don't you take some private lessons to get you ready for tryouts?" I say.

Immediately, I wish I could take it back. Now I am unabashedly buying my child's adoration because I feel guilty about something she knows nothing about. Three out-of-character moves in a few days. Shit. But it's already out there.

"Really? Are you serious?" She looks to Collin, who shrugs in agreement. "Oh my God!" She flings her arms around me. "I'm gonna go and call Katie and tell her, can I?" She's almost across the parking lot before I nod. She leans against the car, gesturing wildly as she talks to her friend.

"You're feeling pretty generous today, huh?" Collin asks lightheartedly. I redden.

"I guess. I'm not sure why I said that. I just hate seeing her down on herself… I don't know."

"I think I know why you said it," he says. The blood in my face drains.

"Sorry?" I ask.

"I think this writing group stuff has really boosted your confidence—made you—I don't know…happier. You need the time away, you know, just to have something that's just yours. I think it's great. You seem different."

"I do?"

"In like a really good way."

"Oh." I smile at him, and then look down, picking at the paper corners of Rachel's list on the table. Ben saves me from having to respond. The tower of wadded up wrappers he's constructed on top of the trash can was knocked down by some asshole kid, and Collin leaps into dad mode, distracting him, showing him the elaborate ice cream cakes in the display case. I gather up our things quickly and meet them near the front door so there is no danger of resuming our conversation. I can't stop thinking about Luke Ellison, and I'm afraid that it's showing—that my behavior seems off—even though it's just an innocent fantasy.

When we get home, I tiptoe into Claire's room. The canned laughter from her sitcom underscores her snoring. She's fallen asleep in her wheelchair with her head back, mouth agape. I remember a Mother's Day, years ago, when Collin took the two mothers in his life to Woodhaven Country Club. Claire and I sat sipping Brandy Alexanders in sundresses while Collin swam in the pool with the kids.

Claire had held a long white Marlboro in her thin fingers, and through threads of exhaled smoke, she spoke about her work at the university. She taught anthropology, and was explaining all of her exciting research and her upcoming trip to Uganda. She was lovely. I aspired to be like her. Whenever she visited us from Santa Fe, I doted on her. I was captivated by her stories, her worldliness. She was charming, sophisticated. And not the big house, ugly charm bracelet, married into fortune, fake sort of sophisticated I'm often surrounded by. She'd earned it.

Now, when I take off her soiled diaper, I try not to think about that woman who jetted around the world and told dirty

49

stories we laughed and shrieked over on the deck at night, pinot grigios in hand. I clean the mess and shift her into her bed. When her eyes are closed, I slip a surgical mask over my mouth, for the smell. No matter how much disinfectant one can use, dying is a smell that just refuses to be cleaned. I hate to offend her, so I only cover my nose when she is fast asleep.

When I place a clean sheet over her and turn off the television, I notice it's faintly dark now. The kids must be in their rooms because the only sound is ESPN on in the living room and Collin on another call about the hospital that's too close to the goddamn train track.

I slip out onto the deck for the fresh air. The light over the door attracts masses of insects. Thick beetles drop onto the thin concrete stoop and collect themselves. The temperate dusk air is dense with mosquitoes and the chatter of crickets sound from the tall prairie grass and the jungle of weeds in the wooded area just beyond my view. It's peaceful.

I sit at the edge of the pool, looking ahead, past the rusted-through jungle gym set, focusing on a dilapidated pool table in one of the storage sheds along the long, fenced yard. Boxes of Christmas ornaments, a calcified fish aquarium, and last autumn's garbage bags of leaves with pumpkin faces are all piled up on a worktable, brittle with neglect.

I try to understand the reason for this finger of pain pressing against my throat. I'm not the only one to have felt this. I'm sure this sort of thing happens all the time. "Get it together," I say softly to myself, and then go inside to start Ben's bedtime routine.

5

Write about your own life. that's what one of the bullet points in Jonathan's handout said, so throughout the week, I have stolen pockets of time, here and there, to try to get my thoughts down on paper. I'm using my notebook to jot things down as they come. I have no time to sit in front of a computer right now: by the time the laptop booted up, I would inevitably be interrupted, so I'm…outlining. It's…a start.

I write about Claire and the life that was robbed from her, about how I secretly lay a damp towel beneath her door at night so the smell of decay doesn't spill into the hall and reach the children. I write about how I married the kindest man in the world, only to find that I almost never see him and how my whole world revolves around behaviors, de-escalations, meltdowns, doctors, medicines. It's raw and honest and I'm nervous to put it out into the world, even though it's just a few people at a bookstore.

I stand in the full-length mirror in our bedroom. It's so strange for the house to feel quiet. Collin is really committed to taking the load on Thursdays for me. He took Ben with him to pick up Rachel from dance practice, and then took both of them out to dinner. I pull a couple of dresses I haven't worn in a while out of the closet and hold them in front of me as I look in the mirror, scrutinizing each for a different reason. A dress to writing group? It's humid outside, I tell myself. Nothing wrong with a summer dress. I choose a yellow sundress with a wisp of a sleeve. I slip on sandals, the fancy sort that have straps winding up the ankle. And then I apply mascara and look at myself a moment.

Collin said that the reason he'd told the bartender to buy me and all my friends a round at that college bar all those years ago was because of my long, chestnut hair. He said he hadn't even seen my face yet, just the back of my head from across the bar, and he'd known. The kids love that story, but I tell him he's full of crap and I saw him looking over all night. My hair is still long, but I haven't seen it out of a messy bun on the top of my head in ages. And not the sexy, trendy, messy bun. The exhausted, droopy mom sort. Not flattering.

I release my hair from its knot. While I hold a flat iron to it, I wonder if Luke Ellison *was* flirting, which surely he was not, but *if* he were—what would he see in me? Constant stress has kept me thin, I'll give myself that. I'm pushing forty, but as I examine myself in a fitted dress with my hair down around my shoulders, I feel almost sexy for the first time in… I could not begin to guess how long. Or maybe not sexy exactly, but slightly less thrown together and frazzled. I'll take it. I realize I need a massive amount of cover-up under my eyes to match the rest of my face. My age and fatigue are evident in the circles beneath them, but nothing some industrial-strength concealer can't fix.

I run my fingers through my hair, smooth my dress with my hands and smile at myself in the mirror. I have a notebook with something resembling a story, and I have been excited for this all week. When I get in my car though, the ignition doesn't turn over.

"Shit." I hit the steering wheel with the palm of my hand a few times, willing it to work. We've only had to replace so much as the windshield wipers since we got this thing. It's never broken down. I feel like the universe is conspiring against me for the hedonistic thoughts I've allowed myself to have. I try a few more times, but it just makes a clacking noise. When I smell gas, I know I've flooded it, trying too many times. Sonofabitch.

I call Collin, even though there's nothing he can do. Maybe if they haven't gotten to a restaurant yet, they can grab takeout and come back so I can use his car. He promised them "restaurant Thursday" while Mom is at her group, and changing a promise on Ben does not go over well. I decide not to ask him.

"Do you know how long you'll be?" I say, and I can hear a group of waiters singing happy birthday to some poor sap at another table in the background. Rachel must have chosen the place this time. It's clearly Barney's Burger Barn.

"We just sat down, but we could probably get it to go, hon," he suggests. He's so sweet.

"No. No, no. That's okay."

"I hate for you to miss it. Take an Uber."

"Really?" I hadn't even thought of that. It's not a flight I'm late for. It's just a writing group. An Uber seems kind of…desperate. It should be easy to say that it's not a big deal, and that I could use a little quiet time anyway, but I don't. I find that, instead, I actually switch him to speaker so I can simultaneously open my Uber app while we're talking.

"Yeah, why not?"

"I'll think about it," I say, casually. "Might be an option. You guys have fun. I'll text if I end up going."

"Okay. Love ya."

After we hang up, the Uber takes less than five minutes to arrive. I feel a flutter in my stomach as I walk into the bookstore, a little more confident this week, but when I arrive I get half-hearted, mumbled greetings from the table—an anticlimactic moment—as everyone is busy passing out copies and offering disclaimers about their work to one another.

"Do you have copies?" Jonathan asks.

"Oh, I thought I'd just read mine, save a tree, ya know."

"That's fine, though it's easier for us to read along so we can make notes as we go. Can't guarantee you'll get detailed feedback this way."

"I'll take my chances," I say, smiling. Then I see him. Luke Ellison is cornered by about a half dozen women. The bookstore has moved his reading to the back of the store, and I'm pretty sure it's because Jonathan complained about the noise. Luke looks past the women, his eyes darting around the bookstore; he pauses and cocks his head a moment, straining to see into the café. Who is he looking for?

Then his eyes meet mine and his face lights up. Or did I imagine that? I look behind me to make sure he's not waving at someone else, but he smiles and points at me, making a "you" gesture so I know it's me. I smile and wave back. Then I quickly drop my head and sit in my place at the table, feeling distracted and confused. Did I really wear this dress because it's hot outside? Now is not the time to question myself. I am confident. I can let these strangers hear my writing and not crawl into a hole and chug a bottle of wine when it's over. I take a deep breath and refocus.

I can hear a faint, low rumble of a male voice from across the bookstore when Luke's reading starts, but it's not upstaging Jonathan and his feedback this time, so after letting everyone else go first, I finally agree to read my story. My hands are trembling involuntarily, so I keep my pages on the wooden tabletop and hold my hands in my lap as I read without touching the paper.

Before the house and Collin and kids, I never thought that writing about my life was an option. There was nothing to write. A teacher once told me, *only write what you know*. I'll never understand that so-called rule. If J. K. Rowling wrote about her own life—about what she "knows," then goddamn it, I'll have what she's having.

For lack of imagination though, I take the advice and write what I know, and it's cathartic. I am not writing about magic and fantasy or the meaning of life, but what I am writing is relatable, honest. I read my story about Collin's dad's funeral. I didn't know where else to start. I remember how Collin hadn't known how to weep and simultaneously be strong for his family. He was so afraid that if he let himself crack, the cancer of his sorrow would spread and damage his kids, so he never shed a tear. Claire was led up to the casket first, and she'd made a wailing sound I'll never forget and tried to get into the casket to lie next to her husband one more time. Ben had begun screaming and run out of the funeral home. Claire never really spoke much again. Her health had seemed stable before that moment. Rachel says she's dying of a broken heart. None of us have ever been the same, really.

I'd turned all of this into a sort of short story. When I finish reading, I see Vanessa wipe away a tear. CJ does a weird slow-clap, and I'm elated that I wasn't laughed out of the bookstore. I can't believe that I just poured out the ugliness of my own life and...they liked it. It's not *New Yorker* bound, but it's a start. I smile shyly, but inside I'm so excited I'm freaking out a bit. I feel accomplished. Accomplished in a way that's not the same as motherhood. I listen to a few notes they offer, but we've gone overtime tonight. It's almost ten and they're closing up.

I'm still riding the high after everyone else has left. I sit at the table a moment in the semidarkness, taking it all in. Then I take out my phone to order an Uber home. In a normal household, Rachel might be old enough, at thirteen, to hold down the fort for a half hour while Collin picks me up, but Ben's behavior can be unpredictable and Claire scares her even though she'd never say it, so I won't ask Collin to get me. Loading up the kids at this hour would be ridiculous.

Before I can punch my location into the app, I hear a voice behind me.

"Fancy seeing you again." Luke is there, on his way out it looks like.

"Hi."

"You came back."

"I came back, yes."

"I wasn't eavesdropping, but it gets quiet in here close to closing. I may have heard a bit of your story from the café."

"Oh my God. Really? No." I am mortified.

"It was really good."

"No." I gather my things, not knowing what else to do, trying to brush off the compliment I don't know how to take.

"Can I buy you a drink across the street?" He nods in the direction of a tavern a few doors down. I freeze.

"I'm married," I blurt out, like a total basket case, but he doesn't react the way I thought he would.

"That's okay. I was just intrigued by your story."

"Oh." I'm embarrassed. Was I being presumptuous? "Sorry. That's so…that's nice of you to say."

"No funny business," he says, holding up his hands. "The offer stands if you ever want any help with it." He starts to go.

"No. I mean, yes. I'm sorry. Of course. I would love to hear what you have to say, I mean that would be…"

I don't say "a total dream come true." I am high from the reaction I already received tonight. I have not done something for myself since I don't even know when. To be praised for work that has nothing to do with how much you are able to take as a caregiver seems like…well, for a moment it seems like I'm living someone else's life. Why would I turn this opportunity down?

I call Collin. I tell him that a few of us are gonna grab a drink after group and chat. That's not a lie. That's perfectly honest. That's what I'm doing. Maybe not a "few" of us, but that's just semantics. It's professional. He tells me to have fun, that he's thrilled for me, and he'll be in bed catching up on a golf thing he DVR'd when I get in.

I sit nervously across from Luke at a pub called Stella's. It's a place I've been many times over the years, but tonight the familiar wooden booths and sticky rows of bottles behind the dark bar seem unfamiliar, intimidating.

He tells me about his years trying to write the great American novel, but no one wanted it, so he tried his hand at sex, and—

"What do ya know? Sex sells."

I sip at my vodka gimlet and we talk about the authors we love. I don't talk about my kids or Claire. It feels like a betrayal somehow, and I don't know why. But we have plenty to say regardless.

It feels like a teenage romance as we go back and forth emphatically about music, showing each other videos on our phones when we come across one the other hasn't seen. I'm tipsy as I exclaim that anyone who can't admit Ray LaMontagne is a genius doesn't deserve to live, and he puts my number in his phone and texts me a few book titles I *have* to read. We order a couple more drinks, and he laughs at my jokes. They're not that funny, but the alcohol has loosened me up and I have little inhibitions at the moment. He tells me he's leaving for Florence sometime in the fall.

"Like…moving there?" I ask. "To Italy?"

"Just spending six or so weeks writing."

"In *Italy*," I repeat.

"Yeah, why not?"

"Why not!" I sort of slur, gesturing widely with my arms. *"Why not?"*

"Have you ever been?" he asks, and I'm quiet a moment.

"I almost went once. During college. Didn't work out."

"Oh, I'm sorry."

"So. So you can just, like, you can just decide you feel like *writing in Italy* for a while, and just like that, you go do it."

"I guess."

"Wow."

"Well, it's my full-time job, if you look at it that way. Obviously it's a mobile line of work, so I like to go where the inspiration strikes."

"That—wow—I just…I can't imagine that life. When do you leave?"

"Not sure yet. I'll feel it out."

"Really? Just whenever the mood strikes?" I ask. Perhaps it comes out bitterly.

"I suppose you could say that, yeah. Right now I like being here." He looks in my eyes and gives a shy smile. I swallow down a lump rising in my throat at the sudden realization, that no matter how long I keep a tiny sliver of hope alive that one day I could be a writer, hanging out in Italy or wherever I fancied, that is no longer any sort of possibility. I have children. Ben's school is my top priority and Rachel has sports and friends. Collin hates to fly. Two-hour flights max. Not to mention that I haven't written anything and I'm not independently wealthy, so there's that. It's ridiculous to even entertain for a second. I stare at Luke, wondering if he appreciates his exotic life and freedom.

"I mean, I know you have responsibilities here, of course. But if you ever needed a writing getaway, my place is open. I hope you don't take that the wrong way, just sayin'."

"No, I mean...that's very nice of you."

I think a moment of how the conversation would go, asking Collin if he can work full-time and also take care of Ben (a full-time job by itself) and Claire (also a full-time job by itself) while I go find myself in Italy for a month, and laugh to myself a little. Fantasies are nice sometimes. But when they are so far from reality, they're just depressing.

"I should probably get going," I say, and start to get my things together.

"Of course. Um, you're...driving?" he asks, and pulls my chair out as I stand.

"I...didn't drive. Actually. No."

"Oh."

"I planned to just hop in a cab."

"Well, let me give you a ride." He sees the look on my face that says I'm about to protest, and adds, "I insist." I nod, gratefully, and follow him out.

The humid air is rich with the hum of crickets as we walk the couple blocks to his car. We are chatting away so it takes me a few minutes to realize how far we've walked.

"Parked kind of far away, huh?"

"I walked. Actually—" he points ahead "—I'm just there, around the corner."

"Oh my gosh, now I feel terrible. You live this close. You're already home, I can just get a cab."

Then I see his place. A gorgeous house. It's one I've always seen in passing—a stunning two-story French Creole mansion, with a broad roofline and a stately wrought iron fence around the property. It's been empty forever. I stare at the beautiful columns.

"This is where you're staying?"

"Believe it or not, I rented it for a steal because it sat empty so long."

"Probably since no one in this town can afford it."

"Well, the price was right. I certainly don't need all this space, but I really wanted a pool."

"Wow. I've always wanted to see what it looks like. Is it updated? Does it still have the original molding and hardwood?"

"Well, come on," he says, and he's walking ahead before I can really say no.

I follow, admiring the manicured lawn. In this town, one block off the main street can feel like a rural ghost town. Even though we're just a ten-minute walk from the main strip the property is private, butted up against a huge ravine and wooded area. The sprinklers hiss on and we duck in the front door, laughing, dodging them.

"Sorry." He turns a handle near the front door and the water stops. He walks me through and I point out the original French doors and wraparound mantels. The drinks are buzzing between my ears, and I feel like I'm in someone else's life right now. I don't even feel like I'm in my own hometown. I feel like a character in a book.

"It's just beautiful," I say.

"It is. It's nice to find someone who really appreciates the old character and history it has to offer."

"What a life you live," I say, and look at him as we stand at the bottom of a grand staircase. I eye the door, and I should say that we should probably go, but when I feel that he hasn't taken his gaze away from me, I look back and we just let ourselves stare a moment, each deciding what we should do. If this is happening.

He steps closer. I let him. In one move, he runs his fingers through my hair and pulls my face close, and he kisses me. Again, I let him. In moments, we're fumbling with buttons and I land on top of him as we let ourselves fall to the stairs. I pull his shirt off of his shoulders and he takes me by the hand and leads me upstairs. We don't take our hands or mouths off of each other the whole way. It happens so fast. I don't think about how late it is, the great sin I'm committing, my children, my future regret, none of it.

I don't stop myself; there is somehow not even a moment of hesitation. I squeeze him between my thighs, I push him into me. I hold the slats on the iron bed frame behind me as we make the ancient floorboards creak and moan. I wrap my legs around him as he picks me up, shoving everything off the nearby dresser, and sits me down on it. I'm not self-conscious about my nakedness, my breasts in his face. I hold him closer and kiss every part of him that I can reach, sweating, as we make love in every inch of this room, and I feel nothing but exhilaration. I don't care about anything else in this moment.

When the Uber drops me off in front of my house, it's dark and silent. I take off my shoes and hold them in my hand as I quietly slip in the side door. I click the door shut behind me, trying not to make any noise and then I hear myself let out a bloodcurdling scream when I see what's in front of me.

There is a gun and a figure. I hold my hands up, gasping for air. Then I see that it's Collin, standing across the kitchen with a handgun pointed at me. I breathe in short panicky bursts, my hands in the air.

"What are you doing?" I scream hysterically.

"Mel?" He flips on the light. "What the fuck?" He puts down the gun and rushes to me, but I pull away, shaking frantically. In that flash of horror, I thought he knew.

"I thought you were a goddamn prowler or something!"

"I said I'd be late."

"Well, Jesus, Mel. Babe, I'm so sorry." He tries to hold me, but I don't want him to smell the sex on my clothes or another man's cologne, so I turn the attention to the footsteps we hear coming down the stairs.

"Mom?" Rachel calls, clearly too scared to come down. Collin hides the gun and stands at the bottom, looking up at her.

"It's okay, hon, your mom saw that possum. Must have gotten in the back door tonight." He looks to me for approval for the lie. I nod.

"Oh my God, eeew."

"We got him out. Go back to bed before Ben wakes up, okay?"

We hear her trudge back to her room and close the door. "I'm sorry," he repeats. "I heard someone in the kitchen earlier, and the TV was on. I was sure it was you a couple hours ago, so when I heard the door open, I thought it wa...I don't know."

"Rachel always comes down for TV when she can't sleep.

God, Collin. A little overboard with the gun, don't you think?" I say, and he sits at the counter and sighs.

"I thought I heard something last night too."

"Really? Like what?"

"I don't know. You were asleep. I checked on Mom and the kids. Just a noise. Something."

"You should have told me." I take off my earrings and pull up my hair while we talk, trying to appear normal.

"It was nothing, apparently. But when I thought I heard it again tonight, I was trying to protect us. It's after midnight. I had no idea it would be you."

"Sorry. We all just got to talking and I didn't even notice how late it was. I wasn't gonna call and wake you."

"No, it's fine, just…God. You scared the shit out of me."

"Likewise. Sorry."

"No, I'm sorry."

We both sit there a moment.

"Well, if you're not gonna shoot me, I'm gonna take a shower. We all went to Stella's so I reek like cigar smoke."

"Yeah, okay," he says mindlessly, already busy putting the gun away and getting ready to go back to bed.

I sit on the floor of the shower while the water pours over me. I try to cry as quietly as possible. If the last hour of emptiness and regret is any indication of how the coming days will be, I've created a kind of hell for myself. But just underneath the weight of my insurmountable shame, I feel the rush, the pleasure, the lust.

6

It's Saturday. A couple weeks have gone by and I tell Collin I skipped out of writing group the last two weeks because I'm working on a big story and I need a little time to write it before I share it with the group. I said I could spend the next couple Thursdays just writing and that I'd go back to the group in a few weeks. I couldn't go back until I knew Luke's reading series was over. He was only meant to be there one more Thursday, but I couldn't chance it. I had given him my number, but I told him never to contact me after I left his house. He promised. And he hasn't.

This morning Ben is in the pool with Pink Panther floaties on his arms. He's whipping the surface of the water with a pool noodle, which has Rachel yelling at him and guarding her phone. She lies on a beach towel, tanning herself. Ben seems upset the last couple of days. He's withdrawn and agitated, and I can't help but think he senses my sins— my active role in potentially destroying my family, but I don't really know why he's on edge. It could be anything.

I've wheeled Claire out to sit with us, but she stares off until she falls asleep sitting up in her chair. I dab the drool on the side of her mouth with my breakfast napkin as I clear the outdoor table. Rachel sees this, then looks away, swallowing hard. I give a breezy smile like it's no big deal.

"Will you eat this watermelon if I leave it out?" I call to Ben.

He doesn't answer. My hands are unsteady. Before I drop the plates I'm carrying, I stop and take a deep breath. Collin is lounging on the other side of the table with his feet resting on a kids' foldout chair. He looks up from scrolling through news stories on his tablet.

"You okay, hon?"

"Oh yeah. Yes. Of course. Just clumsy today."

I realize that I lack the ability to know if my guilt is transparent. Am I forcing prolonged eye contact with Collin for fear of involuntarily avoiding it? Is my voice strangely high-pitched, am I trying obviously hard to be upbeat and excessively friendly?

Collin doesn't really seem to be aware that I'm acting shifty. Maybe I'm not. Then again, what does that say about me, that I could do something this unforgivable and not be crippled under the weight of it? It's strange how incapable I am of having a clear idea if I'm playing the role of the person I was only weeks ago with any authenticity. For a moment I think about confessing to him. He's the kind of man who would probably forgive me. Not that it wouldn't be the cruelest thing I could ever do to him. The fallout would be too devastating to even think about.

It seems kinder to promise myself to never do anything like that again, and keep Collin's world intact.

"Why don't you let me get that," he says, as I come back to clear the coffee cups. "Relax a little." He pulls me down on his lap playfully and kisses me.

"Eeew," Rachel says, covering her head with a towel.

"So when do I get to read it?" Collin asks.

"Read what?" I ask sharply, my face reddening. I fear, momentarily, that he is talking about Luke's book, hidden away in my bedside table.

"This story of yours that's got your head in the clouds," he says, cheerfully.

"I'm sorry. I don't mean to be…distracted with…"

"No. Babe. That wasn't a complaint. I think I put that the wrong way. I love that you're doing this. It's actually…" he pulls me closer and whispers "…kinda sexy."

I laugh playfully in response, pushing him away.

"I don't know about that." I stand and continue to gather the breakfast dishes into a pile at the edge of the table. He glances down at his phone, furrowing his brow. No doubt more news about their recent investment tanking. Ben runs up, dripping water everywhere, and grabs some watermelon. Collin stands to take a work call and steps away from the racket. The topic is officially behind us.

Ralph only moves when necessary, and he takes the opportunity to eat the piece of fruit dangling from Bennett's hand under the table. Ben wails. He throws the rind at the dog, just missing him. Collin, now inside the sliding screen doors, gives an apologetic look, indicating that he can't help because he's on a call, and moves farther away from the noise. I hold Ben's flailing hands and tell him it's not okay to throw things at Ralph—that he's just a little dog and it's not fair to be mean to him.

He growls in frustration, pulls away from me and kicks over his chair. Rachel knows the drill and gets up to help. Ben kicks the chair over and over, screaming that it's not fair. Rachel wheels her grandmother inside because now Claire is awake and the corners of her mouth twitch, her fingers grip the sides of her chair and her breathing quickens. She's fragile, and this sort of chaos unsettles her in her confused state.

Collin has seen that it's a bad one and comes out to help. Ben swings at me but hits Collin in the back. He's small so Collin isn't hurt, but it never gets easier to be hit by your son. For either of us. I have to remember each time that it's not his fault. Each time I take a moment after it's over to recite all of the reasons I love him and remind myself that he's going through something inside that hurts him too, something I'll never understand. I pray for patience. Each time.

I've studied the difference between a meltdown and a temper tantrum. If he's melting down, he's completely overwhelmed, and he can't turn off the emotion. "Usually a tantrum will stop if the child gets what he wants," I read in one of the dozens of books I bought when we learned Ben was on the spectrum. I admit that I don't usually know if I'm getting played and he's having a tantrum to get what he wants, or if it's out of his control. I ask Collin to grab some more watermelon to test the theory this time. When I try to give it to Ben, he throws it and cries. I guess that means that we are in meltdown territory.

Ralph comes over to comfort Ben, but he gets up and moves

to the other side of the deck. Collin gives me a gesture indicating that he'll go deal with it. I go into the kitchen, scraping breakfast plates into the sink and watch them from the window. They're sitting on the deck stairs, Ralph in between and Collin reaching behind to gently pat Ben's back. I love them so much.

I wish that guilt was enough to erase it all. As soon as I dutifully bathe Claire or cuddle with Collin on the couch until he falls asleep and I slip the cell phone from his loose hand and cover him with a blanket—as soon as I make Rachel laugh about something silly before bed and she actually says "I love you, Mom," and especially when Ben sits gleefully in front of his earned video game time, laughing, happy, that's when it creeps back in. I feel like no one has been hurt and things are under control. It's back to the way it was a couple weeks ago, as if nothing happened at all. Then I let myself think about him again. Sometimes late at night, and even though the damage I've caused is invisible, it's there, like the wind.

The rise and fall of Collin's sleeping chest next to me should be the only reason I need to shun all of this from my mind, but just sometimes, safely, in the dark, I let my thoughts wander to fantasies of Luke Ellison. And not always the sex either. Sometimes I have to wonder if that part was real. It feels so otherworldly.

What would a life with Luke look like? A month in Italy writing a book. I see us there together, ordering mimosas from room service, making love in the morning, and spending sunny days on the veranda overlooking the sea. I know how stupid it is. It sounds obnoxious, naive even to say out loud. Does anyone really have that life? It looks like he does. He did exactly the opposite of what I did. He kept after the pipe dream. He didn't marry, buy a house and have kids like the rest of the world. He valued good red wine, world travel and artistic pursuits over the minutiae of the domestic day-to-day.

To him, my world looks like snippets of television commercials. A couple enjoying their new elaborate deck extension behind their town house with friends while the kids play on a jungle gym their father built. Where the ladies wear khaki capris and blouses and carry out bowls of fruit salad and shrimp cocktail while the men stand around a propane grill, holding cans of Budweiser and poking at meat patties on the grill. To him, it's probably a sad cliché. Maybe that's why he did it. It's a life so foreign and far away from his own—why not sleep with a married woman? There are no consequences for him. I feel a sharp prick of anger at this realization. All of those sickly sweet compliments and longing looks. It was likely nothing more than his version of a one-liner, not a real connection.

Collin shifts and drapes a heavy arm sleepily over my hip. I lace his fingers between mine and kiss the top of his hand. The fantasy fades as the remorse resurfaces. How long will this go on?

In the morning, I busy myself with mundane tasks. I empty the dishwasher, fold a basket of laundry and make a fresh pot of coffee. The kids have been back in school a week, and sudden freedom during the day is ill-timed. There are no distractions. Claire is sitting in the sunroom with an afghan. God knows why.

It's ninety-four degrees outside, but she likes to stay covered. As I sit at the counter writing a grocery list and thinking about what Collin would like for dinner, I notice Claire looking at me, staring, actually. I am probably mistaken, but it looks like she's glaring at me. I smile at her. The corners of her mouth turn up in something resembling a smile, and then she looks away. It makes me uneasy. Being in the house is suffocating, so I ask her if she needs anything before heading out, and I hurry out of the house for air.

Driving around town feels dangerous. It's so small that it's very possible I might run into Luke, unless of course he's already flitted off abroad to write his romance novel. I stop at the bank, the cleaners, then sit at a café to eat some lunch. A café dangerously close to the bar we had drinks at only a few weeks ago. Am I looking for him?

I'm sitting outside midday in this heat, so I must be. I must be ill, acting like this—almost involuntarily wanting more. Beads of sweat collect across my shoulders and drip down my back; my dress is becoming translucent with sweat. I feel like a character in one of his books. A housewife, a heaving, sweaty housewife, out on the prowl for hot, anonymous sex. But it wasn't anonymous, was it? We shared laughter, life goals, fears and even family. I ended up telling him about my sweet Ben. It was as intimate as it could possibly be.

And what has he been doing all these weeks? Was I that disposable to him? I can't help but wonder if he never contacted me again because I said never to text or call my number, or if he was just having fun, passing through, and it was just a steamy one-night thing to him and that's all. I should be elated if it's the latter. But I find, instead, that I'm resentful.

I have my trusty notebook open. I try to sort some of this out on paper. It's dangerous, maybe, but I'm just writing fiction. I mean, that's what I'd say if it were ever read, which it won't be. I'm jotting down scattered entries to string together later. It's just fiction, no harm in that. I try to find a way to articulate the anger and guilt and how one could reconcile that with ongoing desire, but my confusion crowds my thoughts. I close my eyes a moment and fan myself with a cocktail menu. Then, I'm startled by my name being spoken.

"Melanie Hale. Hi!" a perky voice says. "Look at you working away."

It's Vanessa from the writing group. She's wearing black skinny jeans and an overabundance of eyeliner, neither of which she's sweating through.

"Oh, hi. No. Just a grocery list. How are you?" I turn my notebook over.

"I'm good. Just going to work." She nods toward the Tipsy Cow Pub. I thank God Luke and I hadn't gone there instead that night.

"We've missed you at the group. Your story." She stops, hand to chest and takes an overdramatic breath. "My goodness, wasn't that something. You're coming back, I hope."

"Oh yeah. I want to. Things just got busy with school starting and all that."

"You're in school?" she asks, matter-of-factly.

"No. My kids."

"Oooooh. Right. Sorry," she says. She's so young that the

whole world is from her twentysomething perspective. She doesn't see other people in her circle as adults with crushing responsibilities. She gets to be a bar hostess, smoking pot and writing bad poetry. *Good for you*, I think. *Hold on to those years.*

"Well, there are no more book readings this month, so we can hear each other talk at least. And it puts Jonathan in a better mood," she jokes. That's what I needed to hear. No more Luke. He's long gone.

"I actually thought I'd come back tomorrow, now that everyone is settled into routine at home."

"Great." She fumbles with a vape pen and exhales a cotton candy-scented puff of smoke. "See you then."

It's Thursday. It's been almost three weeks since I attended the last writing group. I know the reading series is done and I won't see him, but still, I prepare as if I will. I can't help myself. I wear a dove-gray, A-line dress that falls just below my knee. I feel a little like Jackie Kennedy. I'm aiming for classy; I want to feel less like the three-dollar hooker I've been feeling like in recent days. I roll up my hair into a French twist clasped together with a barrette encrusted with faux pearls.

The bookstore is quieter tonight. There are no excited women lined up to hear Luke Ellison read from his new book. The rows of chairs that were filled with eager fans a few weeks ago are now stacked up against a wall behind the café, sad looking in the shadowy corner.

Only three of us show up tonight. Labor Day has thrown

off everyone's schedule this week, so it's a very short meeting.

Mia reads from a story she's working on as Jonathan and I listen. It's an angsty tale of unrequited love and revenge. She's going through a divorce, and so her story is about a woman who poisons her husband slowly and painfully by putting antifreeze into his whiskey every evening so she can kill him and get his life insurance money.

"'And when it was done,'" Mia reads, "'I thought about cutting his nasty T-shirt with the barbecue stain on the chest right off his flabby, hairy body and into bits, and while I had the scissors, maybe cutting off his lips along with that porn mustache I hate, but I knew it needed to look like an accident, so I just dialed 911 and pretended to think it was a heart attack or something.'"

I look around with bulging eyes to see if anyone else thinks this sounds a bit too specific, but everyone is reading along, reactionless. My eyes wander through the café and down to each shelf of stacked books. Did some part of me think he was going to keep coming back every week until he saw me again—just waiting quietly at a café table as if he has nothing more important in his life to do?

I deny to myself that the prickly heat across the back of my neck is a brush of disappointment that he's not here. I don't share the story I'm working on.

"I'm just here to learn. I'm here to keep myself accountable and keep writing," I say. "Maybe next week."

Since there's no pressure to share your work, it's very supportive and everyone is kind to me.

As our small group disperses, I walk out to the parking lot

with Mia. She jokes that if she ever got up the guts to kill her ex-husband, she wouldn't have the patience to do it slowly with antifreeze, she'd just shoot the fucker in the head. I give a courtesy laugh even though the comment makes me a little uneasy because there's something in her eyes that suggests she's thought about this a little too much.

When I open my car door and sit in the driver's seat, I see a flyer flapping from beneath my windshield wiper. Annoyed, I reach my hand around to snatch it. But before I crumple it up, I realize it's handwritten. It's not addressed to anyone and it's not signed by anyone. It just says "Meet me at my place."

I hear my heart pounding in my ears, my pulse racing. I wonder if I've been set up. But nobody else knows, I'm certain of that. I should throw this in the public trash can in front of the doors, I should drive home and pretend I didn't see it. Luke Ellison will be out of the country very shortly and I'll probably never see him again. I have no right to contemplate this another second.

I take a few deep breaths. I'm sweating, I'm panicking. I should go *home*. Instead, I text Collin and tell him I'm hanging out with some of the group members but that I won't be as late as last time.

I leave my car in the bookstore parking lot. I don't dare have it seen anywhere near his house. I walk, casually, down the main street, past the busy bars and restaurants, not pretending to hide something at all, and then I duck into a gas station parking lot. I make the walk across the wooded area that butts up against his house. A few yards from the house, I stop. I decide I need to just turn and go. But then I tell myself that I'm just here to see why he left the note. I knock.

He opens the door almost immediately. The second it closes behind me, he gently pushes me up against it, holding my hands over my head, and kisses me. And just like before, he pulls me up, my legs around him, and we claw at each other's clothes, pulling them off ravenously. When he sets me down on the kitchen island, that's when I know the story I'm quietly telling myself—that I won't let it go too far this time, that I just wanted to see him before he left to say goodbye—is a lie. We make love fast and hard. When it's over, we sit in the dark of his remodeled kitchen. Me, cross-legged on the counter, and him pouring us a drink.

"I don't have long," I say.

"That's too bad, but I understand."

"How did you know that was my car," I ask, "to leave the note on?"

"It's a very small town," he says, smiling, and hands me my drink.

I instantly wonder where he has seen me. Was it schlepping the kids to some practice, running errands with no makeup, wearing an oversize sweater and leggings? Oh my God, did he see me with Collin somewhere? I don't ask, I simply nod in agreement.

"It is."

"Your kids are in school now, during the day, right?" he asks. I don't know why I feel a sense of anger at his mention of my children. It's not rational, it's just that he shouldn't know anything about them. I just nod yes.

76

"I'll be here working. I usually drive into the city or hang out at coffee shops to write, maybe do a little work at home. But I'll stay here, I'll work from my office every day, so we don't have to arrange anything or have any traceable contact. You just show up whenever you want and I'll just be here. It'll be safe."

"I should go," I say, putting down the drink and standing. I bend to slip on my shoes; he moves over to me, running his fingers through the back of my hair, kissing my neck. I let myself lean my head back and feel it. Then he kisses my mouth and looks at my eyes. "It's an open offer."

Just then my phone hums, and I can tell by the happy percussion chime that it's FaceTime. I carry my shoes in my hand as I pull away from Luke and dart through the muddy stretch of field toward my car. I duck under a low-hanging arm of a bald cypress tree and catch my shoulder on a firethorn as I try to slip through a spread of wild pyracantha bushes along a sagging wooden fence at the edge of the property.

"Shit!" I try to cover my shoulder with my hand so blood doesn't drip down onto my dress. When I reach the street, I put my shoes on and try to walk casually. The last thing I need is for someone to see me running out of the bushes, bleeding, barefoot and muddy. I text Collin saying I'll call back in just a second. I try to wipe up the cut on my arm and clean my muddy feet with the only thing I can find, a box of Kleenex rolling around on the back- seat floor. The wispy pieces only stick to the cut, so I give up and toss all the damp, muddy tissue into a soggy pile on the passenger seat. I check my face, smooth my hair in place and FaceTime Collin back.

When he answers, I see they are at Morty's, a restaurant we all love going to. Ben is in the back, trying to push himself into the frame so I see him. I wave to him as Collin tries to refocus him back on his crayons and kids' coloring menu.

"Hey there. We're at Morty's, so Ben wanted to call to tell you."

I hear Ben yell, "It's her favorite!" from the background.

"Oh, how sweet. Sorry I missed you. I was just finishing up a conversation and didn't hear my phone."

"It's fine. We actually just sat down. Rachel's practice went late. But Ben got you…" He has a singsong tone in his voice, then he pauses and pans the phone quickly over to Bennett for dramatic effect.

"Look, Mom. It's lemon meringue!" Ben holds up a small take-out box and beams.

"He saw it in the pastry case on the way in and said we had to get it for you," Collin says, giving Ben a high five. "Sweet kid."

"Sweeeet kid," I repeat in agreement. "Thanks, Benny!"

"Did you eat? Anything else you want us to bring home?"

"Oh, I'm fine. But thanks."

"You can stop by if you're done and meet us if you want." I wonder if he can see the lie as it quickly shapes in my mind. I can't show up like this, obviously.

"You know what, I actually—I cut myself," I say, angling my phone for him to see. It works out well to use this now instead of explaining it later, which I'd have to do anyway.

"Oh my gosh, hon. What happened?"

"That bookstore is about a thousand years old. It was just

a nail sticking out of the wood—I leaned against the wrong ancient wall and snagged it."

"Sheesh. You should sue."

We both laugh because he always says we should sue when any unfortunate little occurrence happens.

"I'm fine. I'll head home and clean it up. I'll see you in a bit."

"Okay. Say bye, kids," he says, maneuvering the phone to show Rachel and Ben behind him, but they don't look up. Rachel stays glued to her phone and Ben is now scratching in the ear of a cartoon cat with a purple crayon. Collin blows me a kiss and we hang up.

I sit a moment, the sudden silence humming in my ears. The evening sun sits like a red mountain on the horizon just before it gives way to dusk. It's getting dark early. It's not even eight yet, and I'm grateful they've just sat down to dinner and that I have time.

I can smell him on my clothes. I'll wrap my dress in a plastic hanging bag left over from the cleaners when I get home—say some blood from my cut got on it and bring it in to get dry-cleaned. My lies are coming too quick, too easily. What am I becoming?

7

I drive through the darkness with the windows down. The air is earthy and heavy; katydid and cricket songs fizz in my ears as I pass the thickets along these otherwise empty roads. My phone startles me. I see Collin's name pop up on the square of light in the passenger seat. When I answer, there is silence.

"Collin?" I say, wondering why he'd call back so soon if they're at dinner. He doesn't respond. I can actually see my heartbeat, it thumps so hard. It pulsates the fabric of my dress.

"Collin. Hello?"

Last time I freaked out over his silence it was a brief bad connection. So I wait, listening. Pinpricks of heat pass between my breastbone and down my spine. He says nothing. I only hear breathing and murmurs of distant conversation in the background. *He knows.*

"Collin," I say again, shakily. He can't even bring himself to speak. Then the call cuts off. I pull over at the next turn, and drive into the parking lot of Bourbon and Spirits; the *I* and the *R* in the word "Spirits" has been burned out so long that everyone calls the place Bourbon and Spits. I'm shaking uncontrollably. I pull to the back of the broad dirt lot against a towering wall of switchgrass and dandelions. I turn off the engine and stare down at the phone in my lap, hunched over in a miserable curve. I try to calm my quivering hands so I can dial him back. I start to hyperventilate, I force myself to take a deep breath. But before I can tap his name on my screen, a text pops up.

BUTT DIAL. SORRY! An emoji shaped like a little butt and another emoji slapping its face in embarrassment follows. The rush of relief is dizzying. I can't force myself to move or text back. I let the phone slip out of my hand and I sob into the steering wheel.

After a few minutes of ugly, hiccup crying, I stop cold when I hear something. The country music and howling from inside the bar is low and muffled, but still obscures the noise I'm certain I heard. A woman, maybe. Calling out for help? I open my car door and step softly. I push my ear forward, straining to hear. It sounded like someone screaming. Just a short, blunt, stiffled scream. I take one of Ben's baseball bats from his equipment bag in the trunk and stand in the wet, still air, waiting for another noise to tell me which direction it came from.

There's a Ford pickup across the lot where the woods meet the dirt clearing. I can make out a man's figure, just a shape in a streetlamp's glare. I see him zip up his pants, and there's a woman. He has her pinned against the side of his truck. I see her more clearly as I edge closer.

"Please," is all I hear her say, and then she cowers as he raises his fist. He laughs at her and hits the metal of the truck bed instead, just missing her face: a warning. She scrambles to pull her shorts back up. She's crying.

What should I do? I should call the police. Shit, no...I shouldn't get involved. His hand is around her neck, he's saying something, inches from her face. I can see the mist of his spit under the cone of light above him from the streetlamp all the way from here. Before I can unfreeze my body and make a run to my phone or run to her or do something, he lets go. She holds her neck and grips the side of the truck, trying to escape him, inching to one side so she can run. Suddenly, he turns away as if he's done tormenting her, then turns back. His fist bashes the side of her face and she falls.

"Think you'll say no to me? Look at you!" he yells, then picks his beer up from the ground and mutters, "Fucking bitch."

When he walks back toward the bar, I swear he sees me. He's looking my way, but he doesn't, somehow. But I see him. I cannot believe who I'm looking at.

It's Joe. Homecoming King Joey. Ben's coach. *Officer* Joe Brooks. When I see he's inside, swallowed up by the patrons and music, I toss the bat in the backseat and run over to the woman.

"Are you okay?" I ask, breathless, kneeling down next to her.

"Who are you? Fuck. Get away from me." She yanks her arm away from my touch. I see that her mouth is bleeding.

"Sorry. Can I help you? I mean—are you—we should call the police. I saw what happened."

After I say it, I realize why she's looking at me the way she is. Joe Brooks *is* the police.

She sits against the truck and buries her head in her hands, crying. I can see she's tipsy.

"Hey, hey, it's okay."

"It's not okay. I need to go home. He was my ride. I got a kid at home."

"Let me take you."

"You don't even know me."

"I saw what happened though. Did he…" I pause, but I need to ask. I need to help. I don't say the words *sexually assault you*. I just look down at her still-unbuttoned shorts and then away. She doesn't answer, but she doesn't have to. She holds herself tighter with one arm wrapped around the opposite elbow and wipes her eyes with her free hand as she looks up, avoiding me.

"We need to get you outta here."

She stumbles a little on the way to my car. When we pull out, I remember the first aid kit in my glove compartment. I open it and tell her to grab the alcohol pads for her lip.

"Thanks." She rips open tiny paper squares and presses the cold pads to her face. Then she lights a cigarette and stares out the window.

"You know, just 'cause he's a cop doesn't mean you shouldn't report him. That's just—I can't even…"

"You know Joey?"

"Yes. Well, I thought I did. I mean what happened? If you don't mind my asking?"

"So, you're fucking him too?"

"What—NO! What? Why? No." I stammer, shocked at the question, feeling accused.

"Well, any girlfriend of Joe's would never say they haven't seen him like that. Is all."

"This has happened before?"

I'm sincerely beside myself in disbelief. She just makes a scoffing sound and sort of laughs, ripping open a bandage with her free hand, puffing on a cigarette with the other.

"So, you're his girlfriend?"

"No."

"Okay."

"I *was* his girlfriend. I finally get out, ya know I finally did it, I stopped comin' back to the bullshit. I was there with a date, even, till I ran into that prick. He got me again. All the sweet-talkin'. Send this loser home, he says. Tells me he's changed. God, and I fucking fell for that bullshit again!"

"You sent your date away?" I ask. She blows a thread of smoke out the window.

"The guy is fuckin' good. He's real good."

"I can't believe Joe Brooks would act—I mean, he hit you. Jesus—I…"

"That? That was nothin'."

When she says this, she blinks back tears. I think of how bad it must be if that was "nothing."

"And you don't report him?" I ask. She tosses her butt out the window and its fiery end skips down the road in the darkness behind us. She looks at me pointedly.

"You gotta promise me you're not gonna say nothin' to no one."

I look at her, at the fear and anger in her swollen eyes.

"Yeah. Okay. I mean…"

"He can make your life hell. Him and all those good ole boys he works with. I made that mistake once—reporting what he done to me. My word against his. All his friends in the department there protecting him. You'll regret it as much as I did if you say anything."

She crosses her arms and leans into the night air that's rushing in the window. I imagine how the he-said, she-said would go. She's a single mom with alcohol on her breath and track marks that I can see on the insides of her arms. Her word against kids' baseball coach and cop Joe Brooks. I feel nauseous.

She points to her street, and I turn in and drop her at the end of Sycamore Street, which leads to the trailer community half a mile down. I don't offer to take her all the way, I'm sure she doesn't want me to know where she lives.

She gets out and closes the door, but leans back in a moment.

"He was there with his friends, celebrating his promotion to detective. For your own good, like, for real, don't be stupid and go reporting anything."

"Okay," I say, and she stares at me, studying, clearly deciding whether I'm telling the truth or not.

"Thanks for the ride."

"Yeah. I'm Melanie, by the way. Melanie Hale." I scribble my phone number down on the back of a gum wrapper I find in the center console and hand it to her.

"In case you ever need it, I don't know," I say, suddenly insecure, wondering if it's too much. She takes it and nods.

"Lacy Dupre," she says as she pulls out another smoke.

"Anyway, I know who you are. Joe pointed you out once at a baseball practice. You're one of the moms he went to school with. Said you were 'fuckable.'"

"He said that to you when you were dating him?"

"Yep."

"Classy," I say, and she lights another cigarette, gives me a final, curt wave and walks unsteadily down the black road toward her home.

8

In the following days, autumn settles slowly as it does in the South, with slight drops in temperature that offer only a small respite from the white-hot sun and merciless humidity. Rachel didn't make cheerleading, so she spends even more time in her room scrutinizing her appearance and general self-worth. The makeup tutorial YouTube channel she started only has nine likes, so that explains why I find a mound of expensive cosmetics congealing in the heat, on top of the garbage next to the garage. I try to rescue a sticky red clump that used to be lipstick, pushing it back into its tube, but it's no use.

Collin suggested we go down to the bayou and fish, maybe charter a boat for the day and camp. Rachel loves being on the water and stopping for boiled peanuts. She doesn't exactly jump for joy, but a half nod and not getting her bedroom door slammed in our faces is a win, so on Saturday, we all pile in the car to drive to Spanish Lake.

The tents and supplies are strapped on the top of the SUV, and we look just like the Griswolds coming down the highway,

I'm sure. I'm like one of the kids, glued to my phone as Collin drives. I skipped Thursday's writing group. I didn't trust myself to go, to risk another note or worse—that I might take Luke up on his offer—and I resist the urge to look up his name on social media. I don't want any record that I even know who he is. But I want so desperately to see the thumbnail of his face bloom on my screen. I want to see candid shots of him at a ball game with friends, or with his toddler nephew on his shoulders at a backyard pool party. I want to see the shameless selfies. I wonder if he takes any. Maybe one on his balcony in Italy—just his face, the subtle duck-lipped expression he doesn't realize he's making, with the vast Mediterranean blue behind him.

I lay naked next to this man while he expressed his fear of dementia—his grandfather had early-onset—while he wrestled with regrets of not having kids, even though he always exclaims how great it is to be free. I laughed under the sheets as he walked through the house naked because he heard Roger, the stray cat, crying at the door and he had to run down and bring him some milk.

He *counts on me*, he joked, leaping back into bed, and rolling me on top of him to make love again that first night. I knew his love for animals. He showed me the locket he always keeps on him, in a pocket somewhere, handed down from his grandmother, which holds a photo of his beloved, deceased dog, Henry.

I knew his body—the body of a man who doesn't work twelve-hour days and come home to kids, who can spend countless hours at the gym between writing chapters at cafés. But then again, I don't really know him at all.

The cut on my left shoulder is almost healed. It's just a wisp of a papery scab now. Collin smiles at me, kisses his finger, then touches it to the cut. I'm pulled out of my fantasy. I put my hand on top of his and kiss it. Because that's what he expects me to do, and I need to act normal. And because I want to. I love him. I don't know why I've done what I've done. He glances in the rearview mirror and then nods for me to look at Ben in back. Ben's face is plastered to the window, asleep, and Rachel has nodded off sitting up, her head bobbing. I'm so grateful for them, and I feel a twinge of pain behind my eyes. Guilt, maybe. I'm angry at myself for letting my thoughts of him take me away from these moments with them.

When we pull into Biff 's boiled peanut and crawfish stand, everyone uses the restroom, and I sit on a picnic table in the shade while the kids get their peanuts. After I call the home health aide who is looking after Claire to check in, I decide to look up Lacy Dupre. There are a few with that name on Facebook, but I see her photo right away. I click on her profile. To my surprise, much of it is public. Her occupation says "Cashier at Lucky's Truck Stop." Her cover photo is her in a slicked-back ponytail and hoop earrings with a toddler on her hip. Her son, I guess. I study him to see if he looks like Joe Brooks. I scroll through dozens of photos, but no trace of Joe in any of them. I get the feeling she's the sort of girlfriend he calls " just some chick he messes around with now and then" when he talks to his friends.

Probably not even that. He's slippery. I bet he doesn't claim her at all. I bet he doesn't take her anywhere in public.

She's just a quick lay to him, in and out, and she waits for him anyway, pretending it's more. If he wanted a fuck the other night, he probably worked it out for himself to meet her later, convince her to ditch the other guy. Maybe she embarrassed him in front of his good-ole-boy friends with the audacity to show affection or act like a couple, and he flipped. I know she said she'd finally broken up with him, but I also know she often goes back to him.

I didn't report what I'd seen, but I can't just do nothing. I know what I saw, but it seems like the smoky ends of a dream you try to keep in your mind as you wake up, the details blurry, evaporating. There has to be a way to expose Joe Brooks. I quickly send her a friend request and put my phone in my purse so I don't keep checking to see if she's accepted.

When evening falls, we sit around a firepit by the water's edge. Collin boils red potatoes and some crawfish the kids collected. The flames dance and pop and silvery ash soars, then falls like summer snow. Mosquitoes force Rachel and Ben into their tent early to watch a movie on Ben's iPad, so Collin and I retrieve bottles of beer from the icy water in the bottom of the cooler and walk down to the dock to put our feet in the water.

There is a hint of a breeze in the air and the glow of fireflies in the trees looks like strings of blinking lights. We kick off our flip-flops before we walk barefoot down the wooden slats to the end of the dock. Collin takes my hand and puts his other hand behind his ear playfully, listening.

"What are you doing?" I laugh. He points up and smiles.

"They're playing our song." He pulls me in to dance to the song of croaking frogs and rustling tree leaves. I play along, and we sway together for a few minutes. Then he picks up our beer to toast "desperately needed away time" and we sit, dangling our toes off the end of the dock.

"Ben asked how fireflies light up like that, and I didn't know how to answer him, so now he thinks they take double-A batteries," Collin says, wiping the light film of sweat from his brow. The humidity is miserable as usual. I laugh.

"You did not tell him that."

"I have no idea how they light up. He asked me how the toaster works once. No idea. It just works when you plug it in. Bam. Superdad." He makes a "mic drop" gesture.

"They're bioluminescent," I say.

"What are?"

"Fireflies. That's how they talk to each other."

"You're so smart. See, you're clearly the superior parent, that's what I love about you so much," he jokes, kissing me, then putting down his drink to kiss me some more. It feels strange kissing him. My husband of fifteen years and it feels so different, new, almost. We haven't made love since…Luke. Things just got busy with school, his late hours, Claire's health. It happens to the best of us. There may have been some avoidance on my part as well, if I'm honest.

"Well, you're good at other things." I pat him, laughing. We both pick up our beers and stare into the bayou.

"Are you okay?" he asks, out of the blue, and I feel a wave of nausea rise in my stomach.

"What do you mean? Of course." I watch the low moon appear now and then between patches of vaporous clouds.

"You just seem…maybe a little distracted. Lately. I know you've taken on a lot, but I just want to make sure…everything is…okay, I guess."

He looks at me with those adoring, hazel eyes and forces a smile. I have no choice. I need to tell him at least one secret so it can all make sense to him—so anything he's sensed from me can be cleared up right now.

"There is something that I want to tell you," I say, crossing my legs and turning to him to highlight the importance of what I'm about to say. The color drains from his face.

"What is it?"

"The only reason I haven't said anything is because I promised someone I wouldn't tell anyone, but if you're feeling like I'm distracted or distant, then it's affecting us and I feel like it's important to just tell you."

"God, Mel. What is it? Is it something with one of the kids?"

"No. No, sorry, I just…I saw something I shouldn't have seen."

"What do you mean? What?"

"We all went for a drink after writing group." I have to add that this was a few weeks ago so it can explain away any strange behavior he's seen in me this whole time. I don't give him time to question why we'd go all the way out there. I don't feel good about adding these details, but I have to. "Mia, from the group, she wanted to go for karaoke, and in the parking lot, I saw a guy assault a woman."

"You saw it."

"Yes, I saw him strike her. But he did more than that, Col. I didn't see that part, but I saw enough to know it happened."

"Like sexually?"

"Yeah. I tried to help her."

I explain about going over to Lacy and giving her a ride home, and how she reacted when I asked what else he'd done to her. "But it gets worse."

"Jesus, Mel. How could it get worse?"

"We know the guy who did it."

"Um...okay? Wha—who?"

"It was Joe Brooks."

"What? Ben's coach?"

"Yeah."

"He's a cop, Mel. I mean, are you absolutely sure? That's—"

"I am absolutely sure. It was fucking awful. I couldn't believe what I was seeing. I promised her, swore to her I would keep this to myself."

"Well, you know you have to report it."

"I can't!"

"Mel, there's no way you can just—"

"This is why I'm freaking out. If I report it, it will be to one of his cop friends."

"I'm sure there are plenty of higher-ups who are not Joe's drinking buddies. I mean..."

"I promised her. It's not my place. I mean, right? She'd get backlash once he finds out. Collin, if you'd seen him, the look on his face—it was horrifying. Who knows what he'd do?" We're both silent for a few moments. "I can't." We pick up our drinks and look out into the water, an oval of moonlight reflecting off the surface.

"Jesus, I can't believe Joe Brooks would do that," Collin says.

"Me either."

"I'm sorry you've had to keep this to yourself. That's gotta be torture. You went to high school with the guy, didn't you?"

"Yeah. Crazy," I say softly, so relieved to tell him and also because he thinks this is what I've been holding in these weeks. He would trust me if I had just said I was sad over Claire's deterioration, which I am, without a doubt, but this monumental ordeal I've witnessed wipes away even the smallest remnant of worry he may have had for me, and now he is an ally in the pursuit of helping find justice for this victim neither of us know.

"Did you know the woman?" he asks.

"No, her name's Lacy. That's about all I really know. She's afraid of him, for sure. I thought maybe if I get to know her, try to befriend her, maybe I can help—get her to report him."

"Be careful. Please. I can see why you want to help, but promise you'll be careful."

"I know. I will."

"We'll get that son of a bitch."

I love that he cares. I love his heart, and how angry someone else's pain makes him. I put my head on his shoulder and he tells me again how sorry he is that I had to deal with all this.

He says, "Men are pigs," and kisses my forehead. Then he goes into a speech about the world his poor daughter has to grow up in.

After a few more beers and exchanges about the injustices

in the world, we find ourselves tipsy and giggling again about fireflies with battery packs. When he kisses me, he pulls my shirt over my head and lays me down on the dock. I kiss him back.

"Race ya!" I say, pulling off the rest of my clothes and jumping into the black water. He strips and jumps in beside me. I squeal at the mush between our toes and we splash each other until that turns into our bodies touching in the murky, shadowed water. Then we make love, and I try to hold him close enough and kiss him hard enough to erase everything I've done.

9

Things feel back to normal at home when we get back from our weekend away. The week is filled with mundane tasks that comfort me: spreading peanut butter on bread, cutting the crusts, stuffing Ziploc bags with carrots and baked chips for the kids' lunches, listening to Rachel figure out what other sports to try out for, helping Ben with his long and short vowels on colorful worksheets.

On Tuesday night, I bathe Claire as usual in her en suite bathroom. It's tough to maneuver her in and out of the shower. When I get her seated on the handicap bench inside the shower, I try to help her hold the sprayer on her own. It helps with her strength and coordination. I smile at her blank face and wrap her hand around it gently when she suddenly grabs my hair with much more strength than I thought she was capable of and pulls. Before I can even react, she's wrenched my head so violently, it crashes into the shower tile.

"Dirty!" she screams.

I sit in shock a moment, now wet, fully clothed, on the

shower floor touching the spot of blood on my head. I call for Collin. I know he can't hear me in the front of the house from way back here, so I don't try again. I want to cry and run out, but I can't leave her by herself like this. Rationally, I know she doesn't know what she's saying, I know that arbitrary, violent outbursts can be part of the disease, but it doesn't make it easier to take. Of course she doesn't know what I've done, but it feels…personal. It feels like she meant to hurt me for hurting Collin. I know it's totally irrational. I blink back tears and take a breath. Now soaked, I stand and squeeze some shampoo into my hand and massage her hair with it.

"It's okay, Miss Claire. We'll get you all clean. No worries. You're okay."

When I finally get her into a clean nightgown and propped in front of her sitcom and box fan, the kids are in their rooms. I peel off my soggy clothes, hang them over the side of the washer to dry out a bit, and go up to slip into a bath and assess how bad my head wound is. I don't tell Collin about it. I'm not sure why. I examine my scalp in the mirror as the bath runs. It's not bad. Cuts on the head are deceiving because they bleed more, but no one will notice it once it's cleaned up. I quickly dab a warm cloth on it and pull my hair up to cover it.

Then I sink to my chin in bubbles and close my eyes. I wish Luke's face would not visit me every time I'm alone. I could go there right now, to his house, say I'm meeting Liz or Karen for a drink. I could say Gillian needs some last-minute help with her fundraiser—doesn't matter what it's for, she's always working on one. There would be no question. I took Ben to the community pool all afternoon in the early autumn heat, so he's out like a light. Collin will be engrossed in work or a game on TV. I sit up sharply at the thought of this.

Right this minute I could simply drive over there and spend an hour in his now-familiar bed on the second floor inside a massive, historic bedroom—the creaky wooden floors and simple white sheets. I imagine the musky sweetness of his breath from the drink he'd fix us, a sultry dampness on his skin from the muggy air.

My phone buzzes. I dry off one hand on the towel hanging on a rod above me, and feel around on the floor outside the tub to pick it up. It's a notification. Lacy accepted my friend request. She sent a message. THANKS FOR YOUR HELP THE OTHER NIGHT…AND FOR NOT SAYING ANYTHING.

I start to type back, then wonder if it's too quick a response and will make me look like I'm just sitting here waiting to hear from her. I get out of the bath, wrap a towel around my head, put on yoga pants and a tank, and sit out on the back deck to take advantage of the evening breeze. I'm grateful the air is actually moving today and it's feeling cooler. I curl up on an Adirondack chair and, feeling I've waited long enough, reply back.

OF COURSE. HOW ARE YOU DOING? I ask, not wanting to invite her to meet too soon. I'll see if she opens communication or shuts me down.

I'M FINE, THANKS. FUCKER CALLED ME A DOZEN TIMES THE NEXT DAY. I JUST DON'T WANT HIM SHOWING UP AT MY PLACE, DRUNK.

I'm glad she feels like she can talk to me about this.

I can't believe he'd call you after that. I'm so sorry you have to deal with it, I text back.

Yeah. Prick, she says.

Hey, do you wanna get coffee or a drink sometime?

I wait, hoping she doesn't think it's weird. Making new friends as an adult is weird in general. I feel like I've asked a boy out and fear he'll reject me. Text bubbles pop up a few times and then disappear. Jeez, she doesn't know how to respond.

Sure, is all she replies.

Great. Just let me know when you're free.

Thurs or Fri are good.

Okay, I have a group at Classics Bookstore Thursday at six. The Local has a good patio happy hour on Friday, starts around five.

That works. Sorry, gotta go. C u then.

Her green dot vanishes off my phone. I have no plan, and I have no earthly idea how I'll help this woman, but how can I just pretend it didn't happen? What sort of person would I be?

I hear the sliding glass door behind me open. Rachel comes out and sits at the patio table.

"Hey, I thought you were in bed," I say.

"Yeah," she says. She turns her phone to show me an image of a girl with French braids forming a round crown on the top of her head. "Pretty, huh?" she asks.

"Yeah. Your hair would look beautiful like that."

"Do you know how to do it?" she asks, hopefully.

"I bet I could figure it out," I say, getting up and sitting behind her. I've braided her hair for years, and I always love this time with her. Just us, without her glued to her phone or rolling her eyes at the burden of having to speak to us because we are so uncool.

"There're auditions tomorrow for *Grease*."

"*Grease?* You're trying out for a musical? Honey, that's great." I'm surprised. She's never shown interest before.

"Katie is trying out for Sandy, but I just want to be one of the dancers in the back."

She wants to do everything her friend Katie does, so this makes more sense now.

"I love it. They'd be crazy not to make you one of the dancers."

She doesn't say anything, but I see the corners of her mouth turn up into a smile as I section her hair to braid.

"Katie has to get Sandy. It's the biggest role," she says with tension in her voice. Then she lets out a sigh.

"There are probably a lot of girls trying out for that."

"Mom. She has to." Her voice breaks.

"Why's that, hon?" I ask, but she doesn't answer right away. I hear her sigh, and her head droops down. "What's wrong?"

"Her dad's been screwing Ms. Mendez."

"What?"

"So she has to get the part."

I don't understand the correlation, but I'm still trying to figure out what she's telling me.

"The gym teacher?"

"Yeah, and the whole school knows. Her mom left and she's trying to pull Katie out and send her to some school wherever she moved to. It's, like, twenty miles away."

I can't believe I haven't heard about this. Stuff like this doesn't stay quiet in this town, but I've been so preoccupied. I should tell her not to say the word *screwing*, but I stop braiding and give her a confused look, unable to think of a response.

"So she has to get the role of Sandy?" I don't know what she's getting at.

"Yeah, we have a plan to fix everything. If she gets the lead, her mom won't be able to take her out of school. Her mom wouldn't do that to her 'cause it's, like, a big part. Plus, maybe kids will stop making fun of her if she's the star."

"The kids make fun of her?" I ask, fixated on this part.

"Everyone says Ms. Mendez is illegal and doesn't have papers. They say Katie is probably her kid if her dad is screwing her."

Again, I resist the urge to scold her for the language. She keeps going.

"That doesn't make any sense," I say.

"Doesn't need to," she adds. "They say she looks more like Ms. Mendez than her mom and that she should go back to Mexico."

"Jesus!" I blurt out.

"Yeah. Someone spray-painted 'build the wall' on her locker." She looks down at her hands. I hate that she even knows about these adult things. A few years back, our neighbor Judy Ainsley's daughter, Mary, was spotted in the cafeteria with a spot of blood on the back of her white jeans. The kids called her "Bloody Mary" for the rest of the year and left tampons in her locker. They were relentless. An Instagram account was created by some anonymous classmate, dedicated to humiliating her with all things menstrual. Mary was hospitalized after a suicide attempt, and the family had to move. They left the state altogether. Rachel was younger then. Mary was in high school, so I don't know if she's heard the story. I hope not.

I want to scoop her up in my arms and shield her from all of this. Instead, I've put her in danger. What would kids find to use and make her life hell if my secret was ever exposed? It could be anything. Luke's writing is provocative, almost pornographic. There would be countless ways they could spin the situation and make it their mission to ruin her.

I take Rachel's hands and hold them inside of mine on her lap. I want to say something magical to fix the situation and transform her mood. A few years ago, I would only need to suggest constructing a tent out of couch cushions and bedsheets and watching *Finding Nemo* with pints of Rocky Road, and no matter what her trouble was, it would be forgotten. It's different now.

"Kids are shitty," I say. Not my best parenting moment, but her eyes widen in surprise, and then she laughs. I laugh with her. I tell her to get her music for her dance number and we can work on it. I push the grill and the patio furniture to the side to clear a space on the deck, and she runs back to her room for her Bluetooth speaker, delighted she's allowed to stay up late, and we get to work.

On Thursday, I am excited to get to the bookstore for our group. I have been working on a story. I don't know the people in this group well, so I finally decide that no one would think it anything but steamy romance, but I'm nervous, so I plan to share just a few pages. I made sure to write in third person and give the protagonist a different and unusual name, keeping as much distance from the truth as I can, in a sense, but I ache to tell someone without telling someone.

I'm not overdressed this time. I'm in skinny jeans, a T-shirt and a Saints ball cap that I have to steal back from Ben's room because he likes to wear it to school. I arrive a little late. As I walk through the lot, I see what I think is Luke's truck. I slow down and peer over as I pass. I leap back, holding my chest when I see he's sitting behind the wheel, looking down at his phone.

"Luke?"

He rolls down the window.

"What are you doing here?" I ask. I am immediately aware of how I look—thrown together.

"You never came to see me," he says, leaning over and pushing open the passenger door.

"It's not safe. Are you kidding?"

"It's dark. No one's around. I'll say I'm hiring you for some local book promotion stuff." He indicates a stack of books in the back that could serve as an excuse if we're caught. I look around, paranoid, making sure there is no one in sight, then slide in and shut the door quickly.

"Hi," I smile, immediately shy and self-conscious in his presence.

"Hi." He moves in to kiss me, but I back away.

"Someone could see."

"Okay, you're right. But they won't see this."

He unbuttons my jeans and moves his hand inside them. I inhale sharply, not expecting his touch. He puts his fingers inside me and we look at one another. I grip the door latch, but force myself not to look suspicious in case anyone were to pass.

"I missed you," he says.

I take off my ball cap and cover his hand, glancing around again outside the window, but then letting myself be overtaken by the pleasure.

"Me too." I'm finding it hard to speak. I stifle a moan. "I thought you'd have gone to Italy by now."

"You make it hard to leave, you know that? Maybe I would be if I hadn't met you."

I keep asking myself, why me? What's so special about me that this perfect man wants me? I don't understand.

"Mel?" a voice calls. Luke and I both start. He pulls back to his side and I straighten my shirt over my open zipper.

"Jesus!"

I see it's Lacy.

"Lacy. Hi. I—" I open the truck door and step out. She must have walked right out of the front door without us knowing. How could I be so careless?

"This is Luke. He's a writer. We're here for a writing event…thing. Well, not him, I mean just me. He already wrote a book." I grab one of the books from the stack in the backseat to emphasize my point. "He was just giving me one." She peers in at Luke and waves.

"Hi, there," he says, and waves back.

"Oh, I'm sorry. I was inside looking for you. I thought we

were meeting here. I'd given up and was gonna head out."

"Oh my gosh, no, I thought that was happy hour tomorrow."

"Did I get it wrong?" She pulls out her phone, and mumbles as she reads my message back. "'I have a group at Classics Bookstore Thursday at six. The Local has a good patio happy hour on Friday, starts around five.' Ohhh gosh. I thought you were inviting me to the Classics group thingy. And I just said 'C U then.' I was in a rush. My fault."

"Oh, it's okay, I thought you were saying 'see you then' to Friday."

"Yes, I can totally see that. I'm an idiot."

"No, please. I'm sure I was probably unclear."

"That's fine. Gives me an excuse to go over to Rodney's and get a drink. I thought I'd be stuck reading all night or something. No offense," she says, and I laugh. "But let's do next week, 'cause I can't get a sitter again for tomorrow."

"Oh, you came all the way out. I can skip the group."

"No, no." She lights a cigarette and rests her other hand on one skinny hip. "It's my stupid fault."

She pulls her phone out, and the light reflects off her face, where I can see the cut on her lip is almost healed. She seems in good spirits. Not in danger, I think.

"Okay, then. Next week." I smile. Then I wave, awkwardly, to Luke. "Thanks for the book." I look like a complete moron right now, visibly jumpy, but I can't seem to control it. Conscious of the need to get to the bathroom so I can do up my still-open zipper, which my T-shirt is barely covering, I finally make myself turn and go in.

I was less than a second away from getting caught. Would I have gone back to his place with him if she hadn't come? Or would I have held to the promise I'd made to myself a thousand times in the last week and walk away, go home, forget him, tell him to leave town?

10

I have nothing in common with Lacy Dupre. We would never come together or form a friendship in any way if I hadn't seen what I'd seen.

She shows up the following weekend, at Rodney's, a bar she suggested, wearing pink cutoffs so short that her butt cheeks peek out the bottom. Her tight tank showcases boobs that are too big for her small frame. She later explains they were a gift from an ex. She sits and I can smell drugstore perfume attempting to mask the heavy odor of cigarettes.

"Hey, what's up?" She drops her phone in her purse and smiles. I see a line of lipstick across her teeth but don't say anything. She pulls out some Tutti Frutti lip gloss and applies a second coat. She reminds me of a Fruit Roll-Up, all pinks and reds and tropical smells. I feel very beige next to her in my skinny jeans and plain white tank.

"Hi, it's crowded, so I just snagged the first table I could. This okay?" I ask.

We're seated at a small two-top in the front of the bar,

near the windows that look out to the sidewalk. The damp, stale urine smell sort of just comes with the territory when you go to a bar in this town. It's the kind of place where shaky addicts and drunks are slumped over the bar before noon, redolent of sour liquor as alcohol leaches from their pores, clinging to the halcyon days of their youth because they haven't got much of a future.

"Sure."

A waitress is quick to place a napkin down in front of Lacy as she passes us, carrying a tub of dirty glasses and empty beer bottles. She orders a beer-rita, and I don't know what that is. I trace the rim of my wineglass with my finger, anxiously, not really having a plan. Not really even knowing why I'm butting into her life. If it weren't Joe Brooks, would I still feel this compulsion to help her, or whatever it is I'm doing?

A giant margarita with a bottle of Corona stuck into it, upside down, arrives at the table.

"Wow," I say, taken aback by the monstrosity.

"Want some?"

"I'm good, thanks."

"I actually bartend here one night a week, so I know all the good drinks."

"I can see that." I try not to sound condescending, but my mom voice is coming out a bit.

"Ronny Lee pissed on me, so I had to change, that's why I'm late. Sorry."

"Oh, is that your…son?"

"Yeah. He should be passed the pissing on me stage by now.

108

I hope he don't end up retarded," she says, sighing, then taking a few gulps of her vat of green beer-rita. I try to make sure my face doesn't show how offended I am by her choice of words.

"Kids always hit milestones in their own time. I'm sure he'll be fine."

"I guess." There is an awkward silence. She probably wonders why I asked her here. A bus lumbers by on the street outside. The paper birch tree outside the front window bends as it surrenders dozens of dead leaves from a heavy gust of wind. I try think of what to say. I have no real plan.

"I thought it was cool of you to ask me to hang out."

When she says this, I feel a rush of relief.

"Really?"

"Yeah, I mean it's hard to be friends with chicks. Don't you think? They're usually nasty to each other. I don't have very many girlfriends."

I do know what she means. I think of Liz, Karen, Gillian, all the women who I see a few hours here and there at social events who I call my friends. They know that Monica Harkins will never lose that baby weight, and that Katherine what's-her-face got fired and might lose her house, and that Tammy's husband is probably gay, but they don't know a damn thing about me. Not really.

I live on Willow Street, I take care of Ben and Claire, my daughter is in honors English classes, and my husband is a riot, well loved by all the other husbands. I sit quietly for most of the PTA meetings and barbecues, and I just sort of blend in. I'm on the invite list—a half of a couple that my neighbors invite places, but I've never had a real conversation with any of them.

"Yeah. Me either," I tell her. "It is hard."

"I'm sorry ya had to see all that, few weeks ago. It's embarrassing. I hope you didn't feel like you had to be nice to me 'causa that."

"No. I mean. I wanted to make sure you were really okay."

"Why do you care?"

"I…" I'm surprised by this, and stutter over a response.

"I didn't mean for that to come out shitty, but I seen online that you got a family, kids and all. You live in the fancy part of town. Just curious, like, why you'd be concerned. Is all." She takes out a cigarette that she can't smoke inside, and taps it on the table, absently.

"I think anyone would be concerned—wanna try to help," I say, and she laughs, a short burst, then she's serious again.

"Nobody I know gives two shits. Ya don't bring it up, ya just deal."

"I understand why you don't feel like you can report it, but you have a witness now. He can't get away with something like this."

"It's over. I'm not goin' back to that bar, I'm not lettin' him come over when he calls anymore. It's done, as far as I'm concerned."

She pulls the beer out of her drink and chugs down the remainder. If it were me I would make a sign that says Joe Brooks Is a Rapist and picket outside the police station if they wouldn't listen. It's not me though. And Lacy Dupre has no credibility. What if he's doing this to other women? He has the gun and badge, and he can really get away with whatever he wants, as it appears.

"I would go with you, if you wanted. He can't get away with—"

"Look. I'm happy right now. Joe's leavin' me alone and I'm not strippin' anymore since my new job at the truck stop. I even met someone…someone I really like, and I can't mess all that up, okay. It's in the past." She looks away, not wanting to deal with any pressure from me. This isn't what she signed up for tonight. She just wanted a new girlfriend, so I let it go.

"You met someone, that's great."

"Yeah, he's really hot. And smart. Like supersmart."

"I'm happy for you. Smart is good." I gesture to the waitress to bring me another rosé. Lacy beams as she talks about her new romance.

"I know it's new, like only a week and all, but I've seen him almost every night, so in regular dating time where you only go out on a weekend, that's like five weeks. That's how I see it."

"Sounds like you're really into him."

"My sister is knocked up, so she's not goin' out anymore, drinkin', so she's staying with Ronny Lee, so I can go see him. It's like a storybook. So romantic. He writes books actually, can you even believe that?" When she says this, all the color drains from my face, I feel dizzy, my heart is in my throat.

"What?"

"Isn't that crazy? I mean maybe it's TMI, but this guy can fuck. God almighty. He makes ya feel like the most important person in the world. It's like love at first sight. Did you feel that way when you met your husband? Is this the way it's supposed to be, and I was just stuck with fuck-face Joe Brooks all this time?" She is genuinely looking to me for an answer, some hopeful words, and I can't speak. I try to swallow down the tears climbing up my throat.

"Are you talking about Luke?"

"Oh yeah! The guy you were buying that book from. So much has happened since then, I forgot you know him too. Do you know him well?"

She's eager for a yes so she can ask me all about him. I feel paralyzed in my chair. When my wine comes, I drink it in a few swallows.

"No, not at all. I just—just from the bookstore. In passing."

"Are you okay?" she asks. I'm not hiding my horror well.

"Yes, I just, I don't feel very well." I know I'm sweating. I can feel it beading on my forehead.

"Ya don't look so good."

"I think it's probably just…something I ate earlier."

"Did you get sushi from the gas station? It'll get you every time." She gives a sympathetic shake of her head, and I stand, feeling my gut betray me, and run to the bathroom. After I throw up in the toilet, I stand in the stall and try to compose myself. I squirt hand sanitizer into my palm and rub it into my hands, then pour a couple of Tic Tacs into my mouth. The jolt of mint is curbing the nausea. I have no right to be this upset. He is not mine to lose.

I take a few deep breaths and return to the table. I don't sit.

"I'm sorry, I need to go home."

"You poor thing. Is there anything I can do?"

"Thanks, no. I just need to rest. Here." I place some money on the table that will cover all our drinks and some change. She stands up as I gather my things, with the look people give when they are powerless to help. "Let's do this again," I add, already headed toward the door.

"Yeah, okay. Feel better!"

I have three hours until I'm expected home, and I know I shouldn't, but I drive directly to Luke Ellison's house.

I park a few blocks away and walk the stretch of land to his door, hugging the tree line so as not to be seen. Just the way he'd suggested I do anytime I *felt like showing up*. He said he'd be waiting. I'm seething with anger, thinking about what I would have found if I did stop by, unannounced. What an absolute fraud. He thinks he's some ladies' man—romance writer who can just come to town and seduce all the women, telling them grand stories, telling them he's never felt this way about anyone before.

I should only be angry with myself for thinking that this was something rare and special, a once-in-a-lifetime bond that we shared. That even when it ended we would have experienced something that I could take away and carry with me—that was just mine—that had nothing to do with caretaking or stay-at-home motherhood or suburbia or anything. It would be this delicious secret that only I knew, and it would keep me going. Because I had proof, in this brief summer of knowing him, that if I said "Yes, I'll come to Italy," I could still take that path I didn't take. This whole other life was still within reach. Even though I wouldn't go, I was shown that I could. But now he's ruined that. I've been had. None of it is special.

His truck is in the dirt drive and the kitchen light is on when I walk up. I knock on the side door and wait in the darkness. When he sees me, his face lights up, then drops after a moment when he can tell I'm upset. He tries to take my hand, but I pull it away and cross my arms. I stand just inside the door, so I don't risk being seen, even though it's too secluded for that to be a concern out here.

"Hi. I'm thrilled to see you, but you don't look happy."

"Is Lacy planning on coming over tonight?" I ask, sharply, and he looks at the ceiling and takes a deep breath.

Then he closes his eyes a moment, probably figuring out how to best lie and get out of this.

"No, not tonight," he says, and I'm surprised he's so forthcoming. "Will you come in, please." He gestures to the kitchen. My eyes rest on the spot on the counter where we had sex last time I was here.

"I think that's all I really needed to know, so I'll just go."

"Please, Mel. Please come in. Just for a minute at least. Don't leave it like this."

I follow him to the kitchen table, reluctantly, where his open laptop and a glass of wine sit. He offers me a glass, but I say no, then we sit at the table under the dim overhead light.

"What is there to say?" I ask.

"I'm leaving in ten days. I don't want this to end with you angry."

"Does she know you're leaving?"

"I don't know. It hasn't come up."

"Really? 'Cause she thinks you're in love—said it was love at first sight."

"What? We hung out a few times, that's it."

"Is that what you call it, hanging out?" I snap, embarrassed at how much I am now realizing I had invested in this.

"Wait. So, you're angry. With me?" he asks, genuinely confused.

"You're good. You acted like this meant the world to you. You invited me to Italy, for fuck's sake. You—"

"And I meant all that. And then you disappeared. When you stop going to your own writing group to avoid me, shouldn't I take a hint? I got the courage up to try a few times—see if you felt the same, but you never came by, never reciprocated my interest. What was I supposed to think?"

"I can't just—So you fuck Lacy and who knows how many other people. I'm an idiot. That's all there is to it." I stand up, as if I'm going to leave, and he counters.

"I told you that after many years in a tough relationship, I was newly single, and I haven't felt the way I did when I met you, never felt that rush—that need to just…be near someone the way I did with you. I meant that. I still mean that. But you're married." When he says the word *married* his voice breaks just a tiny bit.

"I know that." I sit back down, pulling his glass of wine

across the table and taking a sip, buying a few moments of time because this is the last thing I expected him to say and I'm not sure what to do.

"You're the one with a family, and you're the one who doesn't want anyone to know about us. I'd tell the whole world if I could, I'd cancel my trip, I'd be ecstatic."

"Someone who feels that way doesn't go sleeping around. I don't get it. If I were so special, then…"

"I didn't do anything wrong here. You made your position clear from the start."

"I know. I didn't say you did anything wrong. I—"

"Writing is a very solitary life, and I left my friends back in Boston. I met Lacy that night you walked away— walked out of my truck and into the bookstore instead of to my place."

"That's not fair," I say, knowing there was no way I could have gracefully stayed with him, with her standing right there.

"Isn't it? She said something about wasting money on a babysitter and asked if I wanted to grab a drink. Yeah, we had sex a few times. It was just fun, two single, fucking lonely people who had sex a few times. That's it."

"Well, she thinks it's a lot more."

"I don't know how. We said almost nothing to one another. Literally a few words. It was just blowing off steam, just sex." He rubs his hand over his face and sighs. "I'll talk to her."

"Yeah, you probably should." I feel my face redden with shame. He's right. I'm throwing a fit. Somehow I'm asking for monogamy from him, which is absurd.

"If you'd given me any signal that I had a shot here, I

would never do anything to mess that up. But you made your decision. Didn't you?"

The blaze of rage that fueled my trip over here is now extinguished by my longing to be touched by him, to feel adored by him again, and to say the right thing so this isn't over. I'm not ready. I've let it go so far beyond just sex.

If I hadn't come here tonight, he would have left in ten days and I would have remained resentful; his memory would be a fleeting pang of regret now and again, but I did come.

I don't say anything. The silence hangs in the air. I can hear myself swallow. I stand and walk over to him. He's leaning against the counter, staring through the window over the sink, waiting for one of us to speak. When he turns toward me, I kiss him, hard and forcefully. He looks shocked at first, then grabs my face and kisses me back, and we fumble our way to the bedroom.

I glance at the bedside clock, making note that I only have two hours with him, maybe the last two hours I'll spend with him, and we fall into his bed together.

I shower this time, before I leave. As I stand in a towel in his bathroom, fixing my hair back to the way it was, he sits on the edge of the enormous spa bathtub and watches me. I smile at him. I'm holding the image in my mind, trying to collect these memories for when he's gone. He hands me something.

"What's this for?" I ask, looking down at a weird-looking phone—some ancient-looking flip phone.

"It's a pay-as-you-go deal," he says.

"A burner phone?" I ask, horrified. "I think these are exclusively for criminals."

"I got it back when I thought you'd show up at my door again. It's not traceable."

"I know. That's creepy." I hand it back to him.

"It's a way to stay in touch if you want to." He sets it on top of my purse. I nod.

Before I slip back out the side door, he kisses me again.

"You know where I live."

"Bye," I say, turning quickly to go before I am unable to leave.

11

With the kids now at school and Collin busy working on a relocation of the "goddamn vibrating hospital," I find I have many hours a day to myself. There are many things I could be doing. I should actually finish writing the piece I'm working on like I said I would. Collin was gracious in helping me pursue it and now I can't seem to concentrate for more than a few minutes on anything without my mind wandering to forbidden thoughts, Luke's body on mine, the passion I haven't felt in so long.

I should be teaching myself to cook something besides frozen chicken. I should get a head start on Ben's Halloween costume. He wants to be a Ninja Turtle. I should catch up on laundry. I should do anything other than what I decide to do.

On Monday morning, I hire a day nurse and pay her cash to stop in midday and take care of Claire for me. When I think about the fact that Claire can't tell on me and that's the only reason I'm getting away with it, I feel sick. But I do it anyway. Then I show up at Luke's. I can't help myself. I *don't* help myself.

I know he never thought he'd see me again after I left on

Saturday night. It should have been that way. Everything I set into motion by not staying away is my fault. He swallows me in his arms, we spend the day naked in his bed, making love until we are too exhausted to do it again. Then I go back the next two days in a row.

I let him deluge me with care; I take in all of it as if it is deserved. We sun ourselves by the pool, and I read fashion magazines he bought for me. Sometimes, while I fall asleep on a deck chair with my glass of Chablis, he works on his book—leaning over a laptop, just the way I imagined him. We watch documentaries and romantic comedies; he tries to cook for me, but can only produce offerings of burnt pancakes or crunchy spaghetti.

We tell each other everything. I knew about his father, who wanted him to be a navy man like himself and refuses to be proud of his success. He talks about his depression he takes meds for and how it's changed him—how some days he feels the despair encroaching, recognizing the enemy as it approaches, hopeless to battle it, even when he thinks he's perfectly happy. I rest my forehead on his shoulder as I listen. I tell him about my first love, the way the boy kissed me tenderly at first, but never touched my body, only pushed into me, a flat hand on the wall above my head, groaning until he was finished—how it confused me until he came out as gay a few years later. He knows I have a husband I dearly love…just in a different way than whatever this is.

I lie across his bed. A rainstorm has brought in cooler air and it sweeps in through the open window; he leans up on one elbow and traces the contours of my back with the finger of his free hand as I lie facing away, watching the drizzle make trails down the windowpane. He speaks lovers' words and I feel the wet under his eyes when he presses his face into my neck, already mourning the loss of when this will end.

At home in the evenings, the burner phone is on silent and hidden inside a tampon box under my side of the sink. Before bed, I close the bathroom door and run the water, so I have a couple of minutes to read the texted love letters from him. I'm getting very skilled at lying and acting completely normal. It scares me, how Collin and the kids are the same. No odd looks, no suspicion. All because I've become a good liar and cheater. The house is the same, the crack in the front stair that needs repair, the TV always on in the living room as Rachel and Ben fight over the remote and do homework, cross-legged at the coffee table, Ralph begging for food under the dinner table. How can this all be the same when I feel like my life has changed so completely?

One evening, after spending the last four days in his arms, he texts and says he wants to stay through the winter and postpone his trip until spring maybe. I don't know what to say to this.

Rachel comes home in tears, telling me that we absolutely have to let her friend Katie stay over for a few days.

"Honey, what happened?" I hand her a tissue and sit beside her on the sofa.

"Her mom is taking her away."

"What do you mean?"

"It didn't even matter that she got the part, her mom is

so—She ran away. I'm being honest here, okay, so you have to help her and let her come over. She needs somewhere to go. She's, like, freaking out."

My daughter is losing her best friend. I think about the reality of Katie running away. If she really ran, she'd probably be sex-trafficked or in a drug house within a week or two. She'd go to New Orleans, no doubt. This could be Rachel if anyone found out what I was doing and it tore up our family like that.

"Honey, her parents need to know where she is."

"Mom, no!" she sobs.

"We can't hide her from her parents. Do you understand that they would probably file a missing persons report and a police force would be spending time trying to find her? That's a crime. We need to make sure she's safe and her parents know where she is."

"You don't understand!" she screams.

"Rach, I know you want to help her and that this is hard, but that's not the answer. Do you know where she is now?"

"I'm not telling anyone. You were supposed to be cool and help us. This is such bullshit!" She runs into her room and slams the door, violently. Collin comes home and walks in through the garage door just in time to be startled by the slam of her door.

"What's goin' on?" He puts his things down and kisses me on the cheek as I explain about Rachel wanting to harbor a runaway.

"Should I talk to her?" he asks.

"I'd give her a little time."

"I know Katie's dad a little from the country club. Jerry. Sounds like a really ugly situation. His wife drained the joint bank account when she found out. Says he lived in his car for a week before she moved out."

"Wow. Well, Rachel says she's taking the kids away. Thinks she'll never see Katie again," I say, and Rachel comes out of her room to try and manipulate her father. She puts her arms around his waist and pouts. It sometimes works, but he gives me a look like he's got this.

"Daddy," she whines, "can I talk to you?"

And with that she whisks him off to her room to retell the story with extra tears. It hits me, hard, that he's good cop. Not only would the kids probably choose him, he's the breadwinner. I feel weak-kneed, suddenly, and sit. I have no job. All the assets are joint. I would never drain our account and be more selfish and horrible than I've already been. I would single-handedly destroy our family and lose everything if anyone found out. Somewhere in the back of my mind, I have known this, but I'm crippled by how close I am to this blowing up the way it did with Katie's parents.

My phone buzzes on the table. It's Lacy. I pick it up.

"Lacy, hi." I should have sent a text or something the next day, apologizing again for my abrupt departure from the bar, but I've been consumed. I haven't even thought about her. She's crying. "What's wrong?"

"Men are fucking assholes. They're all the same."

I hear her exhale smoke and take another pull off a cigarette.

"Oh no. What happened?" I hate myself. I'm such a liar.

"He called me Sunday and said he couldn't see me anymore. Just like that."

"Oh my gosh, that's—that's terrible. Did he…say why?"

"No! Not even an explanation. He's just not looking for anything right now. What guy is? None. None is the answer. They can all suck it."

"I'm so sorry."

"It's okay," she whimpers, sniffling.

"Is there anything I can do?"

"Tell me not to answer Joe. Fucker keeps calling me, a hundred times a day."

"Lacy. Oh my God. You—" I stop myself, not wanting to upset her more by telling her, once again, to report him. "Do. Not. Answer. You said it was in the past and you were never gonna answer again."

"Yeah, but I always say that. It's not so easy when every other guy you meet just wants a couple a blow jobs then they're gone."

Luke isn't that guy, but she'll never know that.

"They're all the same. I'm so done."

"No, you're not, come on," I try to console her.

"Yes, I am."

"Please, promise me you won't see Joe. Think about it, remember what it's like—what will happen after the apologies wear off."

"I know," she says in a singsong tone, like we're talking about his bad habit of chewing tobacco or something rather than felony assault.

"Can you get a drink at Rodney's this weekend?"

"Yeah, I mean I'll check with Collin, but I'm sure I can sneak away for a bit." As I say this I imagine myself using her by agreeing to plans, and then canceling to go and see Luke. I promise myself I won't do that. I'll be there for her. I go to the stove and poke at the stir-fry I'm heating up.

When Collin comes back out, of course he's somehow persuaded Rachel to tell him where Katie is. He puts his arms around me from behind and steals a piece of broccoli off the top.

"It's frozen!" I try to warn, but he's popped it in his mouth before I can get the words out.

"No, it's good," he says, spitting it into his hand with a disgusted look, and I can't help but laugh. "Turns out Katie's in the food court at the mall, so I'm gonna go call Jerry."

After dinner, we all watch *Survivor*, except for Rachel who's sulking in her room. I must have fallen asleep, because when I wake up, Ben is in bed, and I hear Collin from the kitchen on a work call. He's pulled a blanket over me. I sit in the blue light of the television a moment. I shake off the dream I was having about the wrath of God—a God who looks like he did in all of the picture books from Sunday school. A Gandalf the Grey beard, feathery white hair and a furrowed brow; his mouth open in midcondemnation, lightning extending from his fingers and striking down sinners who run in circles, like ants on the ground, begging for forgiveness, but too late.

I have to do it. I'm ruining everything good in my life. I have to go to Luke's tomorrow and tell him to go to Italy, and that I can't see him again. Ever. I have to.

I look at Collin hunched over his work at the counter, off his call now. I wish I could tell him how sorry I am.

"You're up," he says, seeing me staring at him.

"Sorry, I didn't know I was that tired. You're still working? It's so late."

I go and sit next to him, his computer screen glaring in the dark room. I see a multitude of spreadsheets and hope I didn't open up conversation about his work right now because I'm so very tired and I don't have the wherewithal to mask my sadness.

"I can be done."

"How's Rachel? Actually I should ask, on a scale of one to ten, how much does she hate us for calling Katie's dad— or rather, probably just me?"

"She doesn't hate you. Come on. Let's go to bed."

Later, under the fluffy down comforter, I roll over to Collin, who is fast asleep, and put my arms around his broad shoulders. I hold on so tight and bury my face in his back. I'm so, so sorry. I kiss the back of his head and pray that I can make this right.

The next morning I message Luke and tell him I'll stop by that night. I won't hire care for Claire again even though I want to do it right now, get it over with. I should have never done that. It was dangerous. I try to make it up to her. I bring her lunch and sit next to her while she eats a tough knot of Salisbury steak and some applesauce, and we watch reruns of *Golden Girls*, another of her favorites. I quietly vow to myself to become a better cook. I'm making a mental list of penance.

That night, I say that I need to meet Lacy for an hour, that she's going through something. I cannot let myself think of anything but what I need to do. I can't let myself cave, change my mind, weaken when his face crumples. I'll bring the burner phone to give back to him. No more contact. I will end this for good. He'll move on. I have to think about Collin and my children, I can't care about his feelings. I say this out loud to myself as I drive. Tears blur my vision.

"Goddamn it!" I scream, punching the steering wheel with my fist as I make the familiar drive to my parking spot, blocks away from his hidden house.

When I reach his property, I wipe my tears, but they continue to flood my eyes and fall. I take a minute so I'm composed. I rehearsed what I'll say. It will be short and to the point, so I can turn around and leave without him doing anything to change my mind. I walk up the driveway. I take a deep breath. I will say goodbye. This is goodbye.

12

The door is open when I arrive. I don't think it's strange. I think maybe he left it that way to let in the breezy night air. Perhaps he was enjoying a glass of wine on the porch and had run in for a refill. I didn't know what it would mean that the door was ajar, and I shouldn't have shut it. I shouldn't have touched anything.

I call his name, setting my purse on the counter and cocking my head to listen for maybe a shower running or footsteps upstairs. No answer. No sounds. That's when I notice his phone on the floor of the kitchen. The glass screen is smashed, but it works. That gives me pause. Why would he leave it there like that if he dropped it? When I look through into the living room, I see the couch cushions tossed on the ground. It's so quiet. What the hell is going on?

I call his name again; my heart starts to speed up as I yell for him and throw doors open to find him. Was there a robbery? I chart the stairs and start to panic a bit. He should be home. The television in the upstairs family room is on, but no one is watching it. When I turn it off, the silence rings in my ears.

I see the French doors to the balcony off of the bedroom, which overlooks the pool, are open. When I walk out onto the balcony, I feel a tremor of unease even before I see it.

The backyard is canopied with Spanish moss dripping from the trees and hums with the sound of cicadas, invisible in the branches. The humidity is palpable in the thick night air. I think of calling him, but remember I just saw his phone downstairs. All of a sudden, I wish, desperately, that I could take back every decision I've made over the last couple months that landed me here, witnessing what I can never unsee.

He is there. I see him in the shadowy blue light the swimming pool casts across the patio. He is lying on the concrete slab next to the pool with ribbons of blood making a river from the back of his head down to the pool-deck drain.

I rush down the stairs and kneel next to him. His face has an unmistakable pallor. I can tell from the eerie, lifeless stare and gloss over his eyes that he's dead. I touch the back of my hand to his neck. He's cold.

I don't scream. I immediately understand that no one can ever know that I was here. I want to wail over his body, but the utter shock is helping me through the next few minutes without breaking down and being heard. From the pool deck, I look up to his bedroom balcony. Did he fall? Jump? I can't touch him again. I need to get out. I need to get out of here.

I'm frozen where I stand, wondering if there's evidence of me here. I go into his office and rifle through his desk drawer. Did he ever write down my name or number? Did I leave anything behind in past visits—clothes, an earring? I don't see anything, but I'm trembling, not thinking straight. I look in the bedroom, in the bedside table drawers, in the bathroom. I was careful. Then I spot a condom in the small trash can by the bed. Shit, maybe it's impossible to really be careful anymore. I'm letting myself spin out of control. I take a deep breath, tears streaming down my face as I try to lull the building panic. I take a tissue and pick up the soiled condom like I'm collecting the remains of a smashed insect. I shove it in my pocket. I run, shakily, down the wooden staircase and head for the side door I came in.

His phone! He only called me on the burner number, but I can't take any chances. I grab his phone and put it in my bag, and then I do another thing I shouldn't. I rub my prints off the door handle and shut it. I am tampering with the scene of an accident, a suicide or—and I can't fully let my mind believe this—potentially a homicide. I run back to my car. I didn't even stay with him. I'm a monster.

I take the back roads down to the bay. I'm driving too fast over railroad tracks and dirt roads with the windows down, trying to outrun my pain. When I finally reach a secluded area of the bay, I sit in my car and make the call. I have to, I can't leave him lying there all alone. I use the burner phone so it's untraceable and call 911. I've never called before, I'm scared.

"911. What's your emergency?" the voice asks.

"Uh, I don't—I heard a noise—It just, I think someone should…do a welfare check." I mask my voice using an accent—a thick drawl.

"What's the address of the emergency, ma'am?"

"It's 806 Holland Lane."

"Okay, hon. Did you see anyone, is anyone hurt? What sort of noise exactly?" the operator asks, and I stumble over my words. I say the first thing that comes to mind. I wasn't prepared for any of this. It has to be something that would get them out there, that's all I'm thinking in the moment. Poor, sweet Luke, alone, hurt. Not hurt. Dead.

"I don't know, just like a fight maybe. A scream, I think, or something."

"And what's your name, ma'am, are you there now, you a neighbor?"

My name? I panic and hang up without another word.

The beep of my car door opening echoes into the nothingness around me. I walk down to an abandoned dock and grip the weathered rail to control a surge of nausea. I take his shattered phone out of my bag and hold it together with the burner phone. The water is glassy and still, but just beyond the horizon, it holds away four million miles of a ferocious, consuming sea. I throw them both into its depths. For a moment, the moonlight allows me to watch them feather their way down until they're gone beneath the dark water.

I want to scream until I'm hoarse with his name stuck in my throat, but I cannot spend another moment here. I need to appear normal and calm when I go home. I need to make up a lie about Lacy and some terrible thing she confided in me to explain my red face and swollen eyes. There is no way to hide that at this point.

The police should be there by now. An ambulance will follow. The media, probably. No one dies under strange circumstances in this town. Heart disease and the occasional car wreck are all that happens around here. Will they show his body, the way he looked like he was sleeping— if only there weren't so much blood. As I drive home, I have bouts of light-headedness that make me feel like I'm not really there, like standing up too fast and seeing black for a moment. This can't be happening. I don't even know where to direct my manic thoughts to try to calm myself down because I don't know what happened. My mind is trying to create any scenario to hold on to, to try to make sense of this. I feel a fist of pain in my chest. I want to go home and hold my kids and kiss my husband and pretend that none of this ever happened, and at the same time, I don't know how I can go home. I feel the weight of my sin pressing down on me, and I feel I might collapse under it. There was a flash, a brief second where I thought about slipping quietly off the end of the dock and into the glistening water, all the way under until only the slice of moon, thin as a fingernail clipping above me, and the tree shadows that it brushed across that glossy surface were left.

But I can't. I need to protect my family. They can never know that I knew Luke Ellison.

13

When I pull into the garage at home, I can already hear Ben inside, I know he is in mid-meltdown over something. I sit in the car a few minutes and study my face in the rearview mirror. I use my sleeve to wipe away the smear of mascara under my eyes and take a few deep breaths, telling myself to *act normal, think of your family.* When I come in through the garage and follow the wails to the living room, I see Collin holding Ben, who is slumped over in his lap, crying, "I'm sorry, I'm sorry, Daddy," over and over. This is not an unfamiliar scene. Sometimes, when Ben gets violent, he becomes tearful and repentant when he realizes he's hurt someone. Collin gives me a look, saying it's under control.

"Hey, bud. You okay?" I ask Ben.

He runs to me and puts his arms around my waist, still saying he's sorry.

"It's okay, bud," Collin says. "Why don't you go brush your teeth and put your pajamas on."

"Okay," Ben sobs, and runs off to his room.

"What happened?" I ask, seeing the cut on Collin's lip.

"He got frustrated with a math question."

"Oh no, you okay?"

"Yeah. Fine. A kid in his class called him dumb, so he was determined to work out the problem himself and... yeah. Didn't go well."

"Oh, honey..."

"It's okay, I handled it. He's fine. What happened to you? You look...Mel, you look terrible, no offense. Have you been...crying?"

"I'm fine now. Lacy is going through a rough time. The things that Joe is getting away with, what he's done to her. It's eating me up. I wish I could do something. Sometimes you just need a good cry. It's beyond infuriating, ya know."

"Do you want me to do anything—talk to Joe, or..."

"No! No, I promised. I just—we don't need to talk about it. I'm exhausted."

"Me too."

"Thanks for taking care of things tonight," I say. Collin comes over and gives me a kiss on the cheek and a hug.

"Of course. You hungry?" he asks, and I suddenly remember the condom, wrapped in a tissue, in my pocket. I back away from him, terrified that somehow he'll feel a bulge or slip his hands into my back pockets the way he does sometimes, sweetly, to keep me close after a hug.

"I'm just really tired. I'm gonna run a bath."

I put my purse down and dig in it a moment, to look like I backed away abruptly for a reason, that I'm looking for something. He doesn't notice. It's just me being paranoid. He just walks to the kitchen.

"Okay, I'll bring you a glass of wine."

"I'm sure you could use one yourself after all that," I say, attempting lightness.

"Oh yes."

He smiles and I see him grab a bottle from the rack and dig in the drawer for an opener. Out of his sight line, I rush into the bathroom and run the water for a bath. I take the condom from my pocket and flush it down the toilet. I sit with my head between my knees at the edge of the tub while steam rises from the scorching hot water. I have to keep it together.

Collin gives the door a light tap before coming in to lay a glass of red on the bathtub ledge for me. I used Ben's bubblegum-scented bubble bath and it's filled the room with a candy smell. He makes a scrunched-up face when it hits him.

"Cabernet and bubblegum. Delicious."

He kisses me on the forehead. I force a little laugh at his joke.

"I'm gonna catch the end of the Saints game."

He heads off to the media room, and I'm so relieved I don't have to put on a show anymore tonight. I don't have the strength.

I imagine Luke with medics surrounding him. A coroner, his brother being called to the scene. What happened? Would he have killed himself? Why? That doesn't make sense. He had plans of Italy, and…no. Jumping from the second floor. If his head hadn't hit the concrete the way it did, he may have only broken a leg, if that. I know in my heart that's not what it was. That leaves accident. Did he get drunk? Did he have some fit of rage or frustration in the house? A lovers' quarrel with another lover, maybe?

In many ways I knew everything about him down to his upcoming dentist appointment and favorite childhood memory. In many ways I didn't know him at all. Would anyone be out to hurt him? If he was sleeping with Lacy, am I a total idiot to believe there weren't others? A famous romance writer could be fucking every housewife in town and one may have gotten possessive, jealous.

I think about DNA, if his house were to become a crime scene. Even if mine is all over the sheets, the glasses, on everything, I have never even had a speeding ticket. I would not be in any database for them to check against. I am in disbelief that a thought like this is even crossing my mind. Getting out of volunteering for the fall bake sale was my biggest focus before all of this started and now I'm wiping fingerprints from a potential crime scene.

I need to make it my full-time job to figure out what happened to him, so it's never even suspected that I knew who he was, so it doesn't come back to me. I wasn't there. I never met him. They cannot find one reason to ask for a statement, or for DNA, or even find my name in their mouths.

I remember that I still have his novel that he signed for me. When I get out of the bath, I pull on a light robe and tiptoe downstairs. Collin is in the living room in front of the football game. He's occupied on his phone, so I walk quietly into the front sitting room where I usually write and pull open the credenza where his book sits, no book jacket, just a naked, nondescript green cover, shoved in the back and covered by magazines.

From inside the basket full of sewing supplies, next to a La-Z-Boy, I pull out the pages I've worked so hard on writing—finally I had something I felt was worth writing about—but it describes every seedy detail of this affair. I thought that someday in the future, maybe years from now when this was long behind me, it could be a good novel. None of it true, I could say, just my imagination, of course. Just fiction. I would sell it as steamy romance. No one would ever know what it was based on. Now, fictionalized or not, it can't exist anymore. I'm glad I wrote it on paper and left no trace of it in the computer.

I creep back across the wood floor and grab my gym bag from the mudroom. I cram the book and my manuscript into the bottom of the bag, underneath sneakers and a protruding yoga mat. Then I go upstairs and hide the bag in the back of our closet until tomorrow…when I can take it outside and burn the book and the manuscript to ash.

14

A couple days go by, and I catch Collin looking at me now and again, when I am obviously somewhere far away, zoning out; when I don't know that I'm standing at the kitchen sink, staring through the window, my hands once drying dishes, now at my sides, a towel in one and mug hanging by the handle in the other, still. My mind replaying the moment I saw Luke's lifeless body.

A text pings on my phone. It jolts me back into the present, and I stab a finger at the screen to read it. The writing group has been canceled this week. Mia has sent a group text. I sigh, annoyed at all the texts that will filter in from everyone else, and then I think about Jonathan. How uneasy he made everyone, how much he hated Luke. Why was group canceled all of a sudden? I feel a surge of something that I can't name until I'm abruptly interrupted.

"Want some help with those?" Collin pretends not to notice my distance most of the time, but he also doesn't want the kids to notice, I'm sure. He startles me as he takes the dish towel from my hand. He takes a clean dinner plate from the dishwasher and dries it.

"Oh. No, you don't have to…"

But I see he's already taken the mug from my hand and put it on the counter. "Thanks."

"Are you feeling okay?" he asks, and I know he senses I'm not. I know he sees the bags under my eyes from crying every time I'm alone, but he's kind. He's also becoming concerned, I can tell.

"I'm just really tired. I'm just not sleeping well, sorry."

"This Joe Brooks stuff is getting to you. Maybe you should just, like, do what you think is right even if it pisses off…" He pauses, forgetting her name.

"Lacy."

"Yeah, I think it's really unfair that you're put in this position."

"It's not about pissing her off, it's putting her in danger. And she has a little kid. If Joe is capable of what I saw him do…and that's with people just feet away inside the bar. It was totally risky. He could have been caught…what would he go and do to her in private? He thinks he's God, I guess. I can't be the reason he flips."

Collin puts his arm around my shoulder and pulls me in, kissing my head.

"Well, why don't you go and get a little rest. We can order in tonight if you want."

"Thanks."

I take him up on his offer. I go up into our bedroom and lie across the neatly made bed. I watch the ceiling fan swirl above my head and force myself not to cry. I try not to think of Luke, the back of his skull concave against the pool deck. His arms were sprawled out on either side, his hands limp. I spent time studying his hands, kissing each finger on afternoons in bed together. I quickly try to think about something else so I stay in control, so I don't sit at the dinner table with my children with a red nose and puffy eyes. A light rap on the door, and Rachel pokes her head in.

"Mom?" she whispers, probably instructed by Collin not to wake me. I sit up quickly, turning to her.

"Yeah, honey."

"Dad said to see what you wanted to order for dinner."

"What do you want, sweetie?" I ask, and she looks shocked. I can tell she doesn't know if she can suggest junk food.

"Umm, can we get pizza?"

"Sure," I say quickly, and I see her eyes widen.

"Really?"

"Yeah, go ahead and order. Don't forget to get half sausage for Grandma Claire on one." Rachel runs out the door before I change my mind. I hear her tell Ben that I said yes, and he makes a squeaky, delighted noise. Maybe I am too much of a stickler about health food. In Claire's day, she ate like a queen and drank red wine every day. Rich foods, no regrets. She was a spitfire, a free spirit. We used to be so close, and I miss her.

We have an impromptu movie night with our pizza. I wheel Claire over so she can be seated at the end of the couch and see the TV. Ben brings her a plate with her favorite sausage slice on it. He's in a happy mood tonight and that has made the mood in the house happy too. It makes life so much easier.

Rachel is flopped, long-legged, on the love seat, scrolling on her phone while she eats. Ben sits on the floor against the coffee table, gobbling away and flipping channels, trying to find something we'll all agree to watch, while Collin and I are on the couch, my feet tucked under his leg as I lean against the arm of the couch with a blanket over my legs, picking onions off my slice. I don't deserve him.

When Ben stops at *Toy Story 2*, Rachel yells out a "no way, come on. *Nightmare on Elm Street* is on two channels, can we…" She stops when I give her a look. She knows that Ben is too young.

"Just sayin'. It's Halloween almost. Something scary."

"What about *Ghostbusters*?" Collin tries to offer a neutral selection.

"If it's the one with women, then fine." Rachel puts down her phone, readying herself for this very important argument. Collin is clueless.

"Huh?"

"Uh, hello. The new version with Melissa McCarthy?" Rachel, my budding feminist.

Collin shrugs. I pick up Ben's Ninja Turtle costume that I'm working on, and click on the side-table light. I need to finish his belt, which has the letter *D* embossed in the front because he insists on being Donatello.

"Go to On Demand, Ben," Rachel orders, excited for her female *Ghostbusters* screening. Ben flips around, trying to find the right buttons, and he lands on the local news. Suddenly, Luke's face is in high-def on a seventy-inch television right in front of me.

I go pale. I don't move, I don't look at Collin. We get news out of New Orleans and there are ten stories like this a day. In a second, Rachel will yell at Ben to go to channel 1000 for On Demand and it will be gone. I can't let them see my face. My heart thrums, my ears ring.

"Eeew. Change it," Rachel says, looking up from her phone.

Ben throws her the remote and it falls between the wall and the side of the love seat, unreachable.

"Guys, come on." Collin stands and helps Rachel fish it out while Ben dances around behind him, like a basketball player blocking a shot, ready to steal the remote back when it's retrieved.

I can't take my eyes away from Luke's face. The news anchor cuts to a reporter on the scene. Janelle Johnson is standing in front of Luke's house with a microphone, reading a teleprompter. I catch her comment midsentence.

"It's here in the backyard of his rented home that police found him. The well-known romance writer keeps a residence here part-time to be near family, and police are baffled by the crime." They cut to Luke's brother, Julian, who holds a toddler on his hip. The camera crew lights shine on him in the otherwise dark street shot with police tape flapping in the background. He's holding back tears, his voice breaking.

"We're devastated. We just want to know what happened to my brother. He was the greatest guy on earth."

I've never seen a photo of Julian before, but I know so much about him and now, here he is. He has Luke's square jaw and hazel eyes.

"Mom! Tell Ben to give it!" Rachel yells when Ben runs away with the remote, still fighting for his *Toy Story 2*. I can't move.

"Ben, come on." Collin goes down the hall after him as Ben giggles. I know Collin is trying to be stern, but gentle enough to avoid a fit. Janelle Johnson reappears on the screen.

"At this point we know that there was an anonymous caller who reported that there was some sort of struggle or fight at the residence. We urge whomever it was to get in touch with police. They certainly have more questions for the caller."

Collin lumbers back over with Ben on his back, blocking my view of the TV a moment. He's using the threat of losing pizza privileges to ensure Ben's mood stays positive. Collin grabs the remote and starts to turn the channel.

"No, wait," I say, louder than intended. Collin stops as demanded and looks at me, then to the TV.

"What's up?" he says, still out of breath as Ben is jumping on his lap and laughing. The news anchor continues, but there are parts I missed.

"Police are ruling this a homicide. Anyone with information, please call…" But before she rattles off the number, I cover for myself.

"Nothing, just careful, you're knocking pizza on the floor, Ben."

"Sorrrry," he says, hopping playfully back over to his place at the coffee table and taking another slice of pizza as Rachel finally takes control of the remote and switches it over to order the movie.

Collin twists the cap off a beer and settles back onto the couch next to me.

"Did you know there was an all-female remake of this?" he asks me, tucking my feet back under his leg.

"Um, yeah, I think I saw a preview." My eyes are glazed and my voice is flat. I can't fall to pieces. I force a smile. "Can I have one of those?" I ask, pointing to his beer.

"'Course." He hands me his and goes to the kitchen for another. I press the cool, sweating bottle to my neck and breathe deeply. *Stay strong*, I tell myself. *Keep it together.*

While everyone is engrossed in the movie, my mind reels. I'm devastated, of course, but I'm terrified for myself. I'm not exactly afraid of being a suspect; I'm afraid that something will link me to Luke that will out my relationship with him and destroy my family. The police won't know I was there that day, or that I moved things, took his phone. There is absolutely no evidence. Besides, what motive would I have? I go over and over it in my mind, the play-by-play of my time in that house. I can't think of anything I might have left. They would need to have evidence to arrest me in order to get fingerprints or DNA. It would be there, of course, but there is nothing tying me to the crime, so that can't happen. It can't.

Over the following days, I do my best to busy myself with the day-to-day. I embrace it, actually. It's as if I survived a near-death experience, and each mundane moment now feels precious and invaluable. I spend time on Pinterest searching healthy dinner ideas, and I start to plan meals for the week, making soups in the Crock-Pot and freezing them, testing gluten-free bread recipes and frequenting the local farmers market. I pick four large pumpkins out of the giant boxes in front of the supermarket to carve with the kids. Ben is thrilled as we spread newspaper over the table and scoop out pumpkin guts and bake up the seeds. We put candles in our clumsily carved masterpieces and display them on the stairs in front of the house.

It feels almost normal, but in the afternoons when everyone's gone, I watch the coverage on Luke, carefully. They just keep replaying the same summary. They don't seem to have much else. I start to wonder if the only reason they think foul play was involved is because of my stupid phone call. Why the hell did I panic and say I heard a fight? What if it really was just a drunken accident? The dropped phone, a few things out of place—he could have gotten hammered and simply fallen. A single guy, no kids, nowhere to be every morning, why not get tanked just for the hell of it—just because you have good whiskey handy and finished a chapter you were working on. I breathe a slight sigh of relief, knowing that things seem to be at a standstill with whatever investigation they're doing, and maybe it will prove to be nothing more than bad judgment on his part. I ache at the thought of this. No matter what happened, how it happened, he's gone. I don't want to let myself indulge in these thoughts, so I find a quick distraction. I turn off the news and call Lacy. I've canceled on her twice since this all happened. I should check in, see if she wants to grab a coffee.

When her voice mail picks up, I leave a message and apologize for the last couple of times I had to cancel, and ask if she wants to grab a drink or coffee after my writing group tonight.

I hang up and look at my phone. I haven't wanted to face her since I found out about her and Luke. It infuriates me, but rationally, I know it's not her fault. She has no idea. I'm a happily married woman. I'm the shitty one. She should be angry with me for messing up something that might have been just what she needed to move on from Joe, not the other way around. I have no right to harbor resentment. I wonder how she took the news about Luke. She must know; the whole town knows. I guess if she feels scorned by him, maybe she isn't torn up over it.

I haven't been able to name it—this feeling that everything is moving in slight slow motion. Maybe it's because I am overtly conscious of every moment, I'm not rushing through a task or conversation to get to the next thing, as we all do most of the time. I'm letting myself experience each day, staying in the moment to savor it. Gratitude. That's what it is. I feel fortunate to have this second chance, to not have lost everything that matters to me, and I'm not taking it for granted.

When I go back to the bookstore for the writing group that night I have nothing to share, I'm not writing anything, but I feel like I need to return to routine and Collin thinks this is something I've committed to and love, so I'm going to at least go through the motions right now. I don't see the group gathered, so I buy a cup of hot chamomile tea at the café and sit on a bench in front of the building to wait for people to arrive. The temperature is dipping down into the sixties in the evening and it's a welcome relief from the blistering summer heat. I close my eyes against the breeze and push away any rogue thoughts that try to creep in. After twenty minutes, nobody from the group is here, and I wonder if they relocated or something during my time away. I still have Mia's text, so I message her, asking where everyone is. She calls me right back.

"Hey! Group is canceled again. Sorry nobody told you."

"Oh, that's okay. Canceled tonight, or for good?" I ask.

"Well, I don't know. Jonathan is in the hospital, and frankly, I don't know if anyone else wants the role of leader, organizer, all the crap that comes with that, so I guess we'll see if he comes back, but for now we're on a hiatus."

"Hospital. Is he okay?"

"I think so. He's not in the regular hospital, he's in like a psych ward kinda thing. Steve said he had a nervous breakdown. I don't even really know what that means exactly, but that's all they told me."

"Oh, that's terrible. I hope he's okay."

"Yeah, me too. We're all gonna see him, bring him a card and stuff when he's out. Even though he's a dick, I guess it's the right thing to do."

"Right, well, let me know. I'll send something along."

"Cool. Anyway, everyone was getting busy anyway with the holidays coming up and stuff. I'm sure we'll start up again at some point. Maybe we can start our own, make it less shitty."

"Okay, well, thanks," I say. "Let me know."

"Sure. I'll keep ya posted," Mia says, and we hang up. I've never heard of someone actually having a nervous breakdown in real life, and I wonder what happens to a person to cause such a thing. My phone vibrates in my hand. It's a text from Lacy. Thank God. I was starting to get worried about her, wondering if she was safe. She says she just noticed my message and she's at Rodney's if I want to stop in. Ugh, I detest that place, but I'm already right here with canceled plans, so I tell her I'll be there.

It smells as rancid as I remember it from last time, except there are fewer people on a weeknight. Lacy is in a booth in the back corner, flicking a penny in figure skater spins across the tabletop. As I approach her, she smacks the penny with a loud bang to stop it spinning, and the noise startles me.

"Hi there," I say, trying to appear cheerful, normal. I haven't seen her since she told me she was sleeping with Luke. The thought makes me want to go throw up.

"Hey." She appears a little tipsy. It's two-for-one night, as it turns out, and she has a couple of empty gin and tonics in front of her and two full ones. I see there are scratches on her face, but I don't say anything. When I sit, she pushes one of the drinks across the table to me.

"How are you?" I ask.

"Did you know Luke Ellison is dead? It's all over the news." She doesn't look up at me. There is a coaster made of flimsy cardboard that she absently cracks into four pieces and sticks to the condensation on the sides of her glass. Her voice has a whimpery tone.

"Yeah. That's…horrible."

Then I see that her left foot is sticking out from under the table because it has a brace on it. I look from her ankle to her face. It's visibly scraped.

"What happened to you?" I can't believe that she'd gone

back to Joe Brooks after everything. And maybe it's partly my fault because I took Luke away from her. They could have had a fling at least, that might have kept her away from Joe long enough to get past him and move on.

"Oh, nothin'. I fell at work."

"At the truck stop. You fell?" I ask, but she doesn't meet my eyes.

"No. I got canned from the truck stop, so I went back to Candy's," she says it like it's no big deal, but her eyes don't match her words. Candy's is the strip club. *What did Joe do to get her fired?* is my first thought. I wonder how often he frequents Candy's now, to see her.

"Okay," is all I say, trying not to appear judgmental.

"It's dark in there, it's easy to trip," she says defensively. "It's just a small fracture."

I don't believe her for a second, but I know I can't react. "Sorry about your job at the truck stop."

"Yeah. It's whatever." She makes a dismissive gesture, her words loose in her mouth from the alcohol. I push the drink she gave me away subtly. I don't want it. I don't want to be here, really. I feel like I've betrayed Lacy and I also can't help her because she doesn't want me to, and really, do I want to draw any attention to myself at this point even if she did want help?

I stare past the bar, looking at nothing in particular. Just thinking about how to move this along so I can go. It's not that I don't like Lacy; I actually really do. But I'm suddenly wondering if being seen with her is a good idea. Now that I think of it, did others see her with Luke? I can't believe I have never thought about that. If she's connected to him, and I'm hanging out with her, will they question me too?

I hear the front door of the bar open. I glance over and don't believe what I see. It's a cop, in uniform. He walks right to the bar, all business like he needs to ask the bartender or manager something important. Then he looks over at our table and I see who it is. It's Joe Brooks.

15

His face brightens and transforms into a wide smile upon seeing me. It dawns on me that he has no idea I know all about him. To him, I'm just Bennett's mom from baseball, Mel from high school. He walks right over to me. My heart beats in my throat and my head feels tight.

"Mel, hey there. What are you doing here?" he says jovially. Almost too upbeat. I stand to greet him and he gives me a half hug. He sees Lacy right across from me, but says nothing to her. He pretends he doesn't know her.

"Oh, my Thursday group got canceled, so, ya know, just enjoying a few kid-free hours. What about you?"

"Picking up dinner. Best wings in town." He still doesn't even look at her. She's looking at the table with her head low.

"Oh, I didn't know that."

"Yep. You gotta try 'em. How's Ben doin'?" he asks. Is he trying to punish her in some fucked-up way, or is it a show for me? I decide to introduce her. Maybe it will help because if I act like I don't know they know one another, he will not suspect she's told me anything about him. Which of course, is exactly what he wants.

"Good. He's doin' great at his new school."

"Oh, that's good to hear."

"I'm so sorry. This is Lacy, by the way. I'm so rude." I watch his face as it reddens. He does not want to be forced to acknowledge her.

"Oh, I didn't see you there," he lies, nodding to her out of painful obligation.

"Oh, you know each other?" I ask.

"I come here a lot. It's a small town," he says, and I remember that she mentioned she waitresses here sometimes. He's smart. He's admitting acquaintanceship rather than denying knowing her altogether. I try to reinforce the fact that I don't know her well—that it's a chance thing.

"Right, well I don't get out as much as the single folks, but last time I was here I wasn't looking and I accidentally bumped into her while she had a full tray of drinks, can you believe that? The whole tray just dumped all over her. Poor thing. I forced her to let me make it up to her and buy her a drink next time I came out." I give a little laugh to punctuate my story.

"Well, I'm glad you can sneak out and get some time for yourself now and then. You're the hardest working mom I know." A waitress comes over and hands him a plastic bag, knotted at the top, with foam to-go boxes inside. "Good to see you, Mel," he says, and then leaves with his order. He's good. Smooth. I look at Lacy.

"You okay?"

"I'm fine." She pulls a few napkins out of the dispenser on the table and wipes her eyes, trying to dab gently around her thick mascara so she doesn't streak it.

"I didn't know what to do. I wanted to make sure he didn't think you told me anything."

"Don't worry. He's positive I won't tell anyone. He'd never think that. He's an expert at protecting himself and making everyone think I'm crazy. He knows I learned my lesson the first time…and there's no use. Telling only gets me in trouble." Her voice is flat. She twirls a short straw inside her fizzy drink and a tear drops to the table. She pulls out a tiny compact mirror and examines her face. She dabs again around her eyes, sighing, giving up on trying to fix it.

I want to say that I wasn't worried for myself. Does she think that was a self-motivated move? Maybe it was. I try to erase the last few minutes by handing my card to the waitress and telling her to put all the drinks on me. Lacy's demeanor changes and she looks at me with wide eyes.

"Thanks!" she says, and I try to keep the look of pity out of my eyes as I watch her, bruised and battered, sucking down alcohol at record speed to numb herself, longing for another life. I don't know what it is about her. I guess I see this person just under the surface that was bound for greater things once, like myself. Obligation keeps her here, away from the excitement and opportunity, culture and variety a city could offer. A city full of life, shifting and pulsing, not sedating, like the anesthetic of this sleepy town. I buy her a last round before making an excuse to go home.

* * *

I need to keep it together. It's the night of the big Halloween party at the community center where everyone takes their kids to hit piñatas for their candy instead of trick-or-treating. It's been tradition ever since the media scared everyone with stories of poison and needles showing up in the candy. With a crime like this happening in our safe town, I would be surprised if we see one kid on the streets trick-or-treating.

Over the last few years the tradition went from being just for the young kids to quite the community event. There's a costume contest, a dance for the older kids and cash bar for the adults. I know I'll see all of the neighborhood moms. Gillian and Karen will use it as an excuse to dress like "slutty cats," wearing corsets and headbands with cat ears attached. The last thing I feel like doing is pretending to celebrate while overhearing whispers about the murder, but I need to keep a normal routine. I usually volunteer on the cleanup committee and help with decorations, and I haven't called to offer my time this year, so I certainly have to at least show up.

I stand in the living room with Ben, who is wiggling in his costume as I try to sew on a couple of the last details. Collin has fed Claire tonight, and I hear him put her plate in the dishwasher and come into the living room. He sits and flips channels.

"You look great, sport," he says to Ben. Rachel surprises me when she comes in with a Rosie the Riveter costume.

"Wow, look at you." I smile, impressed.

154

"Cool, Rach. Who are you supposed to be?" Collin says, and Rachel and I roll our eyes at one another.

"Dad."

"What? Lucille Ball?" he says, genuinely thinking he nailed it.

"Who?" Rachel asks.

"I think you need some red lipstick with that outfit," I interrupt.

"Really?" she asks, excited. I take the sewing pin out of my mouth and hold Ben's hem taut, nodding in the direction of our room.

"In my top drawer," I say, and she runs to find it. I find adults dressing up for Halloween obnoxious and I'm glad Collin has no interest either. He smiles at me and shrugs, admitting he truly doesn't understand her costume. He lips to the local news. The meteorologist says there will be scattered showers later in the evening, and then the face of an impossibly thin woman with a nest of strawberry hair that seems to swallow her up appears on the screen. In the corner, the name "Georgia Bouvier" appears, along with the word "witness" underneath it. When she speaks, her words are barely understandable through her thick drawl.

"I was walking my dogs down past the woods behind Main Street there, just near the man's house, I guess. I didn't know no one lived there again. I heard somethin'. Some yellin' I think it was, but I didn't think much of it at the time."

The screen cuts back to the news anchors, who try to decode the woman's statement.

"The police believe that the anonymous 911 call made just before 9 p.m. the night of the murder is suspicious because this witness, Georgia Bouvier—in addition to the victim's estimated time of death, per the coroner's office— indicates that this crime took place a couple of hours *before* the anonymous call was made. When asked exactly what she heard, Bouvier said it sounded like a man yelling at someone to 'get out.' This was closer to 7 p.m. More on this as it develops."

"Mom," Ben complains. I've stopped working on his mask and stand with it in my hands, fixated on the TV. I quickly refocus my attention and make sure my voice sounds light.

"Alllmost done here." I tie on his little mask and he hops off the step stool he was standing on and runs to look at himself in the mirror. Collin has flipped to some sports headline show as he laces up his dress shoes at the edge of the couch. I feel like I could be sick. Who was Luke yelling at to get out? Rachel comes back with bright red lips.

"Are we ready?" she asks impatiently, not looking up from her phone where she texts Katie photos of her costume. It's nice to see they're still friends, despite Katie's move. I suppose that's one thing social media is good for.

"Come on, kiddo," Collin calls to Ben, who is bounding down the hall and directly out the door to the car. As we put on our coats, Collin whispers, "I'll drive so you can get nice and tipsy for later." He raises his eyebrows at me, flirting, and kisses me on the cheek. "I mean, if you want." I try very hard to make my face look the way it's supposed to look, and not drained of blood and apathetic.

"And me without my slutty cat costume," I say back, smiling. I'm trying to resemble the person I was not so long ago.

At the party, Collin stands in a circle of dads who make

chitchat and drink beer near the bar. I spot Liz and Tammy by the punch bowl. They wave and come over.

"Long time, no see," Liz says, sipping a martini. She's dressed like Cher and calls Tammy and me party poopers since we didn't dress up.

"It has been," I say. They never really give me much guff about being busy, since they know the history with Ben and the stress they "could not even imagine," and they think I am " just a saint" to handle it all so well. *Yeah*, I think to myself, *I handled it as poorly as a mother possibly could.*

"We loved having you at the book club. You should come by next week, join us again."

"Okay, I might," I say. My smile is weak and my voice is tired, I can tell.

"Goddamn it," Liz says running over to the barrels where the kids are bobbing for apples and her son is starting to unzip his little fly. "It's not a toilet, Brian!" she yells, picking him up before he pees in the apple water.

Tammy looks at me and giggles. Gillian and Karen are coming over from the beer garden, dressed as twin cats. Behind them I glance over to Collin who mouths an exaggerated *Pineapples?* It's our code word at parties. He's asking if I want him to come and save me. I can't help but smirk at this. It's been a long time since we pulled out that little trick. I mouth back with a laugh, *It's okay.*

"Hey, girls!" Gillian hoots, and after a few minutes of small talk she's already scanning the room for women to make fun of.

"Eleven o'clock. Dear Lord." We all look over to our left.

"Who is it?" Liz asks.

"Elaine Fitch."

"Fattest Wonder Woman I have ever seen," Tammy adds, saying what they were all thinking, and they cackle together. A kid dressed as a ghost walks over to us. A small voice comes from under his white sheet. He looks up at me. I see two blue eyes blink behind the jagged-cut eyeholes.

"Are you Melanie?" he asks. I assume he's one of Ben's friends.

"I am. Who are you?" I kneel down to him. But he doesn't answer, he just hands me a little pumpkin-shaped felt candy bag.

"Why, thank you," I say, but he turns and walks away, disappearing into the crowd of kids around the apple barrels in front of us. Gillian gives an animated "Oh, that's so sweet" look and clasps her hand to her heart.

"Well, does someone have a tiny admirer?" Karen jokes.

"Probably a bribe from Ben to stay out longer." I open it and pick a chocolate coin off the top. Then I see something else in the bag. There is something small and heavy at the bottom. My heart starts to pound. I scan the room, looking for the kid who gave it to me, wanting to go after him, but not wanting to look like a lunatic in front of the gossip squad. I peel the wrapper off the chocolate in my hand and put it in my mouth with a look to the other women like I'm being naughty for eating it. I'm trying to stay calm. We have a brief conversation about how many calories are in a martini, and after an acceptable amount of small talk time, I hurriedly excuse myself to the bathroom.

I go into one of the stalls and sit on the toilet. I'm sweating, trembling. I look inside the bag and pull out a cell phone. I don't understand. It's like the disposable phone Luke gave me, but I know it can't be. That one is on the bottom of the bay. No, this one is a new one. The buttons are different. It's not the one I had, but whose is it and what the hell is it doing in this bag? I flip it open and it has one text message, marked as unread. Who was that kid? Is this meant for me? Maybe it's a mistake. I stare at it before I shakily click open the message. I look at the screen in utter disbelief as I read.

I KNOW WHAT YOU DID, MELANIE HALE.

I almost drop it, my hands are shaking so violently, but I don't. I place it gingerly on top of the metal toilet paper holder and stare at it. I dab the sweat on my forehead and try to catch my breath. Does someone know about the affair, or did someone see me at his house the night he died? Does someone think I killed him? No, that can't be. This can't be happening. I text back, WHO IS THIS?

I wait, but there is no reply.

16

I search the party for the ghost child. Whoever sent this to me is here, but since everyone is in disguise, there is no way to know who sent that kid over. They could have paid a random child in treats to walk over to me anonymously like that—they just chose the most covered-up kid so I couldn't find him later. And I can't. Maybe whoever sent him simply placed a sheet over his head and told him it would be a fun Halloween prank. There are no kids dressed like ghosts. I can't keep making circles around the place. I can't behave strangely. Faking illness to leave early would also be out of the ordinary, so I stand near Collin, who is still in midconversation with the group of husbands near the bar. He slips an arm around my waist. I smile, pretending to listen, but I am thinking, going over and over in my mind how this happened. I was careful.

All the way home, Rachel silently cries with her earbuds in. Despite her giddy text exchanges with Katie, she's still angry her friend has moved away and is making sure we know we didn't do enough to change that fact and have assisted in ruining her life. Ben is listing every single name on each piece of candy in his stash, counting them and grouping them into favorites. By the time we pull into the drive, he's finally sleeping. Collin carries him to bed, and Rachel slams her door, taking her adolescent pain out on everyone around her. I go up to the bathroom and run the shower so I have a minute to hide the phone. There is no text back from whoever sent the first text to me. I need to keep it and wait for an answer. I create a PIN so I can lock it. Then I put it in the bottom of a tampon box, a place Collin would never look, and then stack a box of soap and some wash- cloths on top of it.

The bathroom has filled with steam, so I quickly undress and step into the shower just before Collin comes in. He's telling me about Ben's sugar crash as he carefully takes off his clothes, hanging his dress shirt in the adjacent closet and binding his socks together before he tosses them into the hamper. I can't really hear him over the pounding water. Then I feel the cool draft as he opens the shower door and presses his body against mine from behind. I hold his arms and pull them tightly around me. I need him. I wish I could tell him that I'm in trouble. I wish I hadn't ruined our lives. The steam masks the well of tears in my eyes, and we kiss, slipping into easy, familiar lovemaking before bed.

I lie awake as Collin snores lightly beside me. The windows in the bedroom are open and I relish the sweet, earthy smell the breeze carries in. Our room is decorated with carefully chosen whites and grays, a puffy down comforter and good linens. I wanted it to feel light and airy, soft—a sanctuary. My peaceful surroundings are doing nothing to curb my nauseating anxiety. I don't know him well enough to know who'd want to hurt him, and I suppose, if I'm honest with myself, I wasn't careful. I was too seduced by the white-hot lust and the thrill of it to be as vigilant as I thought I was. Because someone knows.

Suddenly, I remember something. The thought makes me sit straight up in bed with my eyes wide. Jonathan Wilderman. He said it the very first day: he can't stand Luke. That doesn't make a person a murderer, of course, but he thinks Luke stole his story—and therefore his success and potential fortune. Those are high stakes. People kill for much less. All of a sudden he leaves the group right after all this and has a nervous breakdown? Only something very traumatic, I imagine, would give someone a nervous breakdown. *Oh my God.*

The police are keeping the cause of death quiet. I don't know if there was a gunshot or stab wound that I didn't see. It just looked like the fall had smashed his skull, but I can't be sure. I wonder why they haven't released that part. I need to see Jonathan. Just a friendly visit. I should bring a card and make sure he's feeling better. That's innocuous enough. Anyone would do the same. I'll go tomorrow.

The next morning, I text Mia to see which hospital he's in and she replies telling me he's been discharged. I ask for his address, say I want to send a card. On the way, I stop at a coffee shop and spend some time trying to see what I can find out about Jonathan online. He looks like he stepped out of a *Lord of the Rings* film with his long beard and cape-like coats he wears even in the heat of the summer, so I can't imagine he's that social media savvy. He likely hosts basement gatherings to engage in role-playing games or Dungeons and Dragons tournaments. Jonathan Wilderman. A few come up, but can be eliminated immediately. I narrow the search by adding our county after his name. I don't see much: no Instagram, no images when you google him. I do see a nerdy Twitter account. That's him. A close-up of his face taken from a very low and unflattering angle. I scroll through his tweets. All of them are literary quotes. Nothing telling.

On a drizzly late Saturday morning, I walk up a long dirt drive carrying a plastic cone of grocery store flowers. Jonathan's house is in a rural area on the edge of town, and I don't expect what I see when I reach the end of the winding drive. It resembles a shack more than a house. The outside of it looks like somebody emptied a dumpster on top of it. Hub caps decorate the side of the house in massive piles. There's a rusted push mower, a seat that looks like it was pulled from a van and a couple of old oscillating fans with metal blades, all piled on top of one another in front of the house, among many other piles of junk. A few garden gnomes, kind of terrifying with missing noses and fingers, sticking out of a stained twin mattress. This is beyond eclectic. He's a hoarder. I step over the skeletons of discarded furniture that have been invaded with years of damp, and before I reach the front door, I hear a voice.

"Can I help you?"

I jump. There is a bony woman in a housecoat who blends into the clutter, and I didn't see her. She's looking right at me. Her wisp of white hair disappears into the milky gray backdrop on this hazy day, so she appears bald at first. She doesn't get up from her ancient metal deck chair when she calls to me, a long cigarette hanging from her lips.

"Oh. Yes. Hi. I'm—uh, I heard Jonathan was ill."

"Yep."

"So, I—I'm sorry. I'm Mel. From his writing group at Classics Bookstore."

"Oh, you're a writing friend. Come on up." She pushes a wooden chair with the back broken off in my direction, and I sit.

"Thanks. The others said they were gonna stop by when he got back home."

"Yep. They did." *Great*, I think, *this will seem less strange, then.*

"I felt bad I wasn't able to come, so I was out and about today, and I wanted to just drop this off and wish him well."

"That's nice of you. He's sleepin'. I'm not supposed to wake him. He needs his rest."

"Oh, I understand. Are you his…" I never imagined him with a wife, so I almost guess sister.

"Wife. Barbie. Nice to meet ya." She doesn't make eye contact or shake my hand, just rocks back in her chair and smokes. I hand her the flowers. Inside the front window I see stacks and stacks of books piled from floor to ceiling. It reeks like cigarettes and neglect. "Is he going to be okay?"

"Oh, that old fart will be fine. You're a pretty thing, aren't ya?" She changes gears so quickly, I'm taken aback. It sounds like more of an accusation than a compliment.

"Oh. Thanks?"

"You're a writer, then?"

"No, not really. No. I just was dabbling, really. I guess."

"John!" she screams into the house out of nowhere, and a yelp escapes my lips involuntarily. She doesn't acknowledge it, just nods as if she's confirmed something of great importance. "Yep. Sleepin'."

"That's really okay. I just wanted to drop these off."

"Dabbling, huh? John takes it all too seriously."

"Oh, does he?" I ask, hoping to hear more.

"He thinks he should have won at least a Booker Prize, whatever the hell that is, by now. His blood pressure is too high and the goddamn vein in his neck is always popping out anytime someone else gets published who he doesn't respect. It's killin' him. It's his own damn fault." She pushes her feet in and out of her pink, threadbare slippers as she talks. Maybe this is a segue and I can ask more.

"It has to be tough for someone like him when other people steal his ideas, I'm sure."

"Who stole his idea this time?" she yells in a puff of exhaled smoke, then laughs a quick, bitter laugh.

"No, I—I just heard that he thought…"

"Oh, Jesus. He thinks everyone stole his idea. Goddamn Stephen King stole his last idea, didn't you hear? Call the press!" She wheezes and coughs for a short spell.

Well, that's that, I guess. Just a high-strung, failed writer blaming the world for his situation.

"Ya didn't hear? Well, I heard. I heard allll about it for days until he spent a day in bed with chest pain and finally shut up. Ya want a cigarette?"

"Oh, I'm all right. I should go."

"He probably won't sleep all day, you can come back later if ya want."

"You know, if you could just give him the flowers, that should be good. I would have mailed them, but I was in the area." I hope she doesn't start yelling again and wake him up, accidentally. I want to leave. I stand. Thankfully, she doesn't counter, she just picks up a Coors Light bottle full of cigarette butts and jams the one in her hand inside.

"Okay, then." She gives a sharp wave, and I tiptoe through the organized trash and make my way back down the drive. The whole thing was a bit unsettling, but I got my answer. Which is actually disappointing because it was the only lead I had.

I have to take Ben to a swimming lesson at the aquatic center at two, so I head home, taking the route through downtown, using Main. I pull off the side street and go down the alley that separates the heart of town from the dirt clearing and then wooded area that leads to Luke's. I don't know why I stop. I'm not close enough for it to appear suspicious. Main Street looks abandoned anyway in the rain, but I just need a minute. What was I thinking, sneaking back through those trees like that? I must have lost my mind.

I see something in the distance. A figure moving through slanted lines of rain. Someone is running, rounding the wooded area and coming this way through the flat dirt leading to the main road. Coming right toward me. The only thing back there is Luke's place. Who could be running from that direction? Are they coming from his house? I want to put the car in Reverse and leave, but I'm fixated, looking at the figure.

Just when it looks like they will jog directly in front of my car, they duck to the right and out of sight in the alley. They don't notice me. Just when I resolve to back up, there's a tap on my window. I leap back. Then I see a familiar face, under a rain parka, laughing.

"I'm sorry, Mel. I didn't mean to startle you. Jumpy much? I thought you saw me coming." It's Mia.

"Wha-what are you doing here?" I stutter. My mind is searching for any plausible scenario where her running from Luke's house would make sense.

"What do ya mean? I'm running."

"Running?"

"Got a 10K next weekend."

I still look at her blankly. "In the rain?" I ask.

"Rain or shine," she says. I don't see headphones, but some people don't use them for races. It's weird, but if she's covering for something, why would she stop to say hello? If she's covering for something, she sure isn't acting nervous.

"Out here?" I look around and she seems confused by my confusion. I guess she could have been just running *past*, not *into* the trees that lead to his house. I didn't actually see her come through them. She just sort of appeared. I relax a little.

"Uh, yeah. I live just down on Park and Fourth. Close. You okay?"

"Yeah. I'm…yeah."

"Hey, I was thinking, we should talk more about making our own writing group…but like without any psychos like

Jonathan or hotshot writers ruining it with loud readings in the background. Just cool people, maybe some booze involved." She laughs. "You in?"

"Yeah, maybe. I'll think on it."

"I'll text you," she says, before she pulls her rubber hood tighter with two drawstrings and jogs off down Main. What exactly does she have against Jonathan, and was the hotshot writer comment a dig at Luke? There were a few other authors who gave readings at the bookstore over the summer. I'm sure it was a general statement, and I'm sure that she is really just jogging. I didn't know she ran races, but how well do I know her? She didn't look dressed for training, but I guess a runner would throw a rain parka on over running clothes in this weather. There are perfectly reasonable explanations for why Mia was running from Luke Ellison's property.

I remember the story she wrote in for the writing group. She seemed a little too comfortable describing murder and slow revenge in great detail. I feel my stomach turn when I think about the possibility that she was sleeping with him too. If it was easy to have a fling with Lacy, why not her? A single guy stuck in this small town. I take a deep breath and blow it out through my mouth, hard. No. I can't let myself get paranoid.

17

When I get home, Ben is playing a video game—some car racing thing—Rachel is on her laptop with headphones attached, settled into the recliner in the living room, and Collin is napping on the couch between them. Not a bad way to spend a rainy day. I see Collin has made some cinnamon rolls from a tube, the cardboard curl and tub of sugary icing discarded in the sink. I pour a cup of coffee and instinctively check on Claire the way I usually do when I come in. I grab the last cinnamon roll and put it on a small plate to take to her.

"Hey, bub, get your swim stuff together," I say to Ben as I make my way down the hall. I see Claire's door cracked open. That's odd; she always keeps it closed. She prefers her privacy, and she sleeps most of the time. Although I know she doesn't have the capacity to do so, sometimes I think she wants it that way to protect the kids from seeing her waste away, but that's not really possible, I know. I don't think too much of it until I open the door, peering in, and don't see her in her usual spot, propped up in her bed with the TV and fan on. She wanders to the bathroom on her own sometimes. I put the plate down, and I check the bathroom. Then I check all the other rooms in the back of the house, telling myself she's just wandered off down the hall somewhere, before shouting to Collin and running to the living room, looking again inside each door on my way.

"Collin!"

I see him sit up quickly, pretending he wasn't asleep.

"Mel, what's wrong?"

"Where's your mom?"

"What do you mean?" He hasn't registered my panic yet.

"She's not in her room, or any of the back rooms. Kids, go check the rest of the house, look in your rooms."

Ben starts to cry. He cannot handle shouting or any kind of stress or emergency without shutting down. I should have been more careful.

"Mom?" Collin starts calling around the house. I comfort Ben.

"Honey, it's okay. Nobody is upset, it's just not like your grandma to go anywhere on her own." I make my voice overly light. "It's fine, baby."

He calms a little.

"Do you wanna help?"

He nods and goes to check his room. We clear all the rooms, and Rachel even checks behind every shower curtain and behind open doors like it's a deranged game of hide-and-seek. Collin runs down to look in the basement, and I carefully open the sliding glass door as a clap of thunder sounds and the gathering storm inches closer. I'm afraid to look in the backyard. I shudder thinking about Claire wandering off because of our negligence, that I might find her bloated body floating in the backyard pool. The blood around Luke's head flashes in my memory as I walk across the pool deck and peer in. I exhale when I see she's not there.

I meet a panicked Collin back in the living room. He grabs an umbrella from the front closet and starts to put his shoes on.

"When's the last time you saw her?" I ask.

"I don't know. Last night. She was asleep, I thought she was still asleep, right?"

"She was when I checked on her this morning."

"What time?" he demands.

"I guess between six and seven. I left a breakfast tray. I thought she was sleeping late too. Like she usually does." This morning I tiptoed around the kitchen because I was up earlier than everyone. I made up a plate of eggs and toast. She usually wakes up to eat and then naps most of the morning, but she was still out, so I just left it.

I remember this and run back to her room. The food was eaten. Just the crusts left on her bedside tray. The window isn't ajar. I didn't imagine that, distracted as I am. Where could she possibly be?

When I get back to the living room, the kids are slipping rain boots on. Collin is being gentle with the way he handles himself so Ben will want to help and not revert into meltdown mode.

Should we call the cops? I mouth to Collin over Ben, who is sitting on the floor pulling on a sock. He answers out loud because his reply won't scare the kids the way my question would.

"Let's drive around and look for her first. If she slipped out the door, she couldn't have gotten far."

I nod in agreement and we all pile in and drive the tree- lined streets as the sky opens up and the rain falls in torrents, thundering on the metal roof of the car. It's half past noon. I try to think about the window of time she's been gone. She's been unaccounted for for at least five hours. The sliding door was unlocked when I went out to look for her, but it usually is during the day.

Suddenly, I can't help but wonder if that simple sentence on a disposable cell phone, I KNOW WHAT YOU DID, MELANIE HALE, was a threat.

What if someone has taken Claire? It doesn't make sense. They have dirt on me. If they want something in return for keeping quiet, why haven't they asked? I've been going up to the bathroom and checking the phone for a message as often as I safely can. There's been nothing. I feel the bile rise in my stomach as we drive and I think of her scared, hurt…because of me.

After twenty minutes or so, there is a lull in the downpour and we open the car windows.

Ben calls out with hands cupped around his mouth, "Grandmaaaa!"

We've woven through all the streets in a reasonable distance from our house. We stop and ask a few of the neighbors we see sitting out on covered porches. No one has seen her.

"Where is she, Mom? Is she mad at us?" Ben asks, pausing from his steady bellowing of her name.

"No, honey, she just gets mixed up sometimes. You know that. It'll be okay."

I notice that Rachel is quiet. She looks worried, but there's something else too. After about an hour, Collin looks over at me, defeated. I give a nod, and he seems to understand that it means we should go back to the house and call the police.

When we get back, I tell Rachel to occupy Ben with a video game or something so we can talk to the police and he won't get freaked out. She obeys without protest, and they go into his room, where I hear her asking him about his Lego ship and successfully distracting him. Before Collin punches in the numbers to call, I motion for him to wait, and I point out the back sliding door with wide, confused eyes. He puts the phone down and comes over to see what I'm pointing at. It's Claire.

She's sitting on a wrought iron bench in the garden area. She's wearing a white nightgown and her wig is sliding down the side of her head. She's drenched and her hands are covered with mud up the elbow. Her feet are covered too. She stares at the house with a very unsettling look. It makes me shudder. Collin and I stand at the open glass door and stare back a moment. It feels as though she's looking right through us and it's chilling. Then she spits on the ground.

He shakes off the shock of how strange it all is and rushes over to her. I go and grab towels and her robe and hand them to him when he gets her inside.

"Mom, where were you?" he asks, shaken, but he knows that no answer will come. She's looking away, at nothing, her mouth slightly open.

"I'll get her into a bath," I say, knowing that Collin is

eternally grateful that he does not have to see his mother naked, and he knows that she would want it that way too, so I always offer when it comes to things like diapers and bathing. He smiles, gratefully.

"Okay. I'll put some tea on."

"Thanks. Ben missed his swimming thing, so that might take some strategic deflection once he realizes it," I say as I help Claire up the stairs to the bathroom.

"I'm on it." He gives a weak smile and I'm glad we're such a good team with things like this. As I take Claire past Ben's room, Rachel is standing in the doorway, watching us.

"He's playing *Mario Kart*."

"Okay, thanks."

"Need help?" she asks. She doesn't usually volunteer. There is still that same, odd look in her eyes.

"Come on," I say, and she follows to Claire's bathroom. She pulls herself up to sit on the counter while I get Claire into the water.

"Why do you think she walked off like that?" Rachel asks, looking at the tile floor and hooking her hair around her ear.

"Well, sweetie, she gets confused. I don't really know. She hasn't done it before, but maybe she opened the wrong door while everyone was off doing their own thing, and she didn't realize." Rachel nods, tentatively.

"What is it, honey? It's not your fault."

"Okay." She twists her hair around a finger.

"I hope you don't think it is."

"It's just that—it's not the first time."

"What?" I stop washing Claire's back and straighten up, turning to my daughter.

"A week or two ago, I don't remember exactly, I noticed she wasn't in her room. I was the only one home with her, so I panicked. I looked all over and she just showed back up, just like today."

"Why didn't you tell me?"

"You told me to keep an eye on her and I didn't," she says, looking like she may cry.

"Honey, it's not your responsibility to take care of her. That's not fair to you. If we knew she'd ever take off like that I wouldn't have left you alone with her. You should have called me though. One of us would have come home right away. Okay?"

"Yeah. I'm sorry. Where do you think she goes?"

"I don't know, sweetheart, I think she just gets turned around in her mind and she doesn't know what she's doing sometimes." I know that's disturbing to her.

Claire is sitting silently, patiently, in the bathwater with her hairless scalp bobbing slightly, mouth open. She's off somewhere very far away and I can imagine how frightening and ominous that must be for a child to see. It's difficult for *me* still, and each day I handle bodily fluids and discard rancid-smelling linens. I should be used to it, but maybe one never gets accustomed to looking at vacant eyes and a body that has betrayed itself. A soul vacating its body should be reserved for death. This is cruel, a life without memory—without a past or future—she's just existing, and I wonder if living like this is what Claire would have wanted, if she'd had a choice. Or would she have just wanted to go to sleep and not wake up again?

Rachel lowers herself down from the counter and hands me a bath towel for Claire. I hear Ben wailing down the hall. We both know he's realized he missed his swimming lesson he was excited about.

"It's okay, he has a sleepover pizza party thing with his baseball friends tonight. Want me to remind him so he shuts up?" she asks, half out the door, but lingering to wait for my answer.

"Thanks, honey," I say before she disappears into the chaos in the living room. I hear her walk down the hall and call Ben a spaz. But seconds later, his crying is quieted, so I guess it worked.

After I get Claire dressed in a wool nightgown and gently prop her against a heap of pillows in her bed, I hand her a cup of peppermint tea, not too hot, and turn on a channel that plays old, syndicated sitcoms. When I close the door, I go to the kitchen to make the kids some lunch, but Collin has taken care of it. The counter is littered with open pickle jars, ketchup spills and a bag of whole wheat buns that I seal before they go stale. He hands me a turkey burger on a plate, and I smile, exhausted by the task of Claire and grateful the kids have eaten.

"Thank you. This looks great."

"She okay?" he asks as he makes up a plate for her.

"Yeah. She's resting. She's fine as far as I can tell."

"It's so weird that she'd do that." He's cutting a pear into bite-size pieces. "We'll have to figure something out to secure the back door."

"I suppose we will. Like a child lock?" I know it's hard for him, this role reversal with his mother. I try to take the brunt of it so he can maintain a mother-son relationship with her as much as is possible. I really can't imagine seeing my mother like that, so it breaks my heart for him. I don't ask why she'd be muddy up to the elbows—was she digging for something? Where could she have been?

"I guess." He clearly doesn't want to think about it.

I offer to take her plate back, but he says he has it and heads back to her room. Ben bounces into the kitchen holding a Buzz Lightyear sleeping bag. He tosses it next to his overnight bag sitting on a kitchen chair.

"We get to sleep on the floor!" he says excitedly.

"Cool, bud."

"We gotta wear our jerseys."

"I see that. Is it clean?"

But he's already in his number eight baseball jersey. Bless Mrs. Miller for taking on six special needs kids overnight.

"Yeah. Can I wear your Saints cap?"

"Sure, honey. Look in my closet," I say, and he's darting away before I can ask him if he packed his toothbrush. I don't sit to eat; I stop to take bites while I tidy up the kitchen. I scrape plates into the disposal and wipe down the spills on the counter with disinfectant wipes. I don't take for granted the beauty of this simple act—caring after my children. I promise myself not to take anything for granted anymore. I guess guilt offers perspective.

Ben comes back in, minutes later, with an overcome look, giving me a dramatic account of all the places he looked and couldn't find the cap.

"I looked everywheeeere." He drapes himself over the kitchen stool as though the search has drained him and he needs reinforcements. I start to tell him I'll help him look for it, but then I stop cold.

There is no need to look for it, because we won't find it. The doorbell saves me, and I help him on with his backpack and carry his sleeping bag and pillow down the slope of the front yard to meet Sandy Miller at her car and thank her for taking him. I tell her I'll pick him up tomorrow before noon, and then I sit a moment after she drives away, on the front stairs, to collect my thoughts.

The cap isn't here. The night I sat in Luke's truck in the bookstore parking lot, I took it off. Lacy almost caught us, so I rushed out of the car. I left it behind. You'd think that investigators wouldn't look twice at a worn-out Saints cap left in a car. Except that once Ben fell in love with it and kept wearing it to school, I wrote the word *HALE* in Sharpie on the inside of the rim so it wouldn't get lost. My name is literally written somewhere in Luke's property.

18

Collin works from his home office on Monday, and I usually love having him home. It means a long breakfast after the kids leave for school, chatting about nothing in particular over coffee and usually a walk to Edith's Café for lunch, but today I'm fidgety and anxious and I want to be able to catch up on any developments in Luke's case without fear of him seeing me.

I hear him in his office on a work call, talking to Richard, a notoriously high-maintenance client, so I pour a mug of coffee and drop some bread in the toaster. No elaborate breakfast today. The kids had cereal, and I can't concentrate on much more than pouring milk or buttering toast right now. I sit in the window seat next to the dining room table with my coffee, curling my knees to my chest as I watch a fat squirrel balance on a telephone line across the street. Amy Johanson, who lives a few houses down, steps onto her front stoop to collect the morning paper. I watch her clutch her robe at the neck; she's surprised by the chilly wind. The Rodderhams' dog is roaming without a leash again, sniffing his way through the adjacent yards and lifting his leg to every shrub he passes. It's a perfectly normal morning and it seems so hard to believe that Luke is gone and everything just moves ahead as if he were never here.

I think about the Saints cap. I haven't been able to sleep since I remembered it. In Luke's house, which is full of clothes, books, shoes, hats, furniture—a person's whole life, tons of everyday things—why would they notice a ball cap? They don't examine every single item in the house, of course not. They're looking for things that stand out. Why would they even notice it? That is, if he brought it into the house.

Surely he did. He must have seen it on the passenger seat that night, brought it inside, and planned to let me know I'd left it but forgot, so it's sitting on a hook somewhere or on a living room bookshelf, anonymous. I had been in his truck once more since the day I left it there. I'd ducked down in the passenger seat as we drove to a secluded spot near a creek. My toes on the dash, we'd bumped and bobbed through rough terrain, and I'd held on to the door, laughing, as we acted like naive teenagers that day. It shames me to think about now. I would have seen it though, in the cab of his truck, or he would have remembered to return it if it were sitting there on the seat, reminding him every day. It must be tossed somewhere in his house. I need to stay levelheaded. It will not do me any good to start unraveling over the very minute chance it could be noticed.

I notice the smell of burnt toast and see the blackened bread squares smoking in the toaster. Collin comes in, in his T-shirt and flannel pants instead of a shirt and tie; he loves work-from-home days. He won't change into jeans until the kids come home from school if he can help it. He goes to the toaster.

"For me?"

"I'll make some eggs."

"No, I love it like this." He smiles at me, sniffing the charred air. "Like roasted marshmallows. It's perfect." He scrapes some cold butter onto the toast and sits across from me, nibbling at its corners.

I laugh, shaking my head at him.

"Let me make something edible. It's no trouble." I pour him a cup of coffee and place it in front of him, and he pulls me to his lap.

"It's a culinary triumph, seriously." He gives me a bite and we both laugh. He's kind, and he's funny, and I'm lucky. He knows I didn't sleep well.

"A kink in my neck," I lied when he asked again, earlier in the morning, if I was okay. I get them a lot at night, sleeping wrong, so he's trying to make my morning easier.

"Great coffee," he says, and I make a faux-shocked face. He enjoys hating anything brand-name or anything too mainstream, just for the principle of it, so I like to sneak things into his life and not tell him what it is until he admits to liking it. A little game we like to play. He's only been fooled by my trickery once before. He swore whipped cream from scratch was far superior to Cool Whip, so last Thanksgiving I swapped it out and he raved about how good it was. When I pulled out the plastic Cool Whip tub, he knew he'd never live it down. Now I've got him good again, and it's nice to be swept up in a silly moment—a short reprieve from my worrying.

"What?" he asks.

"Nothing?"

"No!" He drops his head into the crook of his arm on the table.

"I didn't say anything." I can't help but laugh a little.

"Just tell me." He's being charmingly overdramatic. I play along and hold my pause before I reveal the source of his coffee.

"Starbucks. Breakfast blend."

"Ahhh." He makes a knife-to-the-heart gesture. I love him. I'm laughing at his antics, but I want to cry at the thought of hurting him. What was I thinking?

He stops goofing around and a serious look comes over his face. I wait for the joke to follow, but it doesn't come. He's looking past me. I turn, following the direction of his gaze. Out the front window, a police car pulls into our driveway.

"Why are the cops here?" he asks, but I'm paralyzed.

Two uniformed men step out of the car and make their way up to our front door, and the fear is making my heart quicken. I can't even set my coffee down. I don't answer, I just watch them, wondering what they'll say, how I'll cover in front of Collin.

"My mom didn't wander off again did she? Is she—?" He starts to move like he's going to run and check on her. I cut him off, quietly, controlled.

"No, she's fine. I was just in there."

The hard rap on the door comes, and I don't move to answer it, so he walks over. The kitchen and living room are one big open-concept space, and I can see him until he gets to the stone archway that separates the front entry from the rest of the house. I stay in the background, but I hear him greet them. I put my coffee down and force myself to take a breath. I can't literally be trembling if they want to talk to me. I smooth my hair with my hands, and as I start toward the front door, Collin is ushering them into the main room. Collin gives me an uneasy look and I immediately know why.

Joe Brooks is standing in my house. *Detective* Joe Brooks now. I can't tell if Collin's pallor is because of our mutual disdain for Joe or because they want to ask me a few questions.

"Uh…come on in. Have a seat," I say.

I think about asking Collin to put another pot of coffee on to get him out of the room, but he would see through that. Joe introduces his partner as Al Davis, a tall man about Joe's age with a military haircut and slender build—a serious, unmoving face, a stark contrast from Joe's floppy, pop-star haircut and bodybuilder physique. They sit on the sofa, careful to perch on the edge of it and not get comfortable. I sit across from them in a green armchair.

"Sorry to come unannounced like this, Mel," Joe says. Collin is hovering somewhere behind me. I wish he'd sit down.

"What's this about?" Collin asks, friendly enough, but I can feel him looking at me. I look back at him and take his hand—I guess an attempt at solidarity, and he sits next to me, on the arm of the chair. Detective Davis starts.

"I'm sure you've heard about our investigation into the murder of a local man. Luke Ellison."

"Sure," Collin says. "It would be impossible not to."

"Right," he says, "but I'm actually asking Mrs. Hale."

183

All three men look at me and wait for a reply. I'm doing my absolute best to keep my breathing steady and keep my voice at a normal pitch.

"Of course," I say, quieter than I meant to. I clear my throat. "Yes."

"Did you know Mr. Ellison?" he asks pointedly. I resist looking over to Collin to gauge his expression.

"Um, I know of him."

"How well do you know *of him*?" he asks, and I know that my answer sounded evasive and sketchy. Do I lie outright, or do they already have the cap?

"I don't know him well, I mean."

"But you have met him?" Joe asks. I have to admit to having met him. Did the person who sent me that disposable phone tip them off? Did they follow me and take photos, do they have proof?

"Yes, just at the bookstore. Classics. I have a writing group that meets there."

"You weren't friends?"

"Friends?" I swallow hard. I feel prickly heat crawling up my back. "No. Why would you think that?"

"Was he a part of this writing group, did you get to know him that way?"

"No, I— He just gave a reading there one night and I met him then. A lot of people did."

"But you chatted with him, exchanged information."

"It was a meet and greet. Like I said a lot of people chatted with him. About his book." I try to keep a look of genuine confusion on my face, but my nervous, fluttery voice betrays me.

"Did you give him your personal info, a business card or anything?"

"Business card? She doesn't have a business card," Collin says, exasperated with their questions, certain they are talking to the wrong person. "Why in the world are you asking her about this guy?"

"Records from his computer show that he searched your name. Quite a bit. He seemed to have scoured your social media pages. If you weren't friends..." the way he says the word implies that he means much more than *friends* "...then can you think of any other reason the man would be looking you up so excessively?" Joe asks, matter-of-factly.

Collin still isn't looking at me with mistrust; he keeps his bunched-up expression pointed at the detectives, baffled as to why they would be questioning me of all people.

"He offers private writing courses—lessons. I signed up at his table for more info. We discussed it, briefly."

"That's all. You didn't take the private lessons?" His emphasis on the word *private* again, is smug and connotative.

"I didn't end up pursuing the lessons." I didn't pull this particular lie out of this air. I've been thinking, incessantly, about how I could dismiss any vague connection if someone had seen me with him. He'd mentioned the private lesson idea once. It made sense. It should explain this.

"So, if you didn't take the lessons, why do you think he would be looking at your photos and searching your name to the extent he did?"

"I imagine that if he was considering taking on a private client, he'd want to search them. Isn't that what everyone does these days? That doesn't seem so odd."

"So you never had any contact besides the bookstore?" Davis is doing the talking now.

"She already told you she didn't." Collin answers for me. "I know you guys have to follow all your leads or whatever, but this is a stretch, don't you think?"

But Davis doesn't respond to Collin, he just waits for an answer from me.

"No, just the bookstore."

"I don't like what you're insinuating." Collin stands, growing angry that he's being ignored.

"We're not insinuating anything. We just need to do our jobs."

"What made you change your mind about lessons with him?" Joe asks. A knot of pain twists in my gut and my pulse is racing.

"Oh, I don't know. I was just starting to get back into writing—nothing too serious. It sounded interesting in the moment after hearing a good reading, but you know how that goes—the excitement fades and you realize you don't want to spend that much money on a hobby."

I can't tell if I'm rambling. I'm trying to offer a solid answer—one that doesn't beg more questions and gives them what they need so they can leave. I wish I hadn't used the word *excitement*.

"I see. Well, there were no records of instant messages or emails between you, so maybe he just had a crush or something. One-sided, of course," Joe adds, looking to Collin. "We just needed to see if you could offer any more insight."

Joe Brooks and Detective Davis stand, and I hate Joe for implying there was a crush and leaving it at that. He hands me a business card.

"If you think of anything else that might be useful, give us a call."

"Okay." I take it, but I don't stand to see them out. I let Collin go instead. He shakes their hands, and Joe turns back to me.

"Say hi to Ben for me."

I nod mutely and force a terse smile. When the front door clicks shut and Collin comes back in, I don't know what to expect. Will he privately have an entirely different demeanor than he had with the cops?

"What a cocksucker," he says, red-faced.

I let out the breath I've been holding. He's still on my side.

"The woman beater, that bully, is gonna come in here and do the same thing. Try to bully you. I cannot believe that prick is walking around in uniform after what he's done, and we just have to accept it. He should be in prison, but instead, hell, let's give him authority and firearms!"

"Yeah, I mean are they going into everyone's house like that? There were a lot of other women at that reading. Jesus." I hate myself, but I have to play the game.

"They're grasping at straws. Hick-town detectives with no experience asking idiotic questions."

"I know. Right?" Is really all I can think to say. "Well, I'm sorry you had to deal with Tweedledee and Tweedledum."

"It's fine. Just weird."

With that, Collin's phone rings. I hear Richard on the other end, talking about some tax form they need to make available for investors. I mime drinking coffee to ask him if he wants me to bring him the rest of his cup. He gives me a smirk, remembering I tricked him into liking Starbucks, but nods and mouths a *thank you* back, and just like that, he has switched gears into work.

But as I walk away from him toward the kitchen, I catch his reflection in the glass of the French door windowpanes, and he is watching me—still on his call—but with his eyes on me, and his face changes when he thinks I don't see. There is something in his expression that resembles…doubt, suspicion. It's subtle, a quick double take at my back as I go, but it's there. I've never seen him look at me like that before.

19

A few days go by and I can't stop checking the disposable phone. It feels like someone is deliberately manipulating me, trying to make me feel crazy by telling me they know what I did, and then letting me sit and agonize instead of just telling me what they want—or who they are.

Tonight, we're taking the kids to dinner to celebrate the A Ben got in his math class—a subject he struggles with. He wants Mexican, so we head to La Haciendas. We go early so we're back early enough on a school night for the kids to have some homework time. From the backseat, Ben is reciting facts about Mexican food. When he really likes something, he tends to memorize everything about it.

"Did you know in traditional Mexican food they use the whole cow, even the testicles and uterus?"

Collin and I look at one another on this one. I turn to look back at Ben.

"Is that what you're ordering tonight?"

He looks at me like I have two heads.

"No. This restaurant isn't traditional."

Well, I guess he told me.

"Good point," I say, but before I turn back around, I notice a truck behind us, driving a bit too close.

A flutter of familiarity brushes over me. I pause and squint to take it in. It looks like Luke's truck. In fact, it is exactly like his, down to the heavily tinted windows and cactus-shaped air freshener hanging from the rearview mirror. I take in a sharp breath. The license plate isn't the same. Maybe it's just a coincidence. Maybe I can't really make out the dangling air freshener shape and I'm just overly paranoid. There are a lot of pickups that look like that, I'm sure.

"What?" Ben asks. Rachel is lost in her headphones, leaning against the car door on the opposite side, paying no attention.

"Nothing, hon. Tell me what you're gonna order." I try to distract him.

"Can I get a margarita?"

"You're a few years away from that, bud." I smile at Collin, trying to share the amusement in our son's witty comment, but he can tell there's something else going on. He's beginning to catch on to my chronic unease.

I try to shake it off and be present for my family during dinner. A mariachi band plays on a weathered wooden platform in the corner. Ben asks if he can say it's his birthday so they will sing to him and he can have free ice cream, but he settles for a round of "La Bamba" and the promise of a *poquito* sundae and seems happy enough.

I push a paste of refried beans around on my plate and listen to Rachel answer Collin's simple question, "How's school?" She's going over every detail.

"Oh my God, so Lindsey Shaw and Celeste Ricke wore the same exact romper to school, and Lindsey told everyone it was Juicy Couture and then she saw Celeste wearing it and everyone knows Celeste is, like, poor, like, no offense, but people just know. Anyway, Celeste said the romper is actually from Target. And then Wendy looked it up, and it *was* from Target and Lindsey stayed home the rest of the week, she was so embarrassed."

She starts to scroll through her phone to find a photo for us, and Collin doesn't ask what the hell Juicy Couture is. He just looks to me to say something relevant.

"Mom," she says, wanting me to look at the romper photos. "I mean, it's not funny, but she's such a bitch, so it's kind of funny."

"Language," I say, without much conviction, and move over to sit next to her in the wraparound booth to look at her phone.

"Sorry," she mumbles under her breath, and then switches gears. She shows me photos of the scandal, giggling. From where I'm now seated, I can see out the windows on the side of the building where the parking lot extends around. The truck is there. This can't be a coincidence. The truck is facing the restaurant windows, and whoever is sitting behind those tinted windows can surely see us.

"Mom, she said 'bitch.'" I am fixated on the truck, and I only partially hear my son.

"Don't say 'bitch,' honey." I dismiss him, barely paying attention.

"I didn't. She did!" he protests, and Collin gives him a look

191

to let it go, which he does because the promise of a sundae is still lingering. I need to go out there. I need to see who is behind the wheel, if it's Luke's truck. Who would have it? But I can't. I can't do a thing except sit here and concentrate on acting normal, keeping calm.

When we finish eating and walk out to the car, it's dusk. I look for the truck, not that I could do anything about it right now, but it's gone. It doesn't matter if it is Luke's truck or not. The fact remains that someone is following me.

On the drive home, Collin turns the radio from his NPR preset to a light pop station. I wonder if he's avoiding the news. But when the song ends, it's the top of the hour and they're summarizing local news headlines. When I hear Luke's name, I want to change the channel, but I wonder if it will make me look like I'm hiding something, so I don't. I wonder though, if Collin wants to switch it off, or if, deep down, he wants to know more—to see if there is any way to connect me to Luke.

"A *new* discovery has been made in the Luke Ellison homicide case. A witness said he saw an SUV screeching away from the Ellison home around the time the crime took place. The witness did not get the plate or model of the vehicle, but did say it was large and black in color. If anyone has any further information that could help the investigation, please notify police." The reporter rattles off more news headlines in an unfeeling voice, but I don't listen. I'm thinking about my Jeep Cherokee. It's dark gray, not black, but close enough to the witness description to be anxiety inducing.

Collin doesn't say anything or look over. We're both

pretending that it's like any other day, listening to any other bits of news headlines. I don't say anything either, and the news fades into a commercial for a mega sale at Benny's Used Cars.

At home, I resist the urge to go directly upstairs and check for a message on the burner phone under the bathroom sink. Not just because I'm becoming obsessive, but because I feel suddenly under the watchful eye of my husband. I entertain the idea that it's my paranoia talking, and maybe he has no suspicion whatsoever, but I can't be sure. I need to be careful.

I sit on the back deck with Ben to help him with his vocabulary worksheet. It's a clear night, finally sweater weather, at least in the evenings and early mornings. The overhead light collects moths and beetles. The buzz of flapping wings in the quiet night air makes me look over to the edge of the pool, where a June bug is stuck on its back and trying to flip itself over. It ends up falling in the water, sending a small ring of ripples across the pool surface. Ben, as if by instinct, goes over and, with one finger, lifts the insect out of the water to safety. His natural kindness is heart melting.

A divorce would destroy him. He doesn't handle change well; he'd be lost and terrified. It's the last thing I want to happen, but if Collin ever found out the extent of my deception, he would leave, I know he would. At the beginning I thought it was a lapse in judgment that he might forgive, but after everything that's happened, I've left him no choice.

Ben is getting sleepy and irritable, so I tell him we can do the last few questions on the worksheet over breakfast and send him to bed. Inside, Collin is in the kitchen, putzing around.

He's pouring a drink, opening some mail on the counter. I need to check the burner phone while he's distracted.

Under the sink in the master bath, I reach back to the tampon box and pull out the phone. This time, there is one unread message. My heart drops to my stomach. I lose my breath. I'm afraid to open it—afraid to find out who's behind these messages. When I click open the text, there is no further clue as to who is sending it, but there is definitely a clear message.

WHAT WOULD YOU DO TO STAY OUT OF NEWS HEADLINES… AND OUT OF JAIL?

Jail? This person thinks I've done something I didn't do. I wish now that I'd called the police the day I found him. I wish I'd stayed and told them the truth, that I found him like this. I could have maintained the story that Luke was giving me private writing lessons. Collin is so trusting; I'm sure I could have spun it in a way where it would seem plausible that I hadn't told him. Maybe that I was really excited about a piece I was working on and Luke was helping me polish it, maybe get it into a small publication, and I wanted to surprise Collin with the end result. Far-fetched perhaps, but it would be better than this—than being suspected of having something to do with a murder.

WHAT DO YOU WANT? I type, and push Send. I wait as long as I can for a response before I hear Collin coming upstairs to get ready for bed. I triple-check that the phone is on silent and push it to the back of the cabinet, closing the door. It keeps me up at night, wondering who this person could possibly be. Is it some stranger who might have seen me parking and then sneaking through the trees behind Luke's house at night? Have they been following me this whole time, looking for an opportunity to blackmail me, and the crowded party was the perfect time?

Before Collin reaches the room, I strip down to my underwear, throw on a T-shirt and slip under the covers, pretending to be asleep so we don't have to mutually pretend not to hear the newscast, so I don't have to see him hide the look of worry and perhaps doubt that I've been noticing in his eyes.

In the morning, with the kids at school and Collin at work, I wheel Claire out to the front porch to sit with me. It's a crisp morning, overcast and hazy, and everyone wants to take advantage of the short few months one can escape the Louisiana heat. I spread a thin quilt over her lap and sit with my coffee and laptop on the porch swing across from her. The weathered slats display peeling yellow paint; they're cool against the backs of my legs. I think about the day we painted it, not long after we moved in. When everything was perfect. I close my eyes against the memory, trying to ward it off, and I open my laptop.

I search for any updates on the case, finding no real details beyond what I heard on the news last night. I stir hot milk into my coffee and curl my knees up to my chest. Tonight I'll cook something special. I need to focus on my family, and make Collin feel like everything is just fine. I go through recipes in my head. There's a Greek chicken thing he likes, maybe shrimp with risotto. As I make a mental grocery list, I'm distracted by the sound of a car approaching. It's just a dot against the horizon at first, but as it gets closer and takes shape, I see that it's a police car.

I sit upright, spilling scalding coffee onto my thighs. I swallow the cussword I want to scream out and wipe my legs with my hand. My heart flutters and I watch, hoping it's just a patrol car passing by. It doesn't seem to be in a hurry. Maybe that's all it is…but then it slows and turns into our drive. I hear the scrape of the underbelly of the vehicle against our steep driveway. I suck in a shallow breath and hold it.

Joe Brooks steps out of the driver's side. He tips his hat to me as he walks toward the porch, with a careless smile as if it's a social call.

"Morning, Mel."

I don't greet him. I concentrate on controlling the look on my face. It can't read shock or guilt. I must unfurrow my brow and turn the corners of my mouth up into something resembling a welcoming smile. At the very least.

"Joe, hi. You're here again."

"Can I take a minute of your time?"

"Of course. Can I get you a cup of coffee?" I ask, hoping my painted expression reads as genuine.

"Sure, thanks."

"Have a seat, I'll grab an extra mug inside." I go inside, rushing, fumbling to get the mug as quickly as I can, wanting him to leave. I want to know what else he could possibly be here for, and at the same time I don't want to know.

I return to the porch and place a colorful "Best Dad" mug in front of him and pick up the French press off the small table. I can see the top of his head from where I hover behind him, pouring him a cup. I see the pale part in his dark shock of hair. I think about finishing the pour, and then slowly dumping the scalding contents of the French press over his head, tiny rivers of boiling coffee running down his face. This dark thought surprises me and I flush a little, momentarily afraid he can read my thoughts, sitting out there on the porch. I have never been the type to wish others harm, and I've raised kind children. But now, after knowing what Joe has done—his abuse of power, his propensity for violence, his almost arrogant remorselessness— and now, his capacity to destroy the life I've built, I wish the coffee was boiling oil. I take pleasure imagining him without any flesh on his face—his eyeballs round and bulging like a photo in an anatomy book, his skeleton jaw like a Halloween decoration.

But of course, I only offer cream and sugar and then sit opposite him, careful not to give away my trembling hands. I glance sideways at Claire a moment, wondering how much of what is said, if any, she is capable of absorbing. She just stares out into the front yard's trees. I envy her for a moment because she's somewhere far away and safe.

"What can I do for you, Detective Brooks?"

"Mel, you can still call me Joe."

I don't say anything back to this, only nod in acknowledgment. I'm not sure what he's playing at, acting overly friendly, but I'm not falling for whatever show he's putting on.

"How's Collin?" he asks, breezily.

"Please, just…what's this about?" I ask, and his smile fades.

"All right, then. Do you recall what you were doing Thursday, September 20?" he asks.

"Uhh, I don't—I can barely remember what I was doing yesterday at this time," I stall, scanning my mind for that date, for what he's getting at. "I usually have a writing group that night, Thursdays, I mean." At least I'm being honest because that was weeks ago and I really don't remember the exact dates.

"So you were at Classics Bookstore that night?" he asks, and I have to think back. Which weeks did I skip? Was I there that day? How will it be significant?

"Probably. I don't go every week, but…"

"We have a witness that says you weren't there."

I shift in my seat.

"Then I guess I wasn't. Like I say, I usually am, but I don't…"

"Were you with Luke Ellison that evening?" he asks.

I think of Luke. It was such a short time ago that he was here, looking at me longingly, whispering lovers' words in my ear. A career and happiness, a holiday in Italy spread out in front of him.

"No." I don't say more because I hear that my voice is husky with the strain of holding back tears.

"No?" he repeats. I don't repeat my response. I wait to see where he's going with this.

"We have a witness who says he saw you get into Luke's truck in the parking lot of the bookstore several weeks ago."

Nausea, something like seasickness, washes over me. The only person who saw me sitting in Luke's truck that night was Lacy. Or so I thought. Could he be using the male pronoun to throw me off? I feel sure that Lacy has gone back to Joe even after saying she was done with him, but I can't believe she'd involve herself in this. Maybe there was someone else passing through the lot.

"Yes, I sat in his truck for a second," I admit.

"But you said you weren't with him." Joe writes something down in a tiny spiral notebook, then looks up and fills the pregnant silence.

"I told you. We spoke about writing, maybe lessons. He was giving me one of his books. I sat in his car for a second, to reach in the back and take a book off the stack— get his card and info. I already told you that."

I want desperately to say that he could corroborate that story with Lacy, because I'd told her the same thing. But I already lied to him in the diner about how I knew her, that I'd met her only once before. I can't change that now— too much rests on my consistency. I suppose, if it becomes necessary for my survival, I'll have to bring Lacy into it, but not now.

"I didn't know he gave private coaching lessons," Joe says, an unyielding look in his eyes.

"How would you?"

"Well, he doesn't have any indication on his website or business card, and no family members have mentioned a side coaching business. He makes plenty of money from his books. Why would he need to?"

"I wouldn't know."

"You wouldn't know."

"No," I say, trying to keep my voice light.

"I met the guy a few times. Didn't strike me as the charitable type, just offering private lessons," he says, and I pause, absorbing that Joe had met Luke before.

"All I know is that he made the offer. I thought about it. And I decided against it."

"Decided against it." He says this like a simple echo, no meaning to be gained from it. Was it a question?

"Is there anything else?" I ask curtly.

"So your statement is that you never met him outside the bookstore." I realize in the moment, when he uses the word *statement* that I don't have to answer any of these questions if I don't want to, and maybe I shouldn't because I can't be absolutely sure that I wasn't seen. Whoever is texting me knows something, but it would likely be my word against theirs if it came down to it. I could always tell the truth about that cap if it were found. Well, part of the truth: that I must have set it down on the seat of his truck the day I sat in it to get his information and grab a book. It correlates with what I just said. The more I act guilty of something or refuse to cooperate, the more attention I'll draw to myself. So I answer.

"Yes, that's right." I hold firm. If he knows more than he's saying, I think he'd tell me, he'd press me for more information. All he knows is Luke looked me up on his computer. That's nothing. I met one of the other moms in Ben's class recently, and I thought she was quite funny and engaging, so I casually googled her name, just to see who she was. It led to Facebook, Twitter, site after site. That's not abnormal. I wasn't stalking the woman. He has nothing.

"Is that all?" I stand as if to escort him off the porch. He puts down his cup and stands too, countering me, but he doesn't make a move to leave.

"You understand I'm not trying to give you a hard time here, Mel. It's just that the guy seemed very interested in you.

Obsessed might be the wrong word, but preoccupied, perhaps. And then we hear that you were seen with him, in his truck. That doesn't exactly look like nothing."

"Well, it is nothing." I swallow hard. I can hear the sound it makes in the quiet morning air. I clear my throat to try and mask the guilty sound.

"I'm just telling you how it looks. The guy seemed like a jerk. If he was harassing you or anything, and you're just trying to remove yourself from this whole thing, that's understandable, but if there is something you're holding back, I'm sure you know that it's important you let me know now—" he pauses "—rather than later."

"I appreciate that. There's nothing to tell," I say. I don't know if playing the "old pal" card back to him and feigning friendliness will help, but I know what he is, and I can't bring myself to pretend with him. I may have done something wrong, but only one of us standing here is a criminal.

"Well." Joe tips his hat, smiling. "Thanks for your time, Melanie." He carries with him none of the Southern charm promised by the singsong way he shapes his words, and I hate the way his lips form around my name. I give a quick, sharp nod back and watch him open his patrol car door. Before he sits, he pauses, holding the top of the door with both hands, looking as if he's going to say something else, but then he looks up at me at the top of the porch stairs. I have my arms crossed, defensively, and I don't welcome any other questions, so he closes the car door and drives off.

When the car is out of sight, I exhale and collapse onto the stairs beneath me. I want to scream. My fingernails have made moon-shaped impressions in my palms from unknowingly clenching my fists. I look to Claire, who leans over the side of her chair and spits. A translucent thread of saliva clings to her lip and stretches near the wooden slats of the porch floor. I like to think it's because she knows the kind of man Joe Brooks is and is disgusted, but I know she can't possibly know that. I'm grateful, anyway, that she can't tell anyone he was here. Collin can't know. This fire I've created grows with each lie I throw on the flame. I am a liar.

20

After I help Claire into her bed to nap, I pace the kitchen floor and try to steady my breath. My eyes land on a picture on the fridge, one that Ben drew. It's our family in periwinkle-blue stick figures. We stand in a line across the bottom of the page, holding hands. One straight vertical line for each of our bodies, with a horizontal line for our arms, a few more strokes at the end of our stick arms to represent four disproportionate fingers on each of us. I'm the only one he drew hair on. Just a butter-yellow swipe, curved up at the end. A red crayon paints a smile on each of our circle faces. Our house, a messy square, stands behind us. And little Ralph is a brown, scratchy circle, curled up next to it. I told him that he was going to be a famous artist one day and he squealed with delight. He drew this just before I met Luke. I pull the paper from underneath the magnet holding it to the side of the fridge. The last months have been so dense with chaos, I scarcely remember what the comfort of prosaic, routine life feels like. I long to go back to that.

Am I causing more damage by concealing my relationship

with Luke? If there are no suspects, and it comes out that I was having an affair with him and lied to the police about knowing him, about being at his house, if there is evidence that I found him, if the person texting me saw me there, I could be a prime suspect for murder. It doesn't matter that I didn't do it. Circumstantially, I fit the bill, and if no one else does, if I'm the only one who lied and covered up evidence, it's very possible that I could be found guilty.

What would they say my motive is? That he threatened to leave me and if I couldn't have him, no one could, so I snapped? That he was going to tell my husband about us and so I had to silence him? It probably wouldn't be too difficult to come up with something that fit if all the evidence pointed to me. But now…it's too late. I already threw away evidence and covered up lies with more deceit and evasion. I thought it was the only way to protect my family, but now I wonder if I've made this so much worse. I've been telling myself that it's not possible for them to arrest or convict an innocent person, but now I am not so sure. I need to find out who would want to hurt him. I can't just sit here and wait for my deception to catch up with me.

Who knows how many lovers he's had over the years, who knows if other failed writers think he stole their ideas, or if he had enemies for any other myriad of reasons. There are so many possibilities to explain his death.

Suddenly, in one crystalizing instant, it hits me. My stomach tightens at the thought: Joe knew him; or, at least, he'd met him more than once, and Lacy was briefly seeing Luke. When she'd talked about Luke to me, she'd spoken as if she'd met "the one." Maybe she flaunted that to Joe, too, on one of the many occasions he stopped by for a quickie, and she thought she had leverage—a way to say no to him. No matter how dismissive and cruel Joe Brooks is with her on the surface, I know he treats her like his property in private. He would not accept rejection in any form. That, I am certain of.

He seems to feel that he can use his badge to get away with anything he wants. What if he found out about them together? If he's capable of rape and physical abuse, is he capable of more? Maybe in a drunken state or jealous rage, or probably both? I need to see Lacy and mine her for information—find out if Joe knew about her relationship with Luke, if she knew where Joe was the night Luke was killed.

It's only 10 a.m., but I remember that Lacy works at the strip club again and may have been up all night. But I can't afford to wait; I need her to meet me, to help clarify things.

"Hello?" she says in a groggy and somewhat annoyed voice.

"Lacy, hi. It's Mel."

"Yeah I know. Cell phones show the person's name these days," she says, which I find unexpectedly witty coming from her.

"Sorry, were you asleep?" I hear a baby in the background.

"We were just napping a little." She says this more to the baby, I think, than me, considering the suddenly light tone.

"I'm so sorry."

"It's fine."

"I just wanted to ask you to lunch, if you're free."

"Today?" I hear her rustling around, a grunting noise as if she picked up the baby, then a faucet turns on.

"If you can."

"I have Ronny Lee," she says, and I'm not sure what she means at first…but then I remember it's her son's name.

"Oh, well, bring…Ronny Lee. It's my treat," I add, knowing that she would be hard-pressed to give up a free meal. I guess that's underhanded in a way, but I need her to be an ally. We need to work together, and she needs to feel like there is no danger of me reporting any of the abuse. She has no idea that it's the last thing I could do in my position. It would look like retaliation for Joe's inquest into my life, especially without proof. And proof is what I need to find.

"Really?" I hear a smile in her tired voice. We decide on Love's Café because she needs good coffee, so I rush to shower and make up a plate for Claire before I leave for a couple of hours. I don't have any clue if Joe's involvement is just fiction I'm creating in my mind, but adrenaline is pumping through my veins, and it's at least a place to start. At least I'm doing something.

Ronny Lee sits in a high chair at the table, cooing and gumming on a saltine cracker with fat little clenched fists. Lacy is hunched over the menu, leaning on one palm, when I arrive. I reiterate that she should get whatever she wants, and I see her carefully making her decision for the most amount of bang for my buck. I wish they served booze, but I settle for the soup of the day and Lacy orders a double cheeseburger and fries with a kids' mac and cheese for Ronny Lee and a Coke. I force myself not to calculate the calories in horror while she speaks to the waiter. I patiently wade my way through small talk about the weather and the Frank Sinatra-themed decor on the walls.

I need to get right to it. It's not like she's going to report the things I'm asking back to Joe. If anything, maybe it will make Lacy more fearful of him and it could actually do some good. It doesn't implicate me in any way, it just plants a seed, so I take the risk.

"I need to ask you something," I say, with determination. Lacy instinctively looks to her child, protectively, thinking it may be about Joe's abuse, no doubt. "It's okay, it's not about that—not really."

"Not really?" she asks, still looking at Ronny Lee, fussing with the wet crumbs on his place mat. Of course he is too little to understand, but I admire that she knows that kids absorb more than we think, even when they're small, and that she wants to protect him. "It's not about what happened…to you…with him, I mean. Something else."

"Okay." She looks like she regrets coming now, and I try to steer the conversation quickly.

"Look, I promised I wouldn't say anything and I won't, okay. It's not that. I actually…I need your help. With something." At this she turns away from Ronny Lee, holding a milk-filled sippy cup, which he's reaching for. She waits for me to continue.

"Did he know about you and Luke Ellison?" I ask, and her eyes fill. She behaves as if they were war-torn lovers over many years and that she'd suffered a great loss.

"Why?" she asks, defensively.

"I know it's none of my business, okay. I just—it would…" I trail off. I don't know how to frame it without telling her exactly what I'm getting at. She interrupts me though, looking down at the table, tracing the rim of her glass with her finger.

"I don't know." Her voice is soft. "I didn't tell him, if that's what you're asking. But he has a way of finding things out. Luke never asked about my past boyfriends."

My heart lurches at the sound of his name on her lips in that intimate way.

"If Joe did find out, he probably would have tried to ruin it for me. Luke never said, but…" She stops as though she's had an epiphany, and makes eye contact with me. "Do you think that's why he quit me? 'Cause stupid Joe got involved or said something?"

I want to tell her that's not the reason. It's because he loved *me*, not you! *How childish. How absurd and hypocritical.* I shake my head in silent protest. How in the world can I even feel that way when I love Collin the way I do—when I feel the depths of remorse the way I do. I don't understand the duplicity of these emotions, existing simultaneously.

"No, I'm sure…" But then I stop myself, because telling her that *I'm sure that's not why he stopped seeing you* implies that the reason was something more personal.

"You think he did somethin' to Luke." It's a statement, not a question. She's still looking down at her cup.

"I just thought, perhaps, if you were seeing Joe again…" I stop a moment, assuming that she'll object, swearing that she wasn't, but she doesn't interrupt. "I thought maybe, considering…" I look to the baby, and become more careful with my phrasing. "Considering his history, he may react… strongly if he found out."

"You don't know how hard it is." She meets my eyes now. They're wet and frightened. "You're so lucky. You have this perfect life and a husband, and—it's hard. It's lonely. He says the right things. And like, you know in your head, like you *know* that it's just a line he says, but when you need to hear it…"

I place my hand on top of hers. She stops and looks up to the dusty hanging lamp above our booth so tears don't fall. She takes a deep breath and when she's blinked them away, she continues.

"When Luke dumped me, I let myself believe what I wanted to believe," she says matter-of-factly.

She's so pretty behind the bad eyeliner and trashy booty shorts. I can see what a man would see in her—what someone like Joe would want to claim as his own. At least behind closed doors. She didn't need to tell me she was seeing him again. It was apparent in the faded purple bruises down her arms and the blue lines around her neck that are either from the erosion of a cheap necklace that stained her skin, or from Joe's hands, cutting off air.

"Do you…do you know where he was September 20, by any chance?" I ask, and she laughs.

"Why? What's September…" she stops when she realizes it's the day Luke died. "Oh. Jesus, I don't even know what day of the week that was. Who the hell remembers what they did weeks ago?"

"It was a Thursday," I say, softly.

"I work Thursdays, so…"

"Does Joe ever come to…see you…at work?" I imagine him and his pervert friends pawing at the dancers, throwing singles at their naked bodies and laughing, going out of their way to humiliate the women. She just shrugs.

"It's important," I add.

"He's been there before. I don't know about that night. Like I said, who can remember? I do the same shit every day, nothing stands out exactly."

"So *maybe*, then?" I try to push without making her shut down. She shrugs again. It's exasperating. Our food comes and she pours copious amounts of ketchup over her fries before spooning cheesy shells into Ronny Lee's little puckered mouth, avoiding eye contact.

"I don't know. He could have been there and I didn't even see him. He pays for lap dances in private rooms with other girls. So do his gross friends. It used to make me crazy and we'd fight about it, but I don't care anymore." I try to imagine sleeping with someone, caring for someone like she does Joe, and watching him take other strippers into private rooms for blow jobs, because that's exactly what a "private lap dance" means depending on how much he pays, I suppose.

"Could you get, like, receipts from that night from the club or something…to see if he used a credit card, if we can place him there?"

She almost chokes on her soda at this.

"How the hell am I supposed to do that? I'm not the manager. I don't know how to do that," she says, through a mouthful of cheeseburger.

I'm growing frustrated.

"Who are the girls he gets private dances from? Can you give me names?" I don't wait for her to reject this. I add, quickly, "I know it seems like I'm invading your life, I'm not trying to, Lacy. I just need your help on this."

Her face is bunched up in an annoyed snarl.

"Cinnamon and Luscious are his favorite two. Good luck."

I don't know why I thought she'd give me real names or want to work with me to nail him. Just as I consider how to change tactics, the waiter comes over. He's a thin, frazzled-looking teenager with a smattering of whiskers that do little to cover his pockmarked face, and he's overwhelmed with the amount of tables he's trying to serve in the understaffed dining room. I think he's going to ask us how everything is, but instead, he apologizes as he places something in front of me. I stare at it. I don't register it right away.

"Sorry, I guess this is yours," he says hurriedly. I look at the silver chain with the oval locket dangling from it.

"I don't think so," I start to say, but then I look at it more closely. As I open the locket, I see what it is.

"What?" Lacy asks, reading my expression.

I look daftly to the waiter and back down to the locket in my hand. Inside is a photo of Henry. Henry, Luke's beloved, deceased dog. It had been handed down from his grandmother, he told me, and he said he always had it on him—in a pocket or on his keys. I lose my breath.

"Mel?" Lacy asks, but I look at the waiter, angrily.

"Is this a joke?"

"Uhhh." He expected gratitude, I'm sure, and is startled by my fury. "No? It's…"

"Why do you have this?"

He's taken aback again by the venom in my voice, but I don't care.

"You dropped it?" He says this like it's a question. He looks frightened of me. Lacy looks a little scared herself.

"No. I didn't. Where did you get it?"

"Uh…" he stutters. "Sorry. I don't—I…A lady gave it to me a little while ago, and said you dropped it when you came in. I was just really busy at the moment. So…yeah. I just—forgot and then, as soon as I had a free second…" He makes a gesture like "there you go."

"Who? Who gave it to you?"

"Look, I got nine tables. I don't know. Some lady."

"What did she look like?" I demand, but he's backing away with his tray, clearly wanting to be rid of me. "It's busy, I don't know. Average. Old."

"How old?" I stand, asking questions lightning-fast so he doesn't walk away before I get answers. It would look unhinged if I were to physically grab him by the collar, but I might if I need to. I'm standing toe to toe with the exasperated waiter now. "How old?" I repeat.

"Like thirty, thirty-five," he says, and then adds quick details before turning to go. "Like brown hair, kinda long. Normal, I don't know. I gotta work." He walks off quickly and greets a new table.

"What the hell?" Lacy says, looking at me with her mouth open and in a slight smile, maybe impressed with the assertiveness she didn't expect from someone she thinks is a rich, suburban lady who has it all. There is no plausible explanation I could give her for my behavior.

"I...this was stolen from me." I shove it in my pocket so she can't examine it. Did Luke share it with her too?

"What do you mean?"

"A while back. It was just missing, so I know I didn't drop it like he said. I haven't had it in weeks."

"That's weird."

"Yeah. I mean whoever gave it to him must have had it. Why give it back?" Am I getting too good at coming up with a quick lie, or do I sound like a lunatic? I can't tell.

"Sounds like someone's messing with you," she says, seemingly less engaged in the problem than I thought. She dips three fries at a time into ketchup and crams them in her mouth. I guess she sees things I can't even imagine at the club every night and this doesn't even warrant a second thought.

"Yeah," I say, because someone is indeed messing with me. Is this a warning? A threat? A woman gave it to him. I didn't expect that. Who could it possibly be? I take my wallet out and lay down some cash on the table. More than enough to cover the bill.

"I'm not feeling all that well. I know I dragged you here, but can we take a rain check? Maybe get together in a few days."

I see her eyeing the sixty dollars, mentally calculating that the bill is probably less than thirty. Her eyes widen a moment.

"Yeah, of course," she says, pretending she's not looking at the money. I don't care if she pockets the rest. I just need to go. I try to slow down so I don't run out of the place. The last thing I need is witnesses discussing my odd behavior with the cops.

"Bye, Ronny Lee." I touch his little hand and his chubby baby fingers wrap around my thumb. "Bye-bye," I repeat, and he coos. I smile at Lacy before I walk, deliberately controlled, out of the café.

In the safety of my car, I scan the parking lot, looking for anyone who might be watching me. Because I *am* being watched. I can't see anything out of the ordinary. I pull the locket out of my pocket and open it. The image of a sweet-faced border collie looks back at me with a black-and-white muzzle and one ear bent. The patina on the metal shows its age, that it's a well-loved keepsake. Who would have this? What do they want?

I will myself not to cry. I will not break down, I will get angry. I will get ferociously enraged, and I will find whoever is doing this.

21

MONEY.

As I crouch under the bathroom sink later that evening, sitting on my heels, I read the text that finally comes through on the burner phone. The last thing I'd texted was What do you want? And now this is the response.

A second text reads, AND DON'T PRETEND YOU DON'T HAVE ANY.

I stuff the phone back to the corner of the cupboard. The kids are on the back deck helping Collin fill the grill with chicken and vegetables. I can't think how to respond and I need to get out to my family.

With the cooler weather, the three of them practically live out there. I can hear Ben yelling, whining that he wants to wrap the onions in foil. I imagine Rachel or Collin have inadvertently taken over his special task. Collin will de-escalate before it becomes an issue, I know. I should be cutting cantaloupe for a fruit salad, but instead, I'm hiding a secret phone, communicating with someone who's blackmailing me and thinks I'm a murderer. How quickly someone's life can change so completely.

In the kitchen, I pull a bottle of red from the wine rack and open it, then I pull out apples and grapes from the fridge and set up a cutting board on the counter in front of the open kitchen window that looks out to the deck. I make sure they see me, so they know I'm present and not acting strangely. I wave to Ben, who holds up his onion slices with pride. I give him a thumbs-up. The breeze from the open window whispers around my ears and brushes my hair back ever so slightly. It's a perfect night with my beautiful family. I hold the sensation in my mind, memorizing it. I'm not sure why. Maybe I see myself in prison orange, only seeing my children through bulletproof glass. Maybe I'm afraid that at the very least, they will find out what I've done and they will opt to live across town with their father and there will never be a night like this again.

Collin opens the sliding door with an elbow, hands full of raw meat juice he's come in to wash off.

"Oh, hey." He kisses my cheek, holding his contaminated hands away from his body. If he is doubting me or suspicious of me, he's electing to let it go. I feel that he truly believes what he said after the police left: that it's just a bunch of "hick-town detectives with no experience asking idiotic questions" because they have no real leads. Once the initial jolt of the whole situation wore off, he softened a bit and seems to be over it, so I'll take it.

"I opened a malbec if you want some." I lean into his kiss and smile.

"Sure. Thanks." He washes his hands. We both see out the window that Ben has opened the grill lid in Collin's brief absence and has dropped a chicken breast. He wails as it hits the deck floor and rolls off into the grass.

"Buddy!" Collin shouts as he runs out to get Ben away from the flame.

"Have him come in and help me with the fruit, hon!" I yell after him, trying to offer a hand. I watch Collin make a show of brushing off the chicken on the ground and telling Ben it's fine, making him break into a smile, and then handing it off to a smirking Rachel to throw away behind Ben's back. I smile at their kind conspiracy. I pour two glasses of wine and carry them to the outdoor table.

"You wanna carry out the fruit bowl, bud?" I ask Ben, and he runs inside to the kitchen to help. "We got those bubbly waters you like if you want one?" I say to Rachel, who is now back in her chair, glued to her phone.

"Okay," she says, absently. Ben carries out the fruit cautiously as if he may spill a very full glass of something, concentrating on not dropping it. I tell him how great he's doing before I go in to pull some flavored water out of the fridge. I notice the TV on in the living room. The squeaky voices of cartoon animals that I don't recognize flit bright colors across the screen. Ben must have left it on. I walk over to switch it off, but before I do, I collect the remote and look back through the kitchen to make sure everyone is still outside before I turn quickly to the news, expecting the same dead-end reporting about Luke. At this point, the coverage is fading and there is less big news about the case. Murders and crises of all kinds in New Orleans commandeer the news feeds. Luke is already disappearing by the day.

When I switch over, I'm right. There is a story about a

new diet trend, and the anchors make jokes that aren't funny as they banter back and forth awkwardly after the clip ends. Before I turn it off though, the female anchor changes gears. The face of a woman I don't recognize is speaking into a mic, being interviewed by the media, but the audio on her is muted as the anchor voices it over, attempting to intrigue the viewing audience to tune back in to hear the full interview.

"Luke Ellison's wife, Valerie Ellison, speaks out for the first time since her husband's tragic death. See the whole exclusive interview with her when you join us at ten. You won't want to miss it. And now, the weather."

I feel as though I've been punched between my shoulder blades, the wind knocked out of me. He was married? No. That's not possible. The hypocrisy in my outrage over this is not lost on me, but I don't care. He knew who *I* was. He knew I wept with guilt, he knew all the times I felt I had to stop. I told him about my children, my life, how my academic dreams were cut short. How could he have not told me? He said he was *newly on the market again*. But he was *married*.

I switch off the TV quickly and think about how I can find a way to watch the interview at ten. I can't record it. Collin might watch TV later on tonight and notice the pending recording before I can delete it. I'm sure they've mentioned his wife before—who he was "survived by" and I'd missed it because I can't have a paper trail of googling his name and I can't watch the coverage in front of my family. I can't even begin to imagine what he would think if he saw me following the case—going out of my way to gain information about something that should

218

be like every other devastating news story…unless of course, I knew the person in this unfortunate headline.

As dusk falls, we eat dinner on the deck. A string of decorative lights are crisscrossed above the table, and a citronella candle burns to keep away mosquitos. I swirl my grilled zucchini around on my plate and try to stay present. Collin sips his wine and Ben spreads his coloring sheets across the table as we all linger in the perfect evening air. Ben is an expert on crayon colors—he's memorized all of them in the huge crayon box— and makes everyone play the crayon game. Collin obliges him. He holds up a green crayon, covering the label.

"Polished Pine," Ben yelps. "No," he corrects himself. "Wintergreen Pine."

"Right!" Then he holds up a silver crayon.

"That one's too easy. Quicksilver. Everyone knows that."

"Everyone, huh?" Collin shoots me a smile, sharing in the knowledge that, of course, not everyone has this skill.

I'm only half listening. I smile back, absently.

"Okay, I'll make it harder on ya." He holds up two reddish crayons.

"Rustic Red and Misty Maroon," Ben says, pointing left, then right.

Collin laughs. "You are unbeatable."

I put a hand on Ben's back, giving him an impressed smile. He takes the red crayons from Collin's hand, pleased with himself, and goes back to coloring. I watch him work on Winnie-the-Pooh's shirt, and I admire him so much. The way he can so effortlessly forget who he is, where he's been, or where he might go, and is utterly engrossed in the simple task of smoothing his hand across the waxy surface of a crayon drawing.

My mind, on the other hand, is fixated on Luke's sheets in that ancient rented house. Had his wife been there with him in that bed? Why was he renting? Did he tell her he had to go away to work and needed to be alone, and she was so naive and blindly in love with him she just accepted it? Surely she wasn't living in town while he was sleeping with other people. The town's too small to easily get away with that. My God. What if there are children involved? If he lied about being married, could he have kids he didn't tell me about? I'm sickened now by the thought that I was a part of this.

Collin nudges me, standing over me with the bottle of wine, offering me a refill. I didn't even notice him get up to go inside and get it. So much for being present. I nod and hold up my glass. He meets my eyes.

"You okay?"

"Yeah. Yes. I was just thinking about Gillian's book club," I lie. "Now that the writing group is on a break, I wonder if it might be worth going back to for a while."

It's the first thing I could think of. Liz mentioned it to me at the Halloween party, and it may actually be nice to be in such vapid company right now.

"Sounds like a good idea," he says, sitting across from me, topping off his glass, as well. "You're in the house too much."

"Well, you know those girls though. They actually don't even read the books," I admit. "It's just an excuse to get away from the husbands and drink." He laughs, and I add, "I'm the only lucky one who doesn't feel the need to do that, apparently." He laughs again at this and raises his glass.

"Good answer."

"I'm serious," I say, laughing back and playfully tossing a tea towel at him from the messy dinner table. "But maybe I could get them to actually read the books. I'm not sure how, but probably not by starting with *The Catcher in the Rye*."

"Suggest smut. Everyone likes smut."

"Oh, do they?" I smile.

"Discussing *Fifty Shades of Grey* over cocktails is better than discussing Karen and Bob's fabulous new boat. Gag."

"They got a boat?"

"Oh, didn't you hear? Everyone needs a boat that sleeps six. I gotta golf with these guys."

"Gotta, huh?" I joke. "You're forced to."

"I'm just saying, why do we have friends we don't like that much?" he asks, not really seeking an answer. We both give something between a scoff and a chuckle.

"'Cause that's the part of being an adult they never tell you about." I stand and start to clear plates. He offers to help, but I tell him I have it.

By ten, Ben is in bed, and I can hear Rachel on her phone, talking to Katie, no doubt, considering the giggles and "whatevers" I can hear muffled from down the hall. Collin is asleep on the couch next to me. His laptop open on the coffee table and half a glass of wine left. His head is rolled back and resting on the back of the couch. His mouth is wide-open; he's snoring lightly, so I can tell he's out. I flip the channel quietly from some show about living in Alaska over to the news. I turn down the volume a bit so the change doesn't startle him awake.

I can't get away with recording it, but I have the remote ready to push the back button if I need to, and if he does wake up suddenly and I don't have time to switch it, it's just the news. I was catching the weather and this popped on. It can be dismissed. I can't help what pops up on the news, after all.

There she is, as promised. Valerie Ellison. A woman roughly my age. Chestnut hair pulled back into a neat ponytail. She has wide-set green eyes and olive skin. She's pretty in her own way. Not the beauty queen I imagined him with. But I guess it's only *after* success that men trade up, so maybe she was on her way out. Maybe he had a slew of twentysomethings, and he made them all feel like they were the only ones he asked to accompany him in Italy. So why me? I quietly chide myself for being so cynical. I know Collin would never do that to me. He gives me the "a woman is like a fine wine" crap and I eat it up every time. But he means it.

"My husband was a good man," she starts. She uses all the clichés you'd expect to hear family say after someone passes away. "He made everyone smile. He didn't have an enemy in the world." There are no tears, I notice. *He must have had at least one enemy*, I think to myself.

This is telling me very little. There is no mention of their life together, where she lives, how long they were married. It's just a plea for anyone who knows something to come forward. She's "just heartsick about the whole thing." It's not a sit-down interview with lighting and multiple cameras in a studio like they made it sound. It's just her in front of her house it looks like, where they caught her for a statement. I guess that's what constitutes an "exclusive interview" these days. I switch back to the Alaska show, a little deflated.

They must be questioning her. They always look at the spouse first. Maybe they are and it's too early to disclose any information. I resist the urge to look her up online. I still fear that if they ever really suspect me and search my computer, that sort of thing could look really bad. Talking to her at all is probably a terrible idea, but I can't help but wonder if she found out about me, and maybe that's the reason Luke is dead. She wasn't shedding a tear during that interview.

I kiss Collin on the forehead to wake him up. He starts with a snort and looks around groggily.

"Huh?" He blinks and rubs his eyes.

"Come to bed. You have an early morning," I say, softly. He shakes his head like a dog shaking out its fur, waking himself up.

"Right." He clicks off the TV and brings his glass to the kitchen to wash. I take the opportunity to beat him upstairs. I pad lightly past the kids' rooms and quickly look in on them, I make sure Claire is asleep and close her door. Then, I go into the bathroom to pull out the disposable phone and respond to the blackmailer. I don't expect a new message when I pick it up, I only expect to send a reply.

YOU LOVE YOUR KIDS, DON'T YOU? YOU CAN MAKE THIS GO AWAY, the message says, and my hands flutter to my mouth. They know who my children are. I know this already because I have been followed and I'm certain I was being watched at the restaurant that night, but to have it written this way— as a threat—I feel nauseous. It's infuriating and terrifying at the same time.

How much do you want? I type and push Send urgently, then tuck the phone away again before Collin comes up. I lie awake, anguished, wondering what sort of amount they will demand. If they know me—if they've looked into my family, my life—they'll know we are comfortable, but not rich. If they ask for some insane number, I'm screwed. If they ask for something they know I can get, which would be the smarter, more reasonable move, I need to find a way to get it. I will do whatever I need to do to get it.

22

In the morning, as I make the thirty-minute drive to Pawn City, I wonder what sort of customer at a pawnshop is going to buy my used Birkin bag. When I called the shop, I didn't think in a million years that they'd buy this sort of item, but then I thought, if they look for watches and jewelry, maybe. The shop owner seemed very excited to have a look at the bag.

The text I got back, when I had tossed and turned to my limit most of the night, and then checked the phone when I got up to pee at 3 a.m., said, $50,000.

It's a number that's heart-stopping, but at least it's not a million. That may be an amount I can come up with, but if I can get only part of it, I'll explain that it's the best I can do. Maybe they'll accept it. At least it's something. If Collin discovers missing money, everything would come out, so I have to find a way without touching the joint account.

I'd texted back that I could come up with ten thousand to start. My Birkin bag was twelve thousand new. It's a despicable amount to pay for a handbag, but it's my only expensive one, and Collin gave it to me as a gift on our tenth wedding anniversary. I had mentioned how cute Gillian's similar bag was at a Christmas party months before, and he had asked her about the details of the bag so he could surprise me with one. I would have liked to have seen his face when he eventually looked up the stats on the bag and saw the price tag.

I would have much rather had a trip together—France or Italy—I never really wanted the bag and I rarely use it. I just mentioned it was lovely to Gillian's face. Of course, he was so proud of himself when he gave it to me, I couldn't tell him that I couldn't care less about a brand-name bag and, call me naive or unsophisticated, but it looks just like the one I got for thirty bucks at H&M, which I actually prefer. Still, it breaks my heart to pawn it, because it was a gift from him, but I have no choice. If ten thousand can keep this person at bay while I figure out the rest, it's necessary.

Inside the pawnshop, a pile of old bikes fills out the center of the room. It smells more like a garage, oily and dusty. Racks of used kitchen gadgets sit beneath a wall of tools, every kind imaginable, hanging messily from hooks on the corkboard wall. Glass cases protect guns and boxes of ammo. Rows of pawned jewelry someone desperately parted with to pay for bills, or more likely meth, are brightly lit and displayed inside the counter that wraps around the checkout area.

I place my bag in front of the man behind the register, who greets me with a smile, not taking his eyes off of it. I run my fingers across the rolled-leather top handles and goatskin exterior, remembering the dinner at Riccio's when Collin pulled a box from the trunk of the car on our way in and made me wait until dessert to open it. It doesn't matter that it isn't something I care for, it is the kindness and incredible thoughtfulness from which it came that makes it so hard to part with.

"You must be Mrs. Hale." The elderly man holds his hand out to shake. I thought about using a false name, but he'd mentioned before during the phone conversation that ID would be required, so I have to take the risk.

"What a lovely piece," he says, examining the bag. "May I?" I let him take it. He looks at it from all angles, examines the inside and frowns at a minute lipstick stain that I can't believe he notices. Then he clicks away on his computer a moment, no doubt looking up what others in the same condition sold for.

"I can offer you seven thousand eight hundred." The papery skin of his hands shows the blue veins beneath, and as I watch them touch my sweet gift from Collin, I think about backing out.

"I need to get ten," I say, meekly, feeling as though I have no control over the situation.

"I'm sorry, but…"

"It was twelve, new. That gives you room to make money," I interrupt.

"Yes, ma'am, but it's not new, it's used, and it has a stain inside. I won't get more than ten myself." I see the small collection of expensive handbags in a case behind him, locked up. I can't imagine he comes across that many, and I still have no idea who would buy one at a pawnshop. Maybe I'm better off selling direct, online, but there's no time. The person demanding money wants to meet today.

"Nine, then," I say in desperation.

"I've given you my best price." He keeps the fake, customer service smile on his face, and I close my eyes a moment and sigh.

"I won't go less than eight thousand," I say. It's only two hundred dollars more, barely worth haggling over, but I want to feel at least a modicum of control over my situation. He nods silently, and pushes some paperwork across the glass case for me to sign.

It's two more hours until I meet this mystery person at the Starlite Motel to hand over the money—two thousand less than I promised. I have imagined every scenario, and I know how profoundly stupid it is to do this alone. They could take the money and shoot me if they know I may not be able to get more. The Starlite is off a desolate frontage road a few miles from the highway. It wouldn't be hard to slit someone's throat and leave them to bleed out until housekeeping discovered the body in the motel bathtub the next morning. I have no true link to this person, no paper trail—just an untraceable phone under the sink that will probably never be found. I also have little choice.

I didn't dare bring the phone with me. It has to stay in one place so I don't get sloppy. The kids are always in my purse for something, or I could drop it, forget it in the car, anything, if I got distracted, so I am not chancing it. This person said 2 p.m. at the Starlite, room 108. So, that's where I'll go. If they're not there… I don't know what, but that's how I need to handle this. I'll wait as long as I have to.

I drive around for a little while. It's a dreary day, dark and wet, and it feels like night outside. I buy a stale coffee from the Shell station and pour packs of powdered cream into it, deciding I'll go and sit outside the motel and wait. I might lose my nerve if I spend too much time thinking about it. I have the upper hand, I think, if I'm there first. If I've scoped out the scene.

Outside the motel, I park under a pecan tree that drops damp leaves on my windshield. I stir my coffee with a tiny red straw and watch the door of 108, that rests underneath the dilapidated Starlite Motel sign. The neon on the sign is alight on this overcast day, and the *S* has come off a screw that's holding it up: it hangs upside down and sways a little. There is no light on inside 108. I don't know why here of all places. Is this person staying here? It would explain why they need to exploit me for money. It's an utter shithole.

My nerve endings feel electric with stress. I recheck my purse to see that the cash in its Pawn City envelope and the gun are still right there where I put them. Just in case, I unlocked the safety box we keep in the bedroom in case of an intruder, and stuffed it down underneath my wallet, pack of tissue and makeup bag. It's been years since I learned how to use it at a shooting range, for my own protection, and I hate touching it. I barely recall how to handle it, truth be told, but coming without any sort of protection seemed beyond foolish. Everything is there. I take a few deep breaths.

After another tension-filled hour of torturing myself with all the worst-case scenarios, a vehicle pulls into the lot. I turn my wipers on to remove the debris from the front window and my ears turn instantly hot when I see it. Luke's truck is pulling into a vacant spot in front of 108. Reflexively, I duck down in my seat a bit, peering over the steering wheel to see who gets out.

I'm relieved to see only one person, so I can rest easier that I won't be ambushed or ganged up on, violently. He's wearing a rain poncho with a hood, and the truck is blocking the rest of his body, so I can't get a handle on who it is. He holds his head down against the drizzle as he opens the motel room door. I see the door shut and a warm light flip on inside. He draws the curtains, so I don't see anything else.

I think about driving away, running away. I should have said I *was* taking private lessons from the start. I wish I had thought of it. It could explain my presence there, but now I'm stuck covering this up. I have to go in. There's no other option.

Standing outside the motel door, I keep my right hand inside my purse, resting on the gun I barely know how to use, just in case I at least need to threaten someone with it. I don't know what to expect when the door opens— could it possibly be someone I know on the other side? I tap a knuckle on the door and step back. When it opens, I'm stunned. I'm more confused than ever.

"Well, get in, for fuck's sake."

I look around one last time and step inside as I'm told. It's a woman. She turns her back to me and pours a splash of bourbon into two motel lowballs and pushes one toward me.

"You're his wife," I stutter.

"Who exactly were you expecting?" She sits at an ugly round table with a wood-paneled top and green vinyl chairs straight out of the 1970s. She motions me to sit. I shake the rainwater out of my hair and reluctantly slide into the chair, holding the drink she gave me with both hands, keeping my purse, and its contents, safe between my legs.

"I didn't know he was married. I swear, I really didn't." I sound more desperate than I wanted to.

"Separated, actually. Soon to be divorced."

When she says this, I feel a little surge of relief. He had said he was newly on the market, so he hadn't really lied. I don't know why any of it matters now, but somehow, it still does.

"I made it hell for him. He's been trying to get rid of me for a long time, so just a little advice—if your husband finds out what you did and kicks your ass to the curb, don't go down easy until you get what's yours."

Up close, she doesn't appear like the grieving wife I saw on TV. Was she putting on an act? She looks like a once-beautiful woman who has been hardened by grief or anger. She wears no makeup and her hair is unkempt. On TV she wore a tight, pained expression, but still had a softer look about her, in her neat blouse, pencil skirt and glossy lips.

"So is that why you have his truck? You got what's yours?" I ask, beginning to feel a bit more relaxed, even though the reason she can spill this much information to me is because she has me completely by the balls in this situation. However, she's actively blackmailing me, so she has plenty to lose herself. Why not answer my questions?

"My name was still on it too, don't get cute," she snaps.

"So if you're his wife, you must be worth a lot of money after he died. What do you want with my piddly fifty K?" I ask, and she gives me a pointed look.

"I thought you'd be mousier. He usually likes the quiet, unassertive chicks…or so I have come to find out."

"How did you find out about me?" I ask, quietly, silently adding that I used to be that mousy, innocent person she just described, but I'm far from that now.

"Easy. I watched the idiot's house. He thinks he can just dismiss me? He's been trying to for a couple of years, but I wouldn't let him just write me off. Fuck him. Then you start sneaking around, and I was like, great. Two idiots. I followed you to your house…"

"You what?" I demand, thinking of her stalking my house with my kids there. That night Collin heard a noise outside and scared me to death with the gun—was it this lunatic lurking around?

"It was pretty easy to learn everything about you after getting your name off your mailbox. Social media, all that crap."

"Why? I didn't know about you. Why are you punishing me?"

"Jesus, you think it has anything to do with you? That jackass went behind my back and drew up all this paperwork with his lawyer, making sure that I wouldn't get a cent of his money if we divorced. He opened a foreign bank account in Italy, moved some money into his brother's name, all kinds of bullshit, just to screw me." She takes a large swallow of her drink.

I can't help but think that that must be why she had to kill him. If she wouldn't get it in the divorce, she would probably get some, at least insurance, upon his death. Louisiana is a community property state. He would have had to work pretty hard to make sure she got nothing. What the hell did she do to him? I wonder. I don't ask this.

"But you didn't get divorced, he died."

"Yeah. And I'm the idiot who signed a pre-nup and now it seems he made sure I'd be screwed completely. He could have left me something," she scoffs, stands up and goes to grab the bottle of bourbon from where it sits on top of a filthy microwave. I think about the truck she's driving, but don't say anything.

"I'm sorry," I murmur, not really knowing what else I can possibly say.

"You're not the only home-wrecker the police questioned. You're just the only one who lied," she says, and I see now how that made me her perfect target.

"Home-wrecker? You said you were in the middle of a divorce."

"I said separated. That's not divorced yet," she snaps.

I won't let myself get in my head about the other women she's referring to. She wants me to ask, but frankly, over two years of her stalking him while he was trying to divorce her, I'm sure there were other women. It's none of my business, and I'm not going to play into her trap on this.

"Where's my money? I gotta get back to the city."

So she lives in New Orleans. Explains why I haven't seen her before. I guess she just rolls into town to exploit people.

"I could only get eight." I take the envelope of money out of my purse, maneuvering it around the gun under the table so she doesn't see, and I place it in front of her.

"Let me get this straight. I tell you to get fifty K, and

you say you can only get ten today, and then you bring me this shit." She seems like someone who is trying to be hard even though it's not really in her nature. Like me, this whole situation has changed her into a character she hasn't figured out how to play just yet.

"That's what I could get. I'll get the rest soon." I try to sound confident.

She stares at me overdramatically, then she pulls her phone out of her raincoat on the bed.

"Here, lemme show you something," she says, turning her phone around for me to see a video. It's dark and hard to make out at first. Then I see it's me. I'm holding my shoes and tiptoeing through the muddy terrain behind Luke's house. When I hit the clearing, I run to my car. The camera moves, so I can tell she's driving slowly behind, following me to get the whole thing, my license plate and all just in case my face can't be recognized in the dark lighting. I feel sick. My chest is hot. My mouth goes dry. She's not just someone who could tell the cops that she saw me there—that might be dismissed as the crazy ex-lover grasping at straws, my word against hers. She has me on a time-stamped video! I'm flush with anger.

"So sending me Luke's locket, and following me and watching me when I'm with my kids... Why the hell did you need to do all of that shit if you have this?" I ask bitterly.

She doesn't react to my increased volume; she just hunches over the envelope of money, counting the bills, and barely looks up when she says, "I like to know how you'll react to things—helps me know who I'm dealing with. Plus, I wanted to make sure you knew who was in control."

"I'm sure they're looking at you. Who else has any motive? You don't want them to know you were stalking around the house. You should be wanting to distance yourself as far as you can from any of this, not blackmailing someone." I force myself not to scream this.

She smiles very calmly. She doesn't look fazed.

"You're cute." She leans back in her chair, like she's enjoying herself.

"I could go to them myself, you know, and say I'm being blackmailed. All I'm guilty of is knowing him. I wasn't a beneficiary of anything."

"You think I'd put myself at risk if I didn't have a rock-solid alibi?" She finishes counting the bills and looks to me for a response, but I just stare at her with my mouth open, letting this sink in. I'm not versed at any of this. I have no idea what I'm doing, and I am starting to suffocate under the weight of all the cunning and dishonesty.

"If I wanted to turn in the video, I could do it anonymously," she adds, giving me a sideways look like I'm the other woman. "I can write a note along with it that says I don't want to get involved BUT I saw something suspicious outside his house." She puts her hand to her mouth, making an O with her lips, a mocking "oh no" gesture.

"What could it be? A burglar. Of course I snapped a video. I was protecting him. But no, it was you. Anyway, I'd rather not release the video, but I will if you force me to."

"It will be suspicious that you didn't say something earlier." The rain outside picks up. It thunders on the roof, and we have to nearly shout over it.

"I didn't think much of it, but then I remembered and brought it to them of my own free will. I think they'd actually appreciate it." She shoves the money in her parka pocket and stands, flipping the hood over her head and aiming toward the door.

"Okay," she says, opening it. The mist from the heavy rain on the sidewalk pops and hisses. I understand the dismissal and go to the door.

"I'll need half by next week. Meet me here. I'll send a time by text. So, seventeen thousand. We'll talk about the rest from there. You should probably have a plan by then."

I look at her in stunned silence, really not knowing what else to say.

"Thank you," she says impatiently, so I walk out into the downpour and run to my car. In the driver's seat, I shake the water off my clothes, and I can see her lock the room door and disappear into the deluge. Why isn't she getting into her car? Where could she possibly be going?

23

Behind Gillian's house is a mother-in-law unit that she's turned into an art studio, even though she isn't an artist. It's still raining when I arrive for book club, after the meeting with Valerie Ellison. All the regular suspects sit in the gloomily lit space where Gill keeps fabric drops covering easels next to buckets of paint supplies in some strange attempt to appear more interesting than she is. The paint streaks staining the artist stool in front of a blank canvas are probably from her kids' watercolors.

Since I'd voiced out loud that I was thinking of going back to the book club and I know it's something Collin would like to see, I made myself go. I welcome any distraction from the bizarre turn my life has taken, even if for only a couple of uninspired hours. I even stopped at Fine Spirits for a couple bottles of wine to bring.

I watch the fingers of rainwater trickle and splinter off the great windowpane that spans the whole north wall of the room. Gillian has left the French doors open to listen to the tapping drizzle outside, and the earthy, damp scent drifting inside is a creature comfort that my mind immediately takes to a dark place: I wonder if I'll miss this in prison.

"Sorry we're stuck out here, girls. Robert insisted on watching some game with his buddies and I didn't want to cancel. Men, am I right?" She says this like we all don't know her house is big enough to host the two parties in separate wings, or that this room she's apologizing for is actually lovely.

"Who wants cake?" She cuts the white cylinder, iced and covered with neat fall decor shaped from sugar.

We sit in a loose circle of white, wingback chairs and exchange the obligatory compliments on one another's hair or outfit. Then, conversation shifts to the weather and morphs into Gillian's humblebrags about her latest gifts from Robert. Karen brings up a couple movies she saw with the family on Netflix over the weekend.

"That movie was an absolute turkey," Karen adds, but I haven't heard which one they're talking about. My gaze rests on the water rushing the gutters down the alley behind the house.

"I suffered through that Ben Affleck puke-bonanza twice. Just because the kids like it." I catch Liz saying this and can't help laughing. She's always been the funniest in the group.

"We're trying to keep it light around our house, so any mindless comedies are welcome, what with a murderer on the loose in town," Tammy says. Now I'm alert, my attention back on the group.

"Yeah, we upped our security system," Karen says. "There are cameras in just about every room and you can see all the rooms in your house from your phone." She pauses. "It's actually really creepy."

"I'd say. How can you *not* be creeped out by that? Every horror movie now has cameras set up and something horrible caught in the footage in the middle of the night. I wouldn't be able to bring myself to look at it," Gill says.

"You think they'll make a movie about this Ellison murder?" Tammy asks eagerly, and Gill rolls her eyes. She often treats Tammy like she's the dummy of the group.

"There are a ton of murders every day, Tammy. Why would they make a movie about this one?"

Tammy shrugs, feeling the condescension in Gillian's voice. She trails her finger across the top of her frosting and licks it off her index finger, looking away.

"Well, I'll tell you why," Karen chimes in. "I heard he was beheaded."

"Who?" Gill asks.

"The dead guy. Luke Ellison."

"I heard that too I think!" Tammy is happy to be validated. "Yeah, beheaded by his own kitchen knife." She seems unsure about this, but still spews out the fiction like it's fact. The news never even divulged the cause of death, let alone these grizzly details. It's suddenly, as if it wasn't already, very clear to me how simple rumors become venomous, life-ruining facts in this town.

"That's not true," Liz snaps, and we all look at her. Her cheeks are flushed and she seems angry at the conversation. The others don't really pay much attention to this outburst. They laugh it off and continue, but I keep my eyes on Liz a moment, wondering why this seems so personal to her. She takes a few swallows of wine and rolls her eyes, then excuses herself to the bathroom.

"What's with her?" Gill asks in her absence.

"Well, there is a killer running loose, maybe she doesn't want to talk about it. It's horrifying," Karen says, and they all give something like a silent agreement, with nods and quiet sips of wine.

"I did hear that they can't find the head though," Tammy adds, "and that's why they won't say how he died."

"That doesn't make any sense," Gill chides her again. "If the media had a juicy fact like that, that's *all* they'd be talking about."

I feel like I could be sick listening to this, but I just stay calm and frown down at my shoes, hoping to remain in the background of the conversation.

When Liz returns, they leave the topic alone and discuss Cassie Duchesne's botched boob job and the seasoning on the deviled eggs Karen brought.

"Subbed Greek yogurt for the mayo. Tangy and healthier." She beams with pride as she passes them around.

Just then, Gillian's husband, Robert, pops his head in the open door. All the women greet him, and he gives a curt nod of acknowledgment, but gestures for Gillian to talk with him privately.

They stay under the awning around the side of the studio, and Karen makes a tasteless joke about her being in trouble for overspending her allowance. Everyone shifts toward the spread of food on the drafting table, but I watch a moment, and see Robert put his finger in Gillian's face. I can't make out what he's saying; I try to read his lips to get the gist, but to no avail. She looks like she's defending herself about something. Then her demeanor changes, and she looks like she gains the upper hand. She heaves some last words at him before storming away without looking back, but I see him rest his straight arm against the side of the house and look up, sighing, as if to say *You gotta be kidding me.*

No one else has paid attention to this. Liz still looks pale, but she's doing her best to fawn over the mini tartlets with everyone else. I shoot Liz a look, silently asking if she's okay. When she catches my eye, she looks away. Then Gillian walks in, chipper as ever, an uncanny ability to shake off whatever just happened and go seamlessly back into hostess mode.

"Oh, aren't they just darling?" She joins the tartlet fan club and the women giggle and poke at more food on the table.

There's a strange intensity in the room, and I have no idea what's going on. I have to remind myself that there's probably nothing going on. I'm highly sensitive right now. Gillian engaged in a very normal disagreement, probably over which side of the house got to use the good vodka for their party or some equally petty feud they always have when they think no one is looking, and Liz *is* probably terrified that there is an unsolved murder, and doesn't want to keep being reminded of it. I can't let unreasonable paranoia hijack my rationality. I pick up a small plate of assorted mini-foods and give a sensationalized account of how good it is, as one does.

At home, Collin sits with Ben on the back deck, playing a card game with a kerosene lamp flickering between them. I pop my head out to let him know I'm back, and I only need to look down at my watch with my mom face on for Collin to tell me they're wrapping it up. It's far past his bedtime, but Collin's joy in spending quiet time with Ben is touching. I smile at them both and then fall into the living room recliner, exhausted from the strange day.

Now that I know who Valerie is—now that I get what she wants and understand that if she turned me in I could say I was researching her because she was blackmailing me—I feel more free to dig into her background online.

There are a zillion Valerie Ellisons on the social media sites I search. This won't be as easy as searching for Lacy, so I pull off my shoes and lean back against the mass of pillows on the bed. I narrow the search by area and click on dozens of photos that don't match up until, forty-five minutes in, I come across a photo that looks like her—somehow her smile even looks smug when she's trying to appear genuine and so it pops out, even from its tiny thumbnail size on the screen. I click.

She half scowls at me from her profile photo, wearing a white, beachy dress and holding a glass of champagne, blue pool water in the background. I try to click through for more photos. Only a few are public. I can't see her occupation or relationship status. In another photo, she's in front of the Space Needle in Seattle, giving a thumbs-up to the camera. Another woman has an arm around her and wears a fanny pack and visor. Nothing that gives me any information. I don't really even know what I'm looking for. Then I see it. We have a friend in common. We both know Joe Brooks.

He's been in the background of my Facebook friends for years. I've known him since we were kids, and he coaches Ben's team, it's to be expected that we would be tied somehow on social media, but I don't log on often, and I'd completely forgotten about Joe being a so-called friend. I click on his profile, shakily.

I flip through all of his photos. Many are of him out on his boat with the guys and a few pretty women in bikinis. Lots of gym selfies, him flexing his muscles. A celebration photo captioned Detective Brooks. That must have been the night I met Lacy. She said he was celebrating his promotion and I can see the kitschy Budweiser signs and coinoperated pool tables behind him in the photo. There is no trace of Lacy anywhere. No photos, and they're not friends.

His page seems to be all selfies and beer with the occasional shared images that are in poor taste, but not overtly offensive. A tray of buns from the oven that look like butts. Super classy. I can't imagine what his page would look like if he didn't have to hold back, his job being in the public eye. I scroll through his posts as the page loads and blooms a new crop of idiotic memes. I stop cold when I see his post from September 20. There's a huge charity event in town every September. Formal dress, overpriced drinks, a silent auction, dancing, the whole nine yards. Collin and I have gone a few times, but we both balk at dressing in black-tie attire, so we haven't bothered in a few years. I didn't realize it had fallen on the twentieth.

I'm looking at a massive group photo, about thirty people scrunched in for the shot. Joe is in the back, in a tux. A few women duck down in the front row in their gowns, balancing as they crouch in heels. One gives another bunny ears. Some of the faces I know from town, a few I haven't seen before. But there, in the second row of the photo, is Valerie Ellison and her rock-solid alibi. She's posing for a group photo time-stamped at 9:23 p.m.

Except that she's not posing, not exactly. It looks as though…she's looking back slightly, not at the camera, but toward Joe Brooks. I throw my phone to the end of the bed, impulsively, when I hear Collin's footfalls coming down the hall. Then, I scramble to pick it up and toss it in my nightstand drawer before he enters the room, and lie back on the bed. He chuckles when he sees me.

"They're that exhausting, huh?"

"Yes." I smile, playing into his assumption.

"Did you discuss a book this time?"

"Does a story in *People* magazine about whether or not Kate Middleton got a new nose count as a book?" I say, and Collin laughs. He sits next to me while he unbuttons his shirt and pushes each shoe off with the other heel. He kisses my cheek.

"You can just use them for research for your novel. Call it *Suburban Wildlife*."

"I like it," I say, and he picks up his shoes and goes into the en suite bathroom to shower. I go in behind him to brush my teeth. In the mirror, I can see his reflection inside the glass panels of the shower. The steam obstructs my view a little, but I feel a heat rising inside me, watching the soapy water slide down his skin and drop into foamy peaks on the shower floor.

Part of my sudden longing for him is remorse, but much of it is the same attraction and feeling of safety and desire we've always felt with one another. I undress and slide into the shower behind him, caressing my hands around his slippery chest. He's surprised, but leans into me as I touch him. He turns and kisses me, passionately. It almost feels like new love, and I realize that I've been neglecting him. He seems almost grateful for my initiating.

When we finish, I lay awake thinking about how I will create a fake Facebook account to friend Valerie, so I can see who she really is and how present Luke is in her documented online history. She has two thousand plus friends, and now that I know we have a mutual friend in common, she probably wouldn't think twice about accepting a request from me as long as I take on a male persona. I can piece one together from stock photos and take my chances.

I try hard to sleep, but I toss and turn. I wonder what it might mean that Joe and Valerie know one another. How? It seems a little too convenient that her alibi involves an event where Joe is also present. She thought she'd get money if Luke died. She didn't know until he was already dead that he'd changed his will and made sure she didn't. She must be pretty proud of herself for this photo, proving she wasn't there. I could just about guarantee that the same photo is displayed, boastfully, on her page, just to make sure it's loud and clear.

My first thought when I found out that they knew one another was that she'd offered to give him a cut of whatever she got if he helped her get rid of Luke. There's no question that she would have needed someone on the inside to help—someone with the connections she'd need to cover something up. And it's also clear that he has no problem abusing his badge to do whatever serves him in the moment. He gets away with it.

But I guess none of that can be true because they're both in the photo on that night. The problem is, I don't trust a coincidence this big.

24

On Monday morning, with everyone away at work and school, I decide to run some errands downtown. Ralph tries to jump into the backseat when I open the car to put my bag down, so I grab his leash, deciding a walk will be good for me. After I finish the mundane task of dropping off dry cleaning and stopping at the post office, I take Ralph around the town center streets. He stops every few feet to sniff something unseen yet fascinating to him. I let him pull me along in fits and starts, not paying much attention.

We pass the little library, rows of small businesses that used to be houses now converted into Knotty Knitters sewing shop and Ye Olde Creamery ice cream parlor, and then a place I used to park to go and see Luke. I dismiss a stitch of guilt trying to rise up and keep walking.

We come up to the quaint police headquarters, which are housed in a small brick building, with eighteenth-century Spanish architecture and wrought iron balconies on the second floor. I always thought it was too pretty to be a police station. Ralph stops right in front to pee on a bed of pale pink snapdragons, and I gaze toward the parking lot on the side of the station. Luke's truck is parked there. An electric surge of hot panic runs through me. Valerie is there. Why? Why would she tell them what she has on me if she knows she can still get money out of me? All the intangible scraps of thoughts that haunted my dreams as I fell into a hard, fitful sleep last night are coming back to me.

I don't care if Joe Brooks is posed in a very public photo the night of the murder. Just because it was posted at 9:23 doesn't mean it was taken then. I have no way to know when it was taken. Luke lives minutes from that downtown venue where the event is always held. Either of them could have left the party for a while and slipped back in. There would be way too many people for someone to really leave unnoticed. Especially—my knuckles go white as I think of it—especially if they were there together. They might be one another's alibi. There would be nobody else, like a date or someone, to miss them if they left for a while.

She had everything to gain, and she'd need help. He has all the connections and clout to never be suspected, and he could protect her. If this overwhelming hunch is right, Joe isn't just casually questioning me. He could be planning to pin this on me. I need to get them before they get me.

I imagine him meeting her at that putrid motel later that night, after I gave her the money, and they probably splurged my Birkin bag spoils on expensive booze and had lewd sex, celebrating what they'd gotten away with—and what they are about to get away with. I can't let that happen.

I hadn't thought of the library before. Probably because coming up with sneaky, devious plots to cover up the lies I've told has not come second nature to me until now. I hook Ralph's leash to a sprinkler spout in a shady spot on the ground and run into the library. The computers are open to the public, so it's better to do this here than use my own IP address.

It's only $19.99 to buy a background check on someone, but when I pull up Valerie's file, there isn't much to see. It mostly just gives criminal background information. It's not that I expected prior arrests for money laundering or fraud, but that would have been nice to see, of course—to have some leverage, something to keep in my back pocket. The only record she has is traffic related—a few petty moving violations, and one DWI. I click on it. It shows that she was arrested on that offense locally. It was only about six months ago. I wonder if Joe happened to be the arresting officer, if that's how she came to know him. I can't find that information out. I see her address is in New Orleans. I write it down with a tiny golf pencil sitting on the computer table and shove it in my coat pocket.

Then I open Facebook and create an account. I call myself Dylan Bisset for no real reason other than we used to have a guinea pig named Dylan and so it was the first thing to come to mind. I type a fake email address and it won't let me continue until I confirm via email. Shit. Now I have to bring up Gmail and create a new account there first. Dylan_Bisset1978_ gets green-lighted after I try a few variations. I go back to Facebook, type in the new email, go back to the email, accept "terms and conditions" and confirm, and I'm in.

I can't steal the photo of someone I actually know because it might be linked back, so I just type HOT GUYS into Google Images, and thousands of options materialize. I cut and paste the photo of a guy who looks around my age, not too model-esque, but not a photo that will scream sleazebag either. I don't know how to populate a history of posts to show that it's not a fake account. All I can do is make an initial post:

WELL, I SAID I'D NEVER DO IT, BUT MY FRIENDS FINALLY GOT ME TO SIGN UP FOR THIS. PROVE ME WRONG, FACEBOOK, Dylan says. A good reason for being a newbie.

I'm pleased with myself for making it sound like a legitimate first post. Then I shamelessly friend request as many people as I can before I have to go. It's amazing how "people you may know" suggestions are abundant, even for a totally made-up person. Before I log off, seven people have accepted my request. Bingo. I add Valerie Ellison, and hope for the best, but I'll need to come back to see if she's accepted. I can't do this from my own devices.

Outside, Ralph leaps to his feet and runs in circles as I approach him. I scratch his ears and walk him back to the car. Luke's truck is gone. Yesterday, my first thought would be that she's back from New Orleans because they wanted to question her further. Now I think she's here for very different reasons.

25

"Gillian and Robert are fighting," I say to Collin over dinner that night. I need a reason to get out of the house and investigate, and so I tell a half-truth because they *were* fighting. I don't really know why I grasp for this when I am about to deceive him. Again. He stabs at a steaming baked potato with his fork.

"Aren't they always fighting?" he asks, resuming the conversation.

"Who's fighting?" Ben asks, wide-eyed. He mostly completely ignores adult conversation and stays lost in his art and coloring books, but he often surprises us and has been paying attention to a conversation we weren't careful enough to have had out of earshot.

"Mom's telling me about a book she's reading, bud," Collin covers. He lifts his eyebrows at me in a self-congratulatory way for thinking of it so quickly.

"What's the story?" he asks matter-of-factly.

Collin pauses, then...

"It's called *The Anesthesiologist and the Gold Digger*."

I choke on my sip of water at his coded description of Gillian and Robert.

"Is it about someone digging for gold?"

"Kind of. It's about someone digging for Prada bags and diamond jewelry," Collin says, trying to keep a straight face.

"Sounds dumb," Ben says.

"It is dumb, bud." He pats Ben on the back and smiles at me sideways.

"Meghan Markle has a Prada bag. It's pink," Ben says.

We both look at him as he picks up his pink crayon and continues his drawing.

"Anyway, you're golfing tomorrow, right?" I ask.

"Yeah, around ten."

"So, would you mind if tonight I grabbed a drink with Gill? Rachel has a paper to write, and Claire is resting."

"Go for it. The boys have plans anyway, right?" he says to Ben who excitedly explains.

"Pacquiao versus Thurman! And we got the good popcorn with the caramel."

"Boxing?" I say, trying to keep the disapproval out of my voice and pick my battles. He gives an overdramatic shrug and goofy look.

"It was the kid's pick this time. He chose Pacquiao and Thurman."

"Mmm-hmm." I kiss Ben's head. "No homework?"

"It's done," Ben says, not looking up from his art.

"Okay then. I'm gonna go change I guess. Thanks for holding down the fort."

Upstairs, I poke my head into Claire's room. She's asleep in her chair. I turn down a *Seinfeld* rerun so I can hear anyone coming up the stairs. I quickly go into her medicine cabinet and look for the bottle I need for my plan. As I stand, looking at the labels, I wish I had brought my readers. I squint at an opaque orange bottle when I hear the creak of a floorboard behind me and drop the pills into the sink.

"Mom?"

"Jesus." I hold my hand to my heart, catching my breath. Rachel has just appeared without a sound. She holds a tampon box in one hand. In the other is my burner phone.

"What are you doing?" she asks. I stop cleaning up the pills and stare at her.

"Nothing. Just—getting Claire's dinner pills ready before I go. Honey…" I don't say anything, I just take the phone from her. "Why were you in our bathroom?"

"I needed…" She stops and looks at the tampon box with a flushed face. "Why do you have a creepy second phone hidden in here? What is this?"

"It's…my phone." I stumble over my words. I was not at all prepared to be on the spot like this.

"It's a flip phone. It looks like 2005 called. That's not yours."

"Keep those," I say, nodding to the box she holds loosely by her side to distract attention from it, "and get ready to go to Katie's."

"I've seen those cheap throwaway phones in movies. Sooo, you're not gonna tell me why you have it?"

"Movies? Rachel. It's just an old phone. I was probably cleaning and got distracted. I put my iPad in the fridge once by mistake. It's nothing. I'll recycle it. Go. You're gonna keep her mom waiting."

Rachel has her hand on one hip and looks at me sideways a few more minutes until she hears Ben yell that Katie's mom pulled up, then she bolts out of the room, seemingly changing moods and forgetting all about it in seconds. I hide the phone in the back of Claire's medicine cabinet for now, not daring to walk across the house with it in my hand. It will be safe until I get home and find a new hiding place when everyone's asleep.

Candy's Strip Club is outside of the county line on a remote road next to a truck stop. That's probably why Joe Brooks goes to that one. Lord knows there are plenty to choose from, but Candy's is full-nude and out of his police jurisdiction. I don't imagine I will run into anyone I know, but if I do, I plan to say that I'm writing a story and this is research. I've never been in a strip club, so I need to see one to accurately write about it. The real reason is that Lacy hasn't returned my last few calls and I'm worried, but selfishly, I also need her help.

Inside, the club is electric with pulses of strobe light. Flashes of laughing faces appear as the spotlight sweeps around the crowd, the light telling a piecemeal story, like hearing snatches of conversation in a crowded restaurant. The light flashes a man tipping back a last swallow of beer, then a girl on a man's lap, taking a cigarette from his lips, then a young man, drunk, with a paper crown, a bachelor party perhaps.

I'm nervous, and I am trying to resist the urge to turn around and leave, so I walk along the back wall, down a sticky hallway to find a restroom. I must be in the wrong corridor because I see the dancers' dressing room. The door stands open, and I watch a moment. I can't turn away from a room full of beautiful women dressing up in heels and gloss, not for a special date, but to walk out and be objectified by a roomful of men.

The bass from the stage speakers rattles glasses, pregnant with ice cubes and colorful cocktails, which rest all along the dressing tables or the floor or on stools. Black plastic ashtrays hold smoldering cigarettes that cloud the small, narrow room. Girls stretch bent legs on stools to fasten garter belts and stockings, covering nipples with tassels, and painting their eyes with beautiful sweeps of purple and glitter. It could almost be mistaken for backstage of a 1930s cabaret. If only they could stay behind that dressing room door and not meet the searing lights of the catwalk.

One of the women, wearing a strappy, glittery wisp of fabric that could fit in the palm of my hand, sees me. I take a step back and look left to right, trying to figure out my escape. She smiles and takes a pull of her cigarette.

"Bathroom's on the other side, honey."

I nod, nervously, and because she was kind and didn't slam the door in my face I ask, "Is Lacy working tonight?"

"Not tonight, sorry."

I find a small table in the back of the room. I didn't put a lot of thought into how it would look, a woman alone in a strip club. Pathetic, I suppose. I don't even know exactly what I plan to do, but maybe if I can find the other girls Joe came to see, I can gain something from talking to them. It surprises me that he can get away with hanging out at strip clubs and paying for sex as a detective, but it's not a crime to come in here, and nobody would ever admit money was exchanged for sexual favors. It's all protected. He's protected. Not just by his badge, but by women too frightened to challenge it—women who, in the eyes of most, have little credibility and are great targets for his type.

I order a vodka tonic and ignore the sideways looks I'm getting from a table of men nearby. I swallow the drink down quickly for liquid courage, and order another. I begin feeling the familiar elasticity in my arms and legs as each sip navigates its way through my blood. I'm slightly more at ease, but still without a plan.

A spotlight illuminates a figure onstage. She's announced as Sugar Cane, and she's sucking on a rainbow lollipop and spinning around a pole. "Feelin' Love" fills the room from speakers hanging in every corner. The moving lights are making me ill. My heart beats in my throat and my head feels light. The room reminds me of going to the roller rink as a kid. It was dark and the lights glittered and danced on the floor like fallen stars. I could never skate over the moving dotted pattern on the floor because it would make me dizzy and I'd fall and trip other passing kids on the rink. I feel like that now, and I decide to just go home, until a woman, almost entirely naked, sits down right next to me, tapping the ash of her cigarette into the tray on my table.

"You here about a job? You gotta talk to George." She

points at a large, sweaty man with a sports coat on, lingering around the bar.

"Oh no. I'm not…I'm just…" I don't have a reason to state why I'm here, so I stop.

"Well, not many girls come in here unless they're looking for a job or to catch their man cheating. You're pretty enough if you want the work. George would put you on a couple weeknights. What's your name, sweets?" She rests her cigarette between her lips to hold her hand out to shake mine, and she squints to keep the smoke from her eyes.

"Uh…Mel." Should I have given a fake name? I don't really see a reason to, and it's too late anyway.

"Cinnamon," she says, confidently. "You must be here to bust your boyfriend, then. Maybe I can help. At least if he's a regular, I might know him."

"Cinnamon?" I repeat, dumbly. That's one of the names Lacy gave me. "Have you seen Joe Brooks here recently?" I ask, and her face goes pale. There is something like anger in her eyes, but she stands, wordlessly, and turns to go. I go after her, grabbing at her elbow, but she pulls it away and turns to me.

"You the wife or somethin'?"

"No! I—I know Lacy. I feel like Joe may be involved in something…I…look, can I buy you a drink or something and talk?"

"You're not an old girlfriend—you're not gonna trick me here 'cause you're pissed at him about something?"

"No, I've never dated him, it has nothing to do with me, I just have a few questions. I think he might have hurt someone, and any help I can get is—it's just really important."

She thinks about this a moment, her face softening a little.

"If you know Lacy, I guess. I was on the early shift, so I'm finishing up soon. You can buy me that drink and meet me over there." She points to the dressing room, and then dissolves into the crowd.

A half hour later, Cinnamon pulls two small wooden chairs out from the dressing room, and we sit with our drinks in the darkness of the oppressively hot back hallway.

"What'd he do now?" she asks, a question I wasn't prepared to hear. I never expected cooperation like this. "Lacy's okay, right?"

"Yeah. She is. I mean, I think. I haven't heard from her in a few days, but I assume she's fine."

I know Joe already has an alibi for the night of the murder, but I ask about it anyway because there was something in Lacy's reaction when I asked her that didn't sit right.

"I know it's a long shot, but you wouldn't remember if he was here the night of September 20, would you?"

"Sure he was," she says right away.

"What?"

"I only remember because I had tickets to Lady Gaga that night in New Orleans. Lacy called, bawling, 'cause little Ronny Lee was sick or something. She was close to getting fired for missing shifts, so she begged me to cover."

"You're kidding. He was here."

"I told her I could only do it if I could scalp the tickets and, man, I got a fortune for them, so it worked out." I try to be patient with her story to get to the part I need.

"What time did he come?"

"Oh, I don't know. Late. I just remember 'cause he usually pays for extra services in the champagne room, but he didn't that night. He was ignoring me, acting weird."

"Weird how?"

"I don't know. He's usually drinking and hootin' and hollerin', ya know. But that night he just sat at a table by himself and didn't look good, didn't talk to nobody."

I think of Joe coming here after the charity event to decompress, maybe still in shock from the crime he'd committed.

"I'm only telling you this 'cause Lacy's messed up with him again and she's my friend. God knows there's plenty of shit he should go to jail for and probably never will, so if you think you got a way to do something, I'm all in."

"Were you ever involved with him? Outside of here?"

She looks off, into the faceless cluster of bodies down the hall inside the main club room, and lights another cigarette.

"I won't say anything to Lacy, if you don't want me to," I say after a minute of quiet.

"She knows already. I'm not proud of it." She wraps one long leg around the other. Her cheekbones are high and her lips are full. Her hair, obviously once blond, now dyed a copper red, falls around her neck and she adjusts a shoe strap, unsure whether to confide in me. "They weren't together at the time, but still. It was a shitty thing to do to a friend. He's good though, I mean you don't know how he can talk his way in." I think of this dual life Joe must live. He poses in photos at charity balls

259

and presents himself as a saint to all the single moms whose kids he coaches. He even dates high-society women now and then and probably treats them like royalty, and then he goes into the slums and lets the devil in him loose. He finds these girls who he thinks of as low-life stripper types he can string along, abuse and keep secret. It makes my stomach flip thinking of it.

"When were you seeing him?"

"Mostly in between when Lacy saw him, the weeks they were on the outs. Then I find out Angela is screwing him too, and—"

"Who's Angela, she work here?"

"Oh. Yeah." She gestures with a twirl of her finger to the dressing room behind us. "Luscious is her name at the club. She's around somewhere. Thing is, we all figured out he's a shit eventually, ya know. But Lacy, she's in trouble. She won't stay away."

"What exactly did he do, what made you stop seeing him?" I ask. Her eyes fill and she sighs.

"He takes his time, ya know? He gets you to trust him real good. He brings you presents and tells you you're beautiful. He doesn't try anything for a good long time. Then, like out of the blue one day he's different. He'd only ever meet me at my apartment or here. After we did our thing, he got up to go home. I was just kidding with him, you know, trying to be cute, and I pulled him back down on the bed a little and told him to stay." She wipes away a tear that's escaped her eye.

"He turned and punched me so hard, he knocked the wind out of me, and while I was trying to get my breath back, he held me down on the bed saying I better never think I can tell him what to do again. I could hear my kids crying in the next room 'cause they heard me scream. He wouldn't let me go, he just held me there awhile. Then, like, just walked out and left." She wipes her nose with the inside of her tiny top and shakes her head softly.

"Was that the last time you saw him…romantically?"

"Ya'd think so, right? But that's what I'm saying. It's like a total *Dr. Phil* show. He comes back with apologies and gifts and I give him another chance, and two weeks later, he fuckin' chokes me 'cause I showed up at Sully's bar. Like I knew he was even there. He thinks I'm following him, trying to get attention or something. Like he owns the town. When you say it afterward, it sounds really bad, but at the time, I thought—I don't know, I thought I was in love. I wanted him not to be the man he actually is."

"How long, then, until you stopped seeing him?"

"It was off and on for a year, maybe."

"Did he ever do anything else, like other sorts of assault?" I ask. She steps on the butt of her cigarette.

"I gotta go. I got kids at home." She stands and reaches inside the dressing room for her handbag. "Maybe ask Angela about that. She got the worst of it."

She hollers inside the door.

"Angie, you got a sec to talk to this lady? She's asking about Joe Brooks." The door slams, violently, in my face, and I hear "Fuck that guy" from inside the dressing room. Cinnamon shrugs.

"Thank you for talking to me," I say.

"Get him," she says, looking right into my eyes, then turns on her heel and leaves.

26

Valerie Ellison seems like a completely normal woman online. She's accepted Dylan Bisset's friend request, and as I sit back at the library again the next day, she doesn't resemble the maniac extortionist I've come to know. In one image, she's posed in a new-looking yoga outfit with an enormous Starbucks cup in hand, and in another she's with girlfriends at a picnic table at a camping site, holding up red plastic cups in a cheers. She's giving close-up duck lips in her car and has captioned it FEELIN' CUTE. She looks like she'd fit right in with Gillian and the neighborhood ladies.

It's not until I scroll all the way down to a year and a half ago that I see photos of her and Luke together. It makes my stomach drop a little at the sight of them looking up to the camera, at whoever is taking the photo, heads touching at a restaurant. He's kissing her on the cheek on the deck of a cruise ship in another. Their wedding photos are from six years ago. I flip through them, forcing myself to look. She was stunning on a beach in Mexico. A barefoot bride next to her striking groom in beachy burlap trousers and a white button-down. In one photo, he is knee-deep in the sea and he lifts her up like a dancer, her legs bent behind her, reaching down to kiss him. They look…in love.

I wonder what happened. Anything, I guess. My own wedding photos look not too different than these, and look what I've done to destroy my marriage. Maybe this greedy, psychopathic side I have seen in her started to show. Maybe one of them cheated. Then I see, around two years back, her activity stops and there are hundreds of posts from friends, people sending "thoughts and prayers" for sweet Lily.

They had a daughter.

A flurry of clicks produces images of a happy child in a wheelchair. When I go all the way back to photos of Lily's birth, Valerie posts a sad announcement explaining the degenerative disease the child was diagnosed with. I wonder if their child's passing was what fractured their marriage. I swallow down the lump in my throat. Why didn't he tell me he had a daughter? We told one another so much. I guess it would mean explaining his ex-wife, but I still feel lied to, which is ridiculous because he had no obligation to tell me anything, truth be told.

Her page is a great disappointment because it tells me nothing I can use to my advantage. She looks like someone I would be friends with. Except that she wants several thousand dollars from me in a few days, and I have no idea how I can get that kind of money without Collin finding out it's missing.

I click to minimize Valerie's profile and search CUBIC ZIRCONIA RINGS, THREE CARAT, QUAD PRINCESS CUT ENGAGEMENT

RINGS. There are pages of them. I stop when I see one that looks closest to my own. My eight-thousand-dollar ring looks almost identical to the fake version worth only ninety-nine bucks. If I pawn my own ring and buy this one, I can't imagine Collin ever noticing. They look so similar, and he's a guy. Why would he even look closely at it? There is nothing else I can sell that wouldn't be missed. It still won't be enough, but as long as I'm paying something, why would she stop the cash flow? I need more time.

There are a few available at a jewelry store in the mall. I pay the ninety-nine dollars in cash and slip the fake diamond on my finger. It's lighter and shinier than my own ring, but no one else would notice that. I can't afford sentimentality right now. This is survival, and I will not get emotional when I hand over the ring that's been on my hand for over fifteen years to the apathetic pawnshop cashier.

A few days later, I find myself in the same motel room. This time it looks like she's stayed the night. The sheets are rumpled up at the end of the bed, and there are two wineglasses, one on each nightstand with a slip of red liquid dotting the bottom of each. Who was she with? I don't see men's things or an overnight bag.

"It's all I could get," I say, handing her the six thousand and feeling a bit of déjà vu from the last time I was here, feeling scolded like an impish child.

"Fuck. Are you kidding me?"

"The whole reason you're getting money at all is so my family doesn't find out about my relationship with Luke. You think that I can just take fifty thousand out of my bank account and my husband won't ask questions? If he finds out, I guess you lose your position and wouldn't get *any* money, so maybe be a little patient."

She stares at me, lips parted, taken off guard.

"Whoa. The housewife is feisty today," she says, amused.

I almost start the words, *I'm not a...* but before I can decide whether to bother, her phone vibrates across the table, and she grabs for it so quickly that I don't see the incoming number before she flips it upside down. What does she want to hide from me?

"Check your phone, and I'll send more instructions soon," she says, opening the door and unmistakably pushing me out with her eyes. I step outside the threshold. I want to ask her about knowing Joe, call her out, gauge her reaction, but I don't. Not yet. She closes the door and I hear the click of the lock behind me.

At home, Ben's just home from swim class, and he and Collin are in the garage changing the oil in Collin's car. Ben can name different parts of the engine like he can crayon colors and likes to boss Collin around as he works, and Collin is a great sport about it. Ben sits in an old office chair we store in the garage and pushes off his heels, flying himself back and forth across the concrete floor between suggestions.

"You should have gotten synthetic. It's better for the engine," Ben says, peering at the container of Pennzoil Collin holds. I twist my new ring as I walk in the open garage door.

"Hey, fellas."

"Mom! Dad waited more than three thousand miles to change the oil and I know that because it's not the right color. He waited too long."

"Well, I'm glad he has you supervising, then."

"Yeah. I put a reminder on my calendar so I can remind him next time."

"Good thinking, bud," I say, and kiss Collin on the cheek as I pass him and go through into the house with the bag of groceries I stopped for.

"Rachel home?" I ask.

"Out with friends," he says, concentrating on curling the remains of a paper bag from the recycling bin into a funnel so he can pour the oil through it. "You goin' to Gillian's pretend book club tonight?"

I'd forgotten it's Saturday, and I dread the idea, but after my odd behavior last week, I feel like I should. I wonder if any of them have heard that I'm being questioned in the murder. I need to put out fires if any small-town gossip has spread.

"Oh right. Yeah, I guess."

"Well, you sound over the moon about it." He winks at me and I roll my eyes before going inside and placing the groceries on the counter.

That evening, I'm almost to Gillian's house when my phone rings. A number I don't recognize illuminates my screen, and I pick up, a tone of defensiveness in my voice, not knowing what to expect.

"Is this Melanie Hale?" a woman's voice with a thick Southern drawl asks.

266

"Who's this?" I try to keep my voice light.

"Well, ma'am. We have a patient here at Park Hospital. Her ID says she's a Miss Lacy Dupre, but we can't reach any family members, and—"

"Oh my God, is she okay?"

"So you do know her."

"Yes. What happened?"

"Well, looks like she's been in some sort of accident, a hit and run, and we found your name and number on a scrap of paper inside her purse. We were hoping you could help us reach her family. Are you her family?"

"Friend. But, yes, I—can I see her? Is she...?" I stop. The woman doesn't offer any more details over the phone, but tells me to come down. I make a sharp U-turn and race to Park Hospital.

In the white, buzzing aesthetic of Lacy's hospital room, I sit, holding Lacy's hand, minding the oximeter clamped to her index finger. A fluid bolus is connected to a needle in the crease of her arm, where it looks like the nurse fought to find a vein. Her right eye is swollen completely closed with purple-and-black bruising, and stitches close a long contusion on her cheek. The ligature marks and bruises around her neck are obvious, even though the nurse has referred to the incident as a hit and run. Lacy's left wrist is broken, bound with a small cast.

"I reached her sister, who promised to stay with her son for the night," I tell the nurse, even though the sister sounded drunk and I didn't feel good about leaving Ronny Lee with her. Of course I didn't say that part. There really weren't any alternatives. I was lucky to recall her sister's name—Lacy had mentioned it one time—and reach her at all.

"Well, poor thing gained consciousness after she arrived at the hospital, so she's just sleeping now," the nurse assures me. "You might want to let her sleep through the night and come back tomorrow if you want to visit with her."

"What did she say happened to her?"

"A motorist found her lyin' on the side of the road out there by Adelia Grove and called it in."

I know where that is, I think. It's out near the strip club.

"She didn't have much more to tell us," the nurse continues. "Says she couldn't remember really—that a car musta come out of nowhere. That's about all I know."

The portly women pushes some buttons on the machine Lacy's connected to and then says, "Don't look like no hit and run if you ask me." She gives Lacy a pitying smile and shakes her head.

"I'll stay just a while longer if that's okay," I say, and the nurse nods before dimming Lacy's room lights and closing the door softly behind her.

After an hour, I decide to message Collin and tell him what happened. I attach a photo of the shape she's in, seizing the opportunity for him to see that I am where I say I am even if the explanation sounds a bit far-fetched—an anchor of truth in my sea of lies.

JESUS CHRIST! JOE BROOKS'S HANDYWORK? he texts back.

THEY SAY IT WAS A HIT AND RUN. I'LL UPDATE YOU MORE WHEN I GET HOME. XXOO

I doze off in a vinyl chair next to her bed, and wake to Lacy, propped up with pillows, sipping a miniature box of orange juice.

"Hey." I wipe a streak of mascara off my cheek and stand at her side.

"Hi. What are you doing here?" She talks with difficulty through her split lip.

"You had my number on you, so they called."

"I'm so sorry you had to come all the way here and deal with this. So embarrassing. I'm fine." Her words are quiet and strained.

"You're not fine. I'm happy they called. Your sister is taking care of Ronny Lee. Is there anything you need? What the hell happened?"

Silent tears stream down her face. I already know what happened.

"I was walking over to Lucky's on my break. I guess I didn't see the car coming down Landry."

I look at my feet and take a slow, deep breath. She watches me, my doubt in her story evident. She touches the blue rings above her collarbone when she sees me looking.

"Well, sounds like they'll discharge you tomorrow. I can take you home then, if you want." I trail her to the door. She looks at the ceiling with her chin quivering and tears welling.

"He came to the club," she says, and waits until I walk over and sit down for her story. "I saw him with a woman—someone I had never seen before. It was a few days ago in town."

"Who?" I ask eagerly.

"I don't know. Brunette with nice shoes."

My heart is racing when she says this and I'm greedy for more information, but I wait.

"He grabs at my stocking when I pass him at the club, tries to get my attention and I ignore him. I'm mad. But you can't ignore Joe Brooks. It's his worst trigger. He tries again later on—tries to buy a lap dance in the back room, and I turn it down. Girls can always turn down those requests. I had a break, and walked over to the truck stop 'cause I remembered I had to get bread and milk for Ronny Lee before I went home later. He followed me out, I didn't know."

"Jesus. Lacy, you didn't tell anyone? The nurse or anything?"

"You still don't understand. There's no point. It will get worse." She tenses up trying to raise her voice, then whimpers in pain, settling herself back.

"I'm sorry. I just—how is this possible? How can he get away with this? It's insane."

"It happens all the time. Not just me."

"So all because you rejected him."

Her answer is in her silence.

"I shouldn't have fought back. He woulda just gone back inside, but I hit him back, and that last blow, he bent my wrist and got a good shot at my face, that's when I got knocked out. He's usually careful not to get a hospital involved, but he just left me there. Some guy driving past called the police, I guess."

I hand her a tissue from the bedside table.

"I don't even know what I can say. I'm so sorry, Lacy."

"Worst part is, he'll be back. He has to apologize now. That's how it goes."

"Did the woman you saw him with—did you see what she drove?"

"No. Why?"

"Did you get her name, or if she was from out of town?"

"I don't know. I've never seen her around. Why?"

I tell Lacy everything I've learned, about the photo linking Val and Joe, about the blackmail, about the flimsy alibi and what Cinnamon said about him being there that night. I tell her that I think he's working with Luke's ex-wife for the inheritance money, and I need to find out more. If I can prove an involvement between them—messages that are damning—I can…expose them. Something. Anything. She sits still, shocked by all of this information I've unloaded on her.

"Well, shit, I can get into his computer. I know the password," she says.

"What?"

"Yeah, he thinks I'm too dumb to notice probably. The password is his birth date. And he stays automatically logged into his email and stuff. I could help you find out."

"No. No way I would put you in a room with that sociopath on purpose."

"Look, you helped me. Besides, he's gonna call until he can apologize, so there's no avoiding seeing him again. Only thing is, if he saw me do it, he'd…" She doesn't have to say he'd kill her. I can tell she's thinking over the details of how it could work. "It would have to be at his place because his computer is there, but I'm never allowed to stay the night at his apartment, so I don't know how I'd do it."

"I have an idea," I say. "This will work. I'll pick you up when you're discharged tomorrow, and we'll talk about it. Yeah?" I place my hand carefully on her arm and squeeze. She places her hand over mine. It feels like a secret handshake we are creating, a bond of trust somehow.

"Yeah," she agrees.

She trusts me, and I can't let one more person in my life down. This has to work.

27

I have waited for the mailman for the last three days since I dropped Lacy off from the hospital, peering through the living room curtains between one and three, his usual times, just to make certain that the package I'm waiting for doesn't get dangerously intercepted by the kids or Collin.

At the library, right after dropping Lacy off and agreeing to our plan, I went again to use the computer anonymously. Even on a public computer, I didn't want to chance an extensive search for which kind of drugs will knock someone unconscious, or leave a trail of clicks from shady websites, so I typed in a name I'd heard before on an episode of *Dateline*: flunitrazepam. Tasteless, dissolves easily in a drink, takes thirty minutes to knock someone on their ass.

Cinnamon told me to "get him." I knew she would help, so I got her number from Lacy. The girls weren't exactly covert about their cocaine use, so I wondered if she might know where to get other things. After she explained to me three times what the dark web was, she gave up and gave me instructions detailing how to order what I wanted online.

It was easier than I expected. The only real hassle was having to first go and buy a prepaid debit card with cash so there wouldn't be a trail. And if the drugs are discovered, I can always claim they'd gone to the wrong house. After all, the sender refused to put my name on the envelope—it will say only "Current Resident." I didn't even give a name at all, just an address, and the service promised the utmost discretion. This is great news for me, but incredibly alarming to know how easy it is for all the Joes of the world to obtain and use these roofies.

A few days later, after the mailman has dropped a handful of envelopes into the metal box on the front porch, I wait until he's walking up the Millers' front stoop and out of sight before I open the door and flip through the pile to find a surprisingly tiny package resting between a piece of junk mail and a utility bill. As promised, it says only "Current Resident." I leave the rest of the mail in the box and go inside. I open the package carefully and drop the tablets into my palm, then slip them inside the zipper pocket in my wallet. They just fit inside the narrow, otherwise useless little pocket.

I call to tell Lacy we're set.

"It's about time," she complains on the other end of the line. "He sent flowers and won't stop calling. I can only get him to let me go to his place when he's still in his apology phase, so we should do it tonight."

"Tonight. Okay."

"Let me text him back and tell him I'll stop by if he wants, but that I can't stay long. He should say yes, the way he is right now, but I can't be sure. If he says to come over, I'll just text you a time, and we can meet beforehand."

"Okay, sounds good. You sure about this? I don't want you to feel—" But Lacy cuts me off.

"I'm sure. Gotta go." She hangs up, and I wait. I pace the kitchen, then take out a bottle of Lysol and spray a mist across the countertop and scrub at it with a scouring pad, trying to keep myself occupied. I wonder how it's possible that the person guilty of a murder could be the one investigating it. Does he get his pick of who he decides to pin it on? If that's really the situation, and he could plant evidence and find someone who would be a perfect candidate to blame, I wonder if it's been decided that that someone is me.

He's always liked me. He's even wanted me. Maybe just in the past, but I have come to learn that he gets what he wants, and I rejected him once. A long time ago. Too long ago for this to be revenge, but the thought flits across my mind, and his current flirtations are not lost on me.

Two hours later, the counters sparkle and I've even pulled the stainless-steel garbage can out on the front lawn to power wash before I finally get the text back that says, 8 PM. I text back to meet in the parking lot of a Shell station a block away before she goes in. It's set.

I need to attend a parent-teacher conference at Ben's school at six while Collin picks Rachel up from JV basketball practice, her new obsession since she decided she hates dance. Ben is chatting away in the backseat after the conference, and I give intermittent "oh, reallys" now and then, only partly listening.

We stop for takeout at a Mediterranean grill and get home in just enough time for me to drop off dinner and head out to meet Lacy.

"Go wash up, bud," I say to Ben's back, but he's already halfway up the stairs, knowing the drill. The house is eerily quiet.

"Anyone home?" I call, but I saw Collin's car, so I know they're here. Collin is standing at the kitchen counter when I round the corner and put the take-out bags down.

"Hey. It's quiet in here. Where's Rach?" I ask, used to the TV blaring and kids perpetually arguing or asking for something. At the very least, blaring music from their rooms at this hour. His face looks fatigued, his eyes dark.

"Rachel's in her room."

"Why? She okay?"

"Yeah, she doesn't want to talk to anyone, and she's skipping dinner, or so she loudly announced."

"What happened? Wha—"

"I don't know, like I said, she's not talking to anyone, but I can only guess it has something to do with the fact that our daughter became a woman today...so I hear."

I don't quite absorb it at first because it's such an odd thing to hear Collin say.

"Uhhh. What?" I ask, daftly.

"Please don't."

"Don't what?"

"Pretend not to know what I'm talking about. I can't take watching you lie right now."

I feel my face go hot and numb. I know she would never tell

276

him about her period in a million years. He must have heard us.

"I, no, I mean yes, you're right, but she wouldn't want you to know that, I—"

"Now you've dragged our child into, I don't even know. Whatever this is."

I look down and see the disposable phone on the countertop in front of him. I back away from him instinctively.

"Why?" he continues. "What reason could you have for owning this—and hiding it? I can't come up with one reason in my mind when I see this. I sure as hell know it's not the nonsense you tried to sell Rachel."

"Yeah, you're right. I was just—taken off guard when she…" But I trail off; there's no hiding, I feel my face flush.

"So what's it for?" he asks, doing little to mask his accusatory tone. When I decided that there was no scenario in which Collin would look inside a tampon box for anything, I never dreamed of this. But Rachel's at that age, so I should have. I should have thought of it, but since it's never come up before, it just wasn't a scenario that ever crossed my mind.

"It's…it's not mine, actually. I know it looks really strange."

"Yeah, it really does." Collin takes a bottle of whiskey from the cabinet and pours the brown liquid into a glass, waiting for my lie, which comes quickly. It's getting easier and easier to spin these tales with only a moment's notice.

"Gillian and Robert, you know—they're on the rocks. She thinks he's cheating, so she hired a private investigator."

Yes, I think. This is a story he can't ask them about to double-check because it's too sensitive. I rest my hip on the stool next to the counter to try to signal that I'm relaxed, not nervous.

"Okay?" he says, impatiently. "So?"

"So, she uses this to communicate with the guy—the investigator—to be careful, ya know. She worries about not getting anything in the divorce if he can accuse her of something, I don't know, so when we met she asked me to keep it. She didn't feel safe keeping it at the house."

Collin turns and fills his glass with ice from the fridge door. The loud clanging makes me jump. He sits down, calmly. He takes his time, and I'm tormented by the long silence.

"So, why would you hide it, then? In a…"

"Oh, well, no, it's just…she gave it to me like that. We were at her place and she shoved the tampon box at me with the phone inside. I guess that's where she hid it, so I just thought I'd leave it there. Out of sight, out of mind."

"Right." He studies my eyes. I receive no indication from his if he believes me or not.

"And she asked me not to tell anyone, of course."

"Of course." He smiles, but it's just his lips that curl up at the ends, his eyes don't match the forced look, and I feel like I could vomit right here. I'm irritatingly aware of the time, and I can't be late to meet Lacy. Who knows what rage Joe might have in store if he's kept waiting by the likes of Lacy Dupre.

"I'm so sorry. I have to meet Lacy in ten minutes."

At least he has empathy for what she's going through and knows that I planned to go and bring Lacy dinner and help out while she heals. He can't be mad at that. If it were anything else, I'd stay. I'd make him feel sure, secure. But I have to go.

"Go, then," is all he says, and I kiss him even though he barely reciprocates.

"I won't be long. Promise." But he doesn't say anything. I turn and go.

As I back out of the driveway, I see him, still at the counter, sitting with his elbows resting on either side of his whiskey. I can't afford the time, but still I wait a couple moments, watching through the window to see if he's okay, if he's accepted what I've said, shaken it off, but he doesn't move. He just stares down into his glass.

28

I'm late. I screech into a parking spot at the gas station across from Joe's apartment building. Lacy is sitting in her car. She crushes out the end of her cigarette and jumps into my passenger's side.

"I'm sorry," I start, but she gets down to business.

"You got the pills?"

I hand them to her in the corner clipped from an envelope, taped at the top.

"I already crushed them up, so all you have to do is puncture the paper and pour it into his drink."

"You sure he can't taste it?"

"Yes, positive. And here." I hand her the pepper spray I've had in my purse for years. "Just in case." She looks down at it, and I can tell she's probably second-guessing this whole bizarre plan.

"Thanks," she says, nodding, sliding it into her bag.

"So, listen. Call as soon as he's out. FaceTime me so I can see the screen as you go through the computer and we can look together. We screenshot anything we can use." I drop her at the door to his building and tell her I will be just feet from the front door with the car running if she needs me.

As she walks to the door, I watch her enter a circle of fluorescent light and push some numbers on a metal box to ring up to him. She props open the front door with a rolled-up newspaper as I instructed, in case she needs me. She charts the stairs just inside the door, and when her feet hit the sixth stair, she's out of my sight line, and I mumble soft pleas to God for this to end well.

If we find anything useful, I don't know if I bring it to his sergeant, as an anonymous tip that one of their own is hiding a secret and needs to be investigated himself? Or do I hold on to it awhile?

Time seems to slow down as my adrenaline speeds up. It's nearly an hour before she calls, and there are a couple times I almost ruin it all by going up and knocking to make sure she's okay.

"Goddamn it. You scared me!" I shout, once her face pops up on my phone.

She shushes me immediately. I don't have time for the details on how it all unfolded, but I see Joe's body on a leather sofa behind her. His arm hangs limp, knuckles brushing the floor. His mouth hangs open like he's about to scream, but he's asleep with his head tilted back on a pillow, and an empty drink sits on a coaster on the coffee table in front of him. She turns the phone so I can see the laptop. She quickly punches in his birth date password, and she's in. Just like that.

First, she noses around a bit in the files on the desktop. Mostly work stuff. She clicks on something that displays dozens of bondage porn images.

"Oh my God," she yelps, looking away and clicking blindly to open to a different page.

"Just try Facebook." I repeat Valerie's full name and have her scroll through his messenger. It's evident, as she scrolls down his recent messages, that he's having multiple intimate conversations with a number of women. She doesn't seem fazed by this. She's used to it, I guess. It appears that he's having a sexual relationship with a dozen women.

When she opens the chat between Valerie and Joe, a long history of communication reveals itself. I tell Lacy to start at the very first date they spoke. It was over two years earlier. He thanks her for accepting his friend request and asks if she remembers him from the Special Olympics Young Athletes event in New Orleans the week before, and he sends her a few photos from the event he thought she'd like to have. There, she is pictured with her wheelchair-bound daughter who proudly holds a basketball in one hand and a medal, hanging from a yellow ribbon around her neck, in the other.

Valerie says that of course she remembers him, and thanks him for the photos and his volunteering with special needs kids.

"Jesus Christ," I mutter.

"What?" Lacy asks, she doesn't know what I have just put together. This is what he does. This is why he volunteers, so he can reel them in by playing the selfless humanitarian card.

Even Lacy says that's how he got her interested, the attention he paid to Ronny Lee.

"Nothing, just take photos of all this with your phone."

She does and as she continues reading down the thread of communication, I see it's eight months later before they make contact again. Her daughter passed away due to complications from her condition, and he just wanted to "reach out to give his condolences." It moved slowly, the bond between the two of them. It was weeks before he talked her into meeting him for a drink, and slowly, the relationship became sexual, as evident in the nude photos exchanged.

Lacy takes the screenshots. It's what I came for, though a sadness starts to well up somewhere deep inside me for Valerie, and even though she is going to great lengths to ruin my life, I feel an overwhelming sense of compassion for her. She was, ultimately, preyed upon herself.

Beyond the computer screen where Lacy has propped the phone for me to see, I have an obscured view of Joe's outstretched legs on the couch. As Lacy exits all the tabs she's opened and closes the laptop, I get a better look at him, and suddenly, he moves. He pulls his knees up and lies on his side, and then reaches his hand around near the coffee table as if feeling for something.

"Go! Get out of there. Now!"

Lacy fumbles, trying to grab her things and run out in a panic. Our call cuts out. I watch the stairs on the other side of the glass door in the entryway and wait to see her feet meeting that sixth stair and run out to me. Her footfalls don't appear.

It should only take seconds before I see her materialize from his second-floor apartment, but she's not there. I can't call the police. I have to go up there. The gun I kept in my purse to meet Valerie is safe back in its lockbox at home. I hadn't even thought about needing it. I should have. But we're not going to shoot a cop. I should have thought of that! Shit!

As I stand outside the building a moment, a tingling whispers through my body, a helpless hollowness keeps me frozen in place. Just before I kick the rolled-up paper out of the way and go in, she is running down the stairs, two at a time, and I turn to run behind her as she whizzes past and we leap into my car and drive away.

"What the hell! What happened?"

"I'm sorry!" she says, an almost-smile on her face, but I'm holding my heart with one hand as I grip the steering wheel with the other, dramatically, waiting for my pulse to slow and my hands to stop shaking.

"God. I thought you were dead!"

"I know, I'm sorry, but he was just turning over. From what you told me about that drug, he wouldn't even be close to waking up, so I still had to get to the date of the murder and see if they spoke around then."

"Did they? What did you see?" I ask in disbelief.

She turns her phone to show me the photo of the conversation. That morning at 10:43 a.m., she says, SEE YOU TONIGHT, with a kiss emoji. He writes back, IS THE PLAN STILL TO MEET BEFORE, AROUND SIX? All I can think about as I read this is how the police think the murder took place a couple hours before the anonymous call—my call—at around 9 p.m. that night. Why were they meeting before the charity event if they'd see each other there?

IF YOU'RE STILL SURE, she replies. IT WILL ONLY GIVE US AN HOUR OR SO, and he answers, THAT'S ENOUGH TIME. SEE YOU THEN.

I release the breath I've been holding and shake my head.

"Can you send me all of these?" I ask, and Lacy forwards all of the messages to me as I drive her back to her car. I promise to let her know what comes of it. There must be a way to get it in front of Joe's superior and frame it in a way that casts undeniable doubt on his character for not disclosing that he's in a romantic relationship with the victim's wife. I drive home, almost giddy, armed with this new power, but then when I pull into the drive, I see that Collin is still sitting in the kitchen, his head slumped low. He's moved to the table, and the whiskey bottle sits half-empty next to him.

I hesitate before I quietly open the garage door that leads into the kitchen and put my things down. He lifts his head from his hands, his bloodshot eyes, rinsed with tears, meet mine.

"So where did you really go tonight?"

29

I don't turn the light on. Only a slice of moonlight illuminates the kitchen, faintly.

"What do you mean?" I ask.

"It's like you've been lying for so long, you don't even know how to tell the truth anymore." He doesn't look at me when he speaks.

My resentment wrestles with my guilt as I feel the sting of this accusation. It doesn't matter that he's right, I still feel irrationally angry that he's saying this to me.

"I was with Lacy."

"So, you're not having another affair, then?" He says it flatly, as if we've already argued about the subject for days and he has no fight left.

"What? No! Collin, wha—"

"I want to save you from whatever ridiculous excuse you're about to make because it's just embarrassing for both of us."

At this, I sit. I slink slowly into the chair across the table from him.

"How did you know?" I whisper.

"I've known all along." There is a long silence, then he continues. "The night the kids FaceTimed you and you were late getting home. That's when I knew."

"How?" My voice breaks a little and my face reddens with shame.

"We thought we'd surprise you and come up to the bookstore when your group was ending." He pauses, closes his eyes a moment. "I saw you. In your car, in the parking lot. At first, I almost pulled up next to you so the kids could see if you wanted to come to dinner, see, we were running late and figured your group might be finishing. But something about the way you looked, so disoriented, told me not to stop, not to let them see." He looks at the ground while he speaks. What I wouldn't give if he'd have stopped that night. I would have made an excuse and maybe said the rest of the group had left early. Maybe it would have been the scare I needed—to be so close to being caught that I wouldn't have done anything wrong.

"Collin, I…"

But he continues, not wanting me to speak yet.

"The kids were glued to their phones, so I followed to see where you were going. I saw you walk into the woods. There's a path to that rented mansion. It really didn't take much to find out who lives in the place." He fills the empty glass in front of him. He doesn't offer it to me, but I pull it toward me. I hold it, looking down, shamefully, into it. He continues.

"I looked at your phone one night while you were sleeping." I exhale audibly when I hear this.

"You searched his name a hundred times. You kept his book poorly hidden. You acted like a completely different person, secretive and paranoid. Did you really not notice how strange you came off?" He spits the last part in a loud whisper because he can't yell—the kids are sleeping—then he stands, abruptly, and twists his body away from me. He leans both arms, elbows locked, against the edge of the counter and hangs his head between them. Saying that I'm sorry feels so far from being enough.

"Why didn't you say anything before now? You seemed happy, normal. You never acted different…I…"

"One of us had to! I thought it would stop. I gave you the benefit of the doubt because I ruined your life, or so it feels like half the time. You're the one who didn't get the career you wanted."

"That was my choice," I start to say, but he doesn't hear me, he's talking to his hands, shaking his head.

"I feel guilty for all you have to handle with Ben and my mom. What you gave up. I could see where maybe someone like him might be exciting, so I made it my job to love you through it. To trust you to do the right thing and not let it destroy us. But you didn't stop."

I walk over to him in the darkness and try to touch his shoulder, but he pulls away from me and moves to the other side of the kitchen island. We stare at one another across it.

"I'm so sorry. I'm…it was such a mistake, and there is nothing I can say to you to justify it. I know you must hate me."

"Well, maybe you should try."

"What?"

"Maybe the least you could do is try...to justify it. Explain why you would do this to me—to us."

Tears flood my eyes, and I know the last thing he wants is to have to comfort me, and the last thing I want is pity, but I can't control them.

"I was weak and so, so fucking stupid. I don't know why. I can't believe it was really me that did it, that allowed it to go so far, and I don't expect you to ever trust me again. Or forgive me, but I am more sorry than you'll ever know. And I love you, and it killed me that I knew I was hurting you even though that sounds so selfish and contradictory, I know, but I do love you." I sob uncontrollably.

He doesn't move from the other side of the kitchen island. He runs his hands through his hair and blows out the air from his lungs in an exasperated exhale.

"I paid him a visit, out there in his big rented mansion. That stupid son of a bitch, I went out there to talk to him."

"No," I whimper, not wanting to know the rest.

"He welcomed me in, knew who I was right away."

"Collin, no. Why didn't you confront me? Why did you go to him?"

But he just continues his story.

"He offered me a drink. He has a pretty good collection of scotch on display in the upstairs study, so we went up, civilized, and shared a scotch on the balcony. He told me he was sorry, but that he was in love with you, and he couldn't promise me to leave you alone if that's what I was there about. That if you wanted to stop, that would be up to you."

"When? Collin. What night did you go over there?" The panic is rising, and my breathing is quick and shallow.

"September 20," he says in a hushed voice, and then sits back at the table and looks at the wall.

"No. Please God. Noooo. That can't—that's not possible! You were here. I left his place. I went to cut things off, I swear to God I did, and came home and you were here, playing with Ben. He was crying, I remember. He hit you in the lip and he was saying he was sorry. I remember exactly. You can't—no."

"You assumed he was crying and saying he was sorry because he hit my lip by accident and was upset that he hurt me. I let you believe that. The cut was from Luke punching me. Ben was crying about something else. I don't even remember, he talked back or something and then got punished and whatever…I was there at Luke's before you. I went straight after work that day."

"I don't believe you. There's no way this is happening. I thought…"

"It was an accident. Whatever you're thinking right now, it was an accident. I had no weapon. I went over to talk to him. Let him know I knew and to stop seeing you."

Now his face streams with tears and an agonizing sob escapes his throat, and I'm doubled over in my chair with my head between my knees, bawling, trying to control my breathing, trying not to scream.

"Oh my God," I cry. I was so sure it was Joe and Val and

that we could finally get out from under this and move on with our lives. The call Val got at the motel could have been anyone, not Joe conspiring with her. The woman Lacy saw Joe with certainly could have been any woman in town. I was so certain of Joe's guilt, I'd strung all of these happenstances together in my mind and created a narrative. I was so sure. It seems impossible that Joe really was just doing his job and following real leads. He's just having an affair with Val like he is with everyone else in town. They were just meeting before a charity event, probably for dinner, quick sex. My head floats, dizzy and airy, and I'm nearly hyperventilating. Collin tells me the rest through tears and the details ground me again, force me to breathe in and out, controlled, slowly. The kids can't hear this. We need to be careful.

"After he said that he refused to leave you alone, he said you were actually thinking of going away with him to Italy, that you loved him and he was sorry, but I'd just have to deal with reality. I threw my scotch in his face." He stands, paces, then leans against the wall and looks at his feet.

"Jesus." I gaze at the ceiling and breathe in short spurts, in through my nose and out through an exaggerated O shape I make with my mouth. I know the scotch collection he's referring to, and next to it, the balcony overlooking the pool. It's impossible to imagine them out there together. They exist in two completely separate worlds in my mind.

"He punched me after I threw the drink and told me to get out. We fought. I swung back, and he lunged at me, so I pushed him." Collin stops a moment and wipes tears away.

"To protect myself. He was coming full force, so I just—I pushed him to get him off me, and he fell backward. He fell over the rail and…" Collin doesn't finish. I know the rest.

"The dark SUV fleeing the scene was my 4Runner. I'm sure of it." He slides down the wall and sits on the floor, cradling his head in his hands.

"No one saw it up close," I point out. I suddenly find my shock and rage turning into protectiveness. I've underestimated my husband this whole time, thinking he was naive, in the dark about it all. He was trying to let me handle it myself, and then, when I didn't, he was trying to protect our family.

"What?" he asks.

"It was an accident."

"Yes. Yes! It was, I swear," he says, almost pleadingly.

I screwed up, more than I'd even thought. I put us in this position—he'd never even have had a reason to be at Luke's house if it weren't for me—but he did something worse. Accident or not, self-defense or not, he covered it up and now there is no going back. We need each other. I sit next to him on the floor. I touch his knee, and he looks at me with a mix of tenderness and surprise as if he never thought I'd touch him again, his sin now worse than mine.

"We can get through this," I say, touching his face and leaning my forehead into his.

"It was an accident," he repeats, and the depth of his pain is too vast for me to come near, so I let him cry. We both cry. We stay on the floor for hours, in the dark, finishing the bottle and talking through every option, worst-case scenarios, how to keep the kids safe no matter what.

Then, just before dawn, we fall into bed, drunk and empty, to meet sleep for a few hours before waking up to our new, dismantled lives.

30

Honesty, from here on out, we both promise. But I don't have the heart to tell him about the ring until a little time has passed. Collin stays home from work on the next day, and we try to keep a regular routine for the kids. I plan to take Claire to the park and run some errands, and Collin needs to catch up on paperwork, but instead we go back to bed after the kids leave for school. Sunlight streams through the east-facing window and we hold each other. We don't talk.

I think about how much DNA Collin must have left. The authorities would have tested the glasses he and Luke were drinking from as well as Luke's body, and the DNA would be found. But, like me, Collin has never been arrested, that I know of, so there won't be a match when they run the unknown DNA through the system. Right now Collin isn't on their radar. I just need to make sure they don't ask any more questions about me. I still have the dirt on Valerie and Joe. It's still valuable.

I told Collin about the phone, the blackmail, the money

she's insisting on, and I told the truth about what Lacy and I were doing and what we found. He didn't ask how I got the money to pay her what I had already. I offered that I sold some old handbags and hadn't figured out how to get her more money yet. There was too much going on for him to press the subject. I'll tell him at some point, but not now.

"Text Valerie the screenshots," Collin said the other night, as we sat on the kitchen floor in the small hours of the morning. "Tell her you're not giving her any more fucking money and that not only is she guilty of blackmail, but she was sleeping with someone else while she was still married, that doesn't look good for her. *That*, coupled with that text about meeting Joe before the charity event puts a big hole in her alibi. Tell her to leave you the hell alone."

We were lying on the kitchen floor by then, hammered, my body draped over his, and so I texted her all of it, right there.

Now, hiding from the morning light, under the covers, my phone buzzes on the nightstand. I keep my head covered as I feel around with one hand and pull my phone in. She replied.

"What?" Collin asks, a pillow pressed over his head.

"Fuck."

Valerie has responded. No text, just the video that blooms open on my screen and shows me tiptoeing away from Luke's place. She's not going away without a fight. Collin peers over my shoulder and sees a snippet of the video before I click it off and sit up, outraged. I throw my phone into the downy comforter and suppress a scream. Collin lies on his back and stares at the ceiling. After a few minutes, I lie back next to him, not knowing what else to do, and we stare at the ceiling together, side by side in our own separate pain.

"There's that house in Panama," Collin says, breaking the silence after several minutes.

"What?" I ask.

"The one we vacationed in, said maybe we'd buy it, retire there one day."

"The kids." I roll over into the fetal position and face him. "Ben's school is doing wonders and Rachel is at the worst age to rip her out of the only school she's known."

"I know all of that, but they can adapt. This is survival."

"How would we do that?"

"We sell the house, we——"

"Claire can't make that trip."

He can't argue against that defense—her well-being. It's not that I wouldn't love to run away to an idyllic beach community and start over, but it's not the solution. At least not yet.

"She could if we absolutely had to. She——"

"And you don't know that you can get work there. We could be screwed," I add.

He rises from the bed, goes quietly into the bathroom and turns the shower on without another word.

We spend the next few days exchanging remorseful, miserable looks. Part of me hates him for what he's done, but I'm the one who put him in the situation. My part was not an accident; it was calculated and planned. His was a moment, a hot flare of anger, an understandable reaction to taunting by Luke, then a mutual fight that ended in a push that was too hard. I put it all in motion. The days pass in a slow fog. We sit close together on the couch in the evenings and let Ben choose the movies to watch while Rachel taps mindlessly on her iPad in the recliner. We share popcorn, and Collin squeezes my hand tightly. Every incoming text makes us jump. We fall hazily into a light tease of sleep at night but can't surrender to its pull. We move around each other on autopilot, but the haze of anxiety is palpable, and we've exhausted talking about the situation. Mostly, we just wait for a knock on the door to take one of us away.

After another week goes by, we start to let ourselves relax ever so slightly and think, just maybe, Joe and Davis had been satisfied with my story.

Then, one evening as cooler weather creeps in, just before dinner, I take a break from cooking and sit in the kitchen window seat, staring at a puckered ring of frost outside the window, drinking a glass of wine and waiting for the rice to cook. I see a police car making its way slowly down our road again. For a very brief moment I'm so lost in my own consuming thoughts that I forget, and I think nothing of it, the way I would before we were criminals, but it only takes a second for me to stand up anxiously and murmur a prayer that it's just an everyday patrol of the area. But then it pulls into our drive and Detectives Davis and Brooks exit their respective squad car doors and walk up to my door. Which one of us are they here for?

I walk to the front door before the kids hear the bell. I see Collin as he walks down the stairs and freezes before he reaches the bottom. We look at each other, fear in our eyes. I crack the door just a slit and peer out with one eye, looking as unwelcoming as I can manage.

"My kids are home. I don't want to scare them by having cops in the house. What's this about?"

"Evening, Melanie." Joe tips his hat. He's clearly going to waste my time with pleasantries. "You remember Detective Davis."

"What can I do for you?" I ask.

"Well, we'd like to ask you to come down to the station with us and answer a few questions."

"The station? I thought I answered your questions."

"We have some additional questions. You're not under arrest or anything like that, but your cooperation would help us out."

"Why not ask me here?"

"I thought you were worried about your kids getting spooked."

"Well, on the porch, then."

"Look, Mel, we need the interview recorded, official. You understand. You don't have to come down, but it would make this easier. I'm sure you could just clarify a few things and be on your way."

I don't know what else they would want to ask me, but I'm relieved that they didn't come for Collin. I look to him to see what he thinks we should do, if I should go. He nods, and I understand because not cooperating would look worse and make them dig more. I open the door wider and tell them I'll get my things.

"Evening, Mr. Hale," Davis says to Collin when the open door reveals him still rooted on the stairs. Collin nods and comes to stand next to me.

"What's this about?" he asks, pretending he didn't eavesdrop.

"We just have a few more questions for your wife about the Luke Ellison case. No need for alarm."

"Can I go with her?"

"It's okay," I say to him. "Please, just stay with the kids. Watch the rice. Dinner is in the oven. Just take it out when the buzzer goes off."

We both observe the other, forcing a calm demeanor. He kisses my cheek as I pull on my coat, and I hold a flat hand up to say goodbye.

The room they question me in isn't like the interrogation rooms on TV. There is no naked light bulb hanging above a shadowy metal table in a dark room. It's unpleasant enough though; it's cramped, with a rectangular fluorescent light recessed into the ceiling panels and plastic chairs, but I keep repeating to myself in my mind, *I don't have to be here. I can leave at any time.*

I breathe and think about Panama. It's starting to sound like a good idea.

When Joe comes in, he doesn't sit on his chair backward or pound his fists like in the TV shows either. He just sits across from me, crosses one leg over the other and pushes his notepad and pen away as if he doesn't need them. The look on his face says, *We're old friends here. No need for all that.*

"Let's just talk," he says.

"Okay."

"It's been reported to me, from a reliable source, that you were involved with Mr. Ellison. Romantically."

"What? What source?"

"I'm not at liberty to say. Anything you want to tell me about that?" he asks.

That bitch. She took my money and told him about me and Luke anyway. I don't believe it.

"No," I say firmly.

He looks me up and down even though he thinks he's being subtle. He even licks his lips a little.

"Now, Mel. If you had something going on the side, that's not a crime. It's best if you just tell me about it. You're a beautiful woman, I'm sure men pursue you. If that's what happened and there was an indiscretion of some sort, now's the time to come clean."

I'm pretty sure that if the interview weren't being recorded, he would have taken his dick out right then and there when he talked about men pursuing me.

"So, one person tells you they think I was involved with him, and you bring me down here? Anyone can say anything they want. Did you look into their motive for telling you that?"

"So, your statement remains that you were not involved, romantically, with Mr. Ellison."

I don't know whether to admit it or not. It disgusts me that he's probably getting off on the visual of it right now, but maybe saying that I was will be enough. Collin can be my alibi, saying I was home with him that night. Clearly, they have nothing on him. I think. But I just don't know, so I sit, silently.

"There's one other thing," he says, and moves to take something out of a bag near his feet. I sit up straighter, straining to see. I feel a mist of sweat break out on my chest. He drops my Saints ball cap on the table and looks to me for my reaction. I look at it blankly, so he flips it over, showing the word *HALE* written in Sharpie.

"This was found in Luke's truck. It wasn't until later the writing on the inside of the rim was noticed. Is this yours?"

"I left it in his truck that day I told you about—when I grabbed a book out of the back and got his info. I remembered later that I set it down on the seat. So what?"

"What if I told you that I had video evidence of you leaving Luke Ellison's residence late at night?"

That absolute bitch. She handed it all over. All of it.

"What if I did have an affair with him?" I ask, I cannot believe this monster has the power to interrogate me about an affair while he has dozens himself.

"Like I said, that's not a crime. But you need to be honest. The evidence is there. Unless you'd like to offer another reason you were running from his house, carrying your shoes, with your dress unzipped."

I hate him in this moment more than I can describe. The way his lips curl when he talks about it—in this wry, amused way. Suddenly, I know what I need to do. I stand up.

"I'd like to leave now," I say, and he counters my movement to the door, standing so close I can feel the heat from his chest.

"That's your decision, but we'll probably have to bring you back in. I hope it's not with a warrant next time. You sure you don't want to talk?"

I shove past him and walk down the corridor that leads

to the parking lot. Once outside, I lean against the door and suck in the fresh air. I could barely handle an hour in that claustrophobic nightmare. I can't go back there. I can't let Collin become even a blip on their radar. I have to preserve my children's innocence in all of this mess.

He has video evidence, does he? I can play that game too. I'll show him what video evidence should look like. I know what I have to do.

31

I don't tell Collin about the ball cap. It's one of those details that will edge into his thoughts and place me even more vividly in Luke's arms, and the fact is, they know about the affair, so I leave it alone. The video and ball cap are just logs on a fire already burning too hot inside of him. His eyes are swollen from grief and the unconvincing smile he wears around the kids is transparent even to them; his words don't match the look in his eyes when he assures them everything is fine.

"I didn't admit to anything," I tell him. "But they know."

I wonder what will come next. If they bring me in on a warrant, they can check my computer and phone. Can they fingerprint me? I'm sure they can, and then it will be all over. It will lead to Collin, surely. The jealous husband theory will not be magically overlooked. Using the messages between Joe and Valerie isn't enough in the situation I find myself. When I truly thought he was involved, it was a revelation. Now it will look like a desperate attempt at revenge. I need more.

Next Saturday night, Ben and Rachel will be staying the

weekend at my mother's house in Baton Rouge, and Collin will be at his friend Kenny's house for poker night. At least that's the plan, but Collin seems to be falling into a depression, so I'm not surprised when he tells me he doesn't feel up to going. But he has to.

When Saturday rolls around, my plans are all laid out. I could tell him another lie, say I'm going to meet friends. I don't know why I can't bring myself to tell such a small lie, which is nothing compared to what I'm about to do. Somehow simply not telling him my plan feels less of a betrayal than another outright lie.

He's more deflated than I've seen him since the kids left for their grandparents' last night. Like they were the only thing bolstering him up enough to function these last weeks. At 10:23 a.m., he's still in bed. I bring him a cup of coffee and scooch over to sit next to him.

"You should go tonight." I stroke his hair.

He sits up and takes the coffee.

"I don't know."

"You go every month. If you start retreating from usual things, it won't look good in the long run. We need to keep up appearances."

He holds his coffee in both hands and stares ahead. His sigh indicates he agrees with me, but he doesn't say anything.

At 8 p.m., he lingers on the couch, slipping on his Converse sneakers slowly. He pulls a sweater over his T-shirt and rubs his eyes. He sits with his elbows resting on his knees, still contemplating whether he really has the mental energy to move. I know he'd rather be in bed. We both want to sleep until Sunday night when the kids get back and then take them and disappear, but we can't.

He hugs me like a soldier going off to war before he clicks open the garage door and pulls down the drive. I spring into action once his taillights disappear down the lane. I go into the bedroom and pull out the black mini-skirt I haven't worn since I dressed up as Madonna for a costume party years ago. Then I squeeze myself into a skintight red tank top. I smooth my hair with a flat iron until it hangs, sleek and glossy, down the middle of my back. I apply an excess of lipstick and false lashes I'd almost forgotten how to put on. I finish the look with alligator-skin stilettos and head to the first of the two places Lacy assures me Joe Brooks will be on any given Saturday if he's not working.

I confirmed his schedule already, with Lacy's help, and now it's either Bourbon and Spits or the strip club. I hope to God it's the first because explaining my presence at the strip club again will be more difficult. I'll drive to every bar in town and his house if I need to, but this is his spot, normally, and she says if he does go to the club, it's usually late, after he's already gotten drunk at Spits, so I drive out to the bar, ready.

I hadn't been back since that first night I met Lacy by witnessing her sexual assault in the parking lot. I suck in a deep breath and park. Inside, country music blares and the place is bursting at the seams. I belly up to the bar and sit on a gummy bar stool with duct tape holding the torn, faux-leather seat together. I order a chardonnay that I plan to nurse slowly so I can play drunk but keep my wits about me. I scan the bar to find him perched on a stool near the pool tables, holding a bottle of Coors between his knees as he uses his arms to tell some animated story to a few drunk buddies standing around him. He's here. My stomach turns over; I watch.

One guy nudges him and pushes a pool cue his way for his turn to shoot. His unsteady gait as he moves to the pool table exposes his level of intoxication, which is exactly what I was hoping to see. I don't act right away. I observe him in his group of friends. One guy, whom I vaguely remember from school and who wears a T-shirt that says Dad Bod, brings another tin bucket of beers to the high-top table they hover around. They jab at each other like high school boys. Dad Bod puts another guy in a playful headlock and rubs a knuckle on his scalp when he misses a shot. They laugh too loudly and have wide stances and folded arms most of the time, asserting their dominance, taking up space.

A couple of them leave an hour later; the dads of the group, I assume. I'm still watching between staving off fumbling, stammering cowboys who elbow their way to the bar for a drink and stay to make passes at me through slurs and spit. When the two remaining friends strike up a conversation with two college-aged girls at an adjacent table, Joe finally comes up to the bar. He's graduated from beer to hard liquor, and turns to his left only after he feels my stare. He doesn't try to hide the shock on his face. Maybe because he's never seen me dressed like this, or in a bar like this, but probably because I'm a married woman not wearing a ring who he's currently trying to prove had an affair.

"Mel." He stands up straight and tries to appear sober.

"Hey, Joe."

He can't help himself. He looks directly at the triangle of space a short skirt leaves between crossed legs, hoping to see more.

"What are you doing here?" he asks, and I shrug.

"Needed some time away, I guess."

"Well, let me buy you a drink, shit." His words are slow and labored. The last thing he needs is another drink.

"Thanks."

And just like that, we move to a small table across the room since there is no extra stool next to me at the crowded bar.

"You look really good. I'm surprised to see you here."

"Moms need some fun every now and then too, ya know. Off the record, right?"

He laughs and moves his chair in. I see him notice the pale circle on my finger where a wedding ring should be.

"I don't judge you, ya know. I mean…"

"Surprised you want to talk to someone you're suspecting."

"Listen, Mel. I'm just doing my job, but I don't think you did anything wrong. Sex ain't a crime."

"Exactly."

"Exactly," he repeats, and leans back with a laugh, one elbow around the back of his chair, taking me in.

"I do a lot at home. I can go out sometimes. No one owns me."

"I like that. God, Mel. You seem so different."

"Clearly there's a side of me you never knew."

"Clearly." He tips back his drink and holds up two fingers, gesturing for another round.

"That's too bad," I say, looking wide-eyed and flirtatious. He leans back, running his hands through his hair, nervously.

"Wow." He sort of pauses and looks at me a moment, and I don't know if I'm pushing this too fast. Then he shakes his head, and holds his drink up to cheers and gives me a wink. "This is unexpected."

We spend the next hour talking about nothing of importance. Like two people on a first date, we flirt and make small talk, and then he lets his hand rest on mine, and looks in my eyes, and he wants it so bad, he's waited for years. But he is really good at this game, so he'll keep the charm coming until I'm ready. I have to be home by midnight, so I move this part along as quickly as I can.

"Listen, Collin and I are staying together for our family, okay, and the only reason I can't let what happened with Luke get out is because it would be all over the news and ruin my kids' lives. We have an arrangement."

"What arrangement? What do you mean?"

"We can see other people, but we'll stay married for now. So, yes, Luke and I had a relationship and I don't regret that. It was good."

"I bet it was," he says, lustfully. "And, I mean, I told you, I never thought you did anything, but I had to cross you off the list and with this affair stuff hanging out there…"

"I know. So I'm telling you now. Sorry I had to lie about it, but you get why. I have a family to protect."

He's too drunk to really process it right now, or maybe he doesn't care all that much about his job at the moment, when potential sex is dangling in front of him, and just thinks that me having one affair means I'll easily have another. With him.

"Anyway, I better get going. Thanks for the drink. And the talk," I say, as sweetly as I can muster. He scrambles to his feet as I stand, trying desperately to hold on to his shot.

"You're going? It's still early."

"Yeah, I should get home. This place is so loud."

"Well, let's get out of here. Take a drive with me. We can get a drink somewhere quieter." He's hammered, trying to fish clumsily in his pocket for his keys.

"Only if I drive," I say, and he doesn't have to think about it. I drive down the same rural road I took when I drove Lacy home that night. Moonlight flashes, dull and pale, through tree branches in the woods that stretch for miles along the road.

"We could stop at the Roadhouse Inn," he says, trying to make it seem like he's just interested in that drink in a quieter place, but of course, I know that it's a motel with a dumpy karaoke bar attached. Technically quieter I guess, since nobody really goes there for the bar.

"Sure," I say, making a right turn to head toward the Roadhouse Inn. We pull up to the one-story strip of building with a pale pink exterior and an empty, calcified swimming pool in front. The sign for Zippy's Liquor store blinks neon red across the street, and the remoteness of the place is making me uneasy, but I came here for a purpose and I need to stay on course. If I make it too easy for him, will that be suspect? Should I play harder to get?

"If you want to have a quiet conversation, I could grab a bottle of wine across the street and we could relax in a room. I mean, if you want," he says, still refraining from touching me, but leaning in seductively. I'm happy he suggested it. It may be a bit unrealistic coming from me.

"I don't know," I say, feigning shyness. "There's a bar, you know."

"Well, I mean that's fine. I just know karaoke gets loud. And you said yourself you just need some fun sometimes. Not that I assume you… I mean, we'd just be hanging out as friends, of course."

"Well, as long as it's just as friends, I guess so."

He tries to play it cool as he walks into the glass encasement where the check-in desk sits. I wait in the car and see him get impatient when nobody is minding the place. He rings a little bell and leans over the desk, stretching to see if there is anyone in the back. A small, tired-looking man trudges to assist him. When he gets the key, he gives it to me and says he'll run across the street for that bottle.

Inside the room, I feel hot tears spring to my eyes. I wipe them away. I tell myself to focus, that this is the only way. I needed a few minutes alone before he came back, so I get myself ready. This is it. I have to follow through.

He forgot a bottle of wine needs a corkscrew, so he shows me his old college trick and pushes the cork down into the bottle with his car key. He pours two glasses into plastic motel cups and the wine bobs around the cork, leaking everywhere as he tries to fill the cups. When he finally succeeds, we toast to "old friends."

"Just goes to show, you never really know people," he says, sitting himself on the king bed. I sit in the desk chair near him.

"What do you mean?"

"Well, I mean, you. You and Luke."

I look at the floor, and he quickly realizes that he brought up something painful. He's so focused on the sex, he's not thinking that I lost someone I actually cared for. He changes gears.

"Well, the arrangement you have with your husband, the fact that you're here. It's just...I would never expect that. From you."

"Well, there's a lot you don't know about me."

"So, tell me." He holds his hand out for mine, so I sit next to him on the bed. I take it, and we sit so close our shoulders squeeze together.

"You want me to tell you my life since, what, when's the last time we really talked, high school?" I laugh, playing into his hands.

"I would listen to the whole story. You look exactly the same, by the way."

"Yeah, right." I give him a dismissive gesture with my hand and take a sip of wine.

"Really, I wouldn't say that if it weren't one hundred percent true. You're really..." He brushes his hand against my cheek. He is a gifted charmer. "Just so beautiful."

Then he kisses me. I'm glad to get this started without too much more painful effort. I kiss him back. His five o'clock shadow burns my cheeks as we kiss harder. He pulls at my tank, but it's impossibly tight, so I help him get it over my head. He tosses it across the floor and pushes me down on the bed. I start to unbutton his shirt, but he pulls it off over his head instead. He kisses down my body and I shimmy out of my skirt. He kneels over me, my body straddled between his legs while he unbuckles his belt and smiles down at me, biting his lip, stopping to slip his hand into my panties a couple of times while he gets himself out of his pants and slides on a condom.

He moans and pushes his way into me, and I can tell he won't last long by the pace he's going.

"I want it hard," I whisper. He doesn't stop but slows a minute and looks at my face.

"Hard?"

"Yeah. Rough. Can you do that?"

"I can do whatever you like," he says, biting my neck softly.

"Rough," I repeat. "Make me tell you to stop."

"Yeah? You want it rough?" he says, trying a little too hard for it to sound sexy.

"More. Punish me." He starts to get into it now, holding my hand, restrained in his grip while he goes at me hard. Then he slaps my face.

"Yes! Do that until I beg you to stop. Then choke me."

"Jesus, Mel. You really do like it kinky."

"Do it," I demand, and it's turning him on. He obeys. He slaps me in the face, then a bit harder.

"No!" I scream, and he's getting off on it. He slaps me again and I holler "no" and "stop." Then he puts his hands around my neck and presses. He holds them there, and I grow light-headed, but he comes and falls to the side before it goes too far. He pants, slapping one limp arm over my waist.

"Jesus, Mel. That was…" He rolls off the condom and ties it in a knot, flicking it into the garbage near the bed. "Hoo-eee."

He pats me, approvingly, then jumps up and goes into

the restroom to pee. I gather my phone and my purse. And I collect my clothes from the floor. When he comes out, naked still, I'm trying to pull my top on by stepping into it and pulling it up around my hips.

"You're getting dressed," he says more as a fact than a question.

"Yeah, I stayed out way later than I should have. I'll take you back," I say, and he walks up to me and holds my breast, kissing me again.

"That's a shame. We could do that a few more times."

"Well, I have some time on Monday. We could meet here." He looks astonished at this suggestion.

"Yeah, shit. I mean I'm on duty Monday, but only till about ten."

"Do you have a lunch break?"

"I do now." He smiles. And with that, he dresses and we drive back to his car. I couldn't give a shit how he gets home from here. As soon as he shuts my car door in the Spits parking lot, I rush back to the motel room. When I arrive, Leonard Cohen sings "Hallelujah" from the speakers in the bar, and it pipes out into the parking lot. I creep back into the room carefully, as if someone might be there, ready to catch me midcrime.

I throw away the cup his lips have touched, and I pick up the soiled condom with a tissue like I'm collecting the remains of a smashed insect. I take out the small, plastic medicine syringe we used for Ben's cough syrup when he had the flu. I suck up the contents of the condom into it and lie on the bed to inject it between my legs. I look at the footage I captured from the video I took on my phone. His run to the liquor store gave me more time than I thought I'd have to hide the camera perfectly out of sight and record. It's all there. All of the slapping and asphyxiation are there, and when I get home, I can edit out the rest, so the only clip I have shows him assaulting me.

Then comes the hard part. I have been taking Claire's prescription Xarelto out of her medicine cabinet for the last few days because it causes easy bruising and will help a lot with this next part. The blue circles around my neck are already starting to surface and look eerily like the ones he gave Lacy. I feel bruised between my legs from the power of his thrusting, so now it's just my face left. Just one blow. Every other bit of evidence is there. I empty the wine bottle and look at myself in the mirror. Tears are already falling, but I have to finish.

I look at myself in the eyes—eyes that look so different than they did six months ago, because now I am a completely different person that I no longer recognize. I take in a deep breath and aim for my cheekbone, just under my eye. I strike it so hard that blood gushes from the cut the glass makes on the side of my eye, and my cheekbone swells and turns purple almost immediately. I let myself weep and scream for all the pain I've caused and the wrong I've done. I sob for what I have just done to Collin, but it's the only way to save him.

Then I walk back to my car as Leonard Cohen turns to Tom Waits puffing out a sad melody into the night air, and I drive myself to the emergency room to report a rape.

32

They take swabs and samples in the ER and bring in a domestic abuse counselor for me to talk to. They take photos of my injuries. I've already taken extensive photos of my own on my phone, and they ask if I want to press charges, and if I will talk about who did this to me. I say I can't say who did it, that he'll come after me, and I'm too scared. Lying to kind, genuine people somehow feels like the worst part of this so far, but I don't need to say his name. Yet. His semen and DNA is safely tucked away from the samples they took, and a police report has been made, noting that the victim is too fearful at this time to offer a name.

Honesty, we said. From here on out. But it's far too late for honesty. Sometimes, the truth will not set you free, but do quite the opposite. I'm the only one who can save us now, and I'll do so by any means necessary. I think of sweet Ben as I drive home, his five-gallon bucket filled with crayons from many Christmases' worth of stockpiling, his kickball game with the neighbor kids at the end of the cul-de-sac on summer nights, the easy way he shows affection and his chapped-lip smile. I think of Rachel's first school dance coming up, of French braiding her hair on the back deck as we drink sweet tea and talk about the boys at school and her future as a veterinarian. We are their whole world. What would happen to them if one of us went away forever?

With that, I drop my fake cubic zirconia ring into a dumpster behind a Denny's. In my car, I push out of my skirt and awkwardly pull on jeans in the driver's seat so my outfit doesn't raise any red flags, and I drive home to explain to Collin what happened.

"Jesus Christ!" He drops his keys and rushes to me when he comes home not long after I get there.

"It's okay, I just. I was attacked, but it's…"

"You didn't call me? What the…Christ, what the hell happened?"

"I'm sorry, I was with the police. I just. I agreed to pick Lacy up at that strip club she works at, she called me, desperate 'cause her kid was gonna be left home alone if she didn't get back before the sitter had to go," I explain. "I was waiting in the parking lot for her to come out, and you know how that area of town is, some guy came up."

"Oh my God, you were robbed?" he asks, his eyes wide, his face still, waiting for more detail. I rub the spot where my ring should be and he looks down and takes my hands. "Oh God, you were…"

"It's okay, really. He only got my ring. I left so quick to pick her up, my purse was still at home on the counter. I thought I'd be back in a half hour, ya know?"

"You made a report."

"Yeah. It's okay, he clocked me, but I'm okay. Really." But tears come, and he holds me to his chest. I let myself break down, and I sob apologies into his shoulder, so sorry for everything I've done, and when he asks what I mean, why I'm sorry, I tell him it's because I can't believe I let them take the ring. He brushes his hands through my hair and holds me tighter. I can feel him shaking his head in disagreement.

"It's not your fault. I'm so sorry this happened to you. My God." He guides me to the sofa, where we sit, the top of my head under his chin, and he rocks me. We don't say anything for a long time, then I pull away.

"It's been a really tough night, I just—I just want to take a bath and lie down."

"I'm here if you need to talk about it. Is there anything I can do? Did they get the bastard?"

"I don't know who he was. I already told the police everything, and I just need to…"

"Okay, yes. Of course. Let me run you a bath. They checked you out though, you're okay?"

"I'm okay," I lie, because I'm not okay. I don't know if I'll ever be okay again.

On Monday, Collin says he'll work from home and we can order takeout and be lazy together, in an attempt to try and take care of me and my battered body, but I insist I'm fine. I tell him that being made to feel like a sick patient just makes things worse, and that I'd like to go about my regular plans. Ben's tree costume from the school play needs to be done by the weekend, and I want to create as much normalcy as possible.

He sweetly kisses my head and tells me he can be home in ten minutes if I need anything at all. When he leaves, I get ready for my one-thirty lunch date with Joe Brooks at the Roadhouse motel.

I arrive early so I can pay for the room and get myself ready before he arrives. I keep the door open a crack, so when he parks, he can't miss my car parked in front of the same room with the door ajar. A soft tap on the door makes me jump even though I'm expecting him.

"Hey." He smiles, still dressed in uniform, eyes sparkling even in the pale winter light. I'm suddenly very aware that he has a gun in a holster, and of course I don't think he'd just up and shoot me for what I'm about to do, but a hot glint of panic still burns in my chest at the thought that he could. He could call it a suicide or something. I think of a last-minute layer to add to my plan, and feel my breath calm a bit. He shuts the door behind him and is already slipping his police belt off his hips.

"Holy shit. What happened to your face?" he asks, tossing the belt on the bed and coming in for a closer look.

"You like to beat up women. It shouldn't be so shocking to you."

"What?" He's still smiling, maybe unsure about whether I'm role-playing and maybe he should play along.

"Sit down."

"What is all this?" he asks, sitting at the tacky, peeling table across from me. He looks at the photos I have spread out on it and doesn't understand.

"A police report." I point to one of the printouts he's looking at.

"For what? What are you talking about?"

"For sexually assaulting me," I say as calmly as I can, so he knows I'm in control now, but my heart beats so fast, I can see my blouse vibrating.

"Is this like foreplay thing, or…"

"No. You like to beat up women and you like to have sex with them even when they beg you not to."

"You fucking told me to make it rough. Are you fucking with me?" He stands, his face hot and red.

"I would sit if I were you." I manage a calm tone.

"Or what?" he screams, dots of spit reaching all the way across the table, a rage I have seen in him before. In the parking lot that night.

"The rape kit they took from me the other night is stored in a crime lab for fifteen years, and your semen is just waiting to have your name attached to it."

"What the actual fuck are you talking about?"

"I didn't say who did this to me. I thought maybe you and I could make an arrangement so I don't have to." I watch him work out in his head that he used a condom and they don't have a name, and for sure he never hit me in the face. There is a moment, just a second, where relief forms around his bulging eyes. The next thing he says is quiet, pointed.

"You're a crazy, fucking bitch."

"Yep."

"Semen? I used—"

I stop him abruptly and tell him about using a syringe so it would be found inside me. His jaw drops so dramatically it's almost cartoonish. He slinks into the chair again, frozen with utter shock and outrage.

"What?" he says, almost in a whisper. "I didn't do anything to you. Why would you do this? That's not proof, by the way, psycho. We had sex, that's all that proves."

I click on my carefully edited video and show him on my phone. It recorded fifty-four minutes of us from when he arrived with the wine to when we left, but I edited it down to a perfect forty-one seconds of him hitting my face and strangling me while I beg him to stop. The rest of the video doesn't exist anymore.

"They'll know you edited that," he argues.

"Nope. There are safe apps that automatically start recording when you press a panic button. They come with key fobs, so I could have pressed it at any time to start the video. See where it starts, right when I move my hand from the nightstand to my face. It looks like I may have reached over right when the recording started." It doesn't matter that I didn't do it this way. Just that it's possible is good enough. The other pieces of evidence don't really need explaining after that. He sees the photos of all my injuries, snapshots I took of my hospital band and the documents I signed in the hospital, the police report.

"Why would you…I didn't do shit to you."

"But you did to Lacy."

"Lacy—wha? What?"

"By the way, I gave her a copy of all this, so if you're thinking of doing anything crazy, you'll be even more fucked," I snap, using the insurance policy I quickly thought about when he walked in.

He looks so defeated and pathetic, I almost feel sorry for him. The way he shakes his head in slow disbelief and lowers his tone as he says, "Why would I do anything to you? Oh my God."

"It's all here. Every detail has been covered."

"What do you want? Why? Because of Lacy? You act like I'm some abuser, some maniac. She hits me all the time, does she tell you that? She provokes a fight, I'm not out there looking for trouble. Jesus, Melanie. Fuck!"

But I don't feel for him. He's a bigger liar than I am. He doesn't know that I not only saw it with my own eyes, I was also the one holding her hand in that hospital after he left her for dead, thinking his coveted position in the community could keep him safe.

"So that's what you want? You want me out of Lacy's life? You don't think there were easier ways to go about that? Fine. That's fine, I was already done with that cow anyway."

"That's part of it, but that's not why we're here."

"Then fuckin' tell me why we're here!" He stands and walks to the opposite wall, punching his fist through the cheap drywall.

"There's one more thing," I say, and push the printouts of all his communication with Valerie toward him on the table. His eyes scan it, trying to make sense of these messages and why they're in my possession.

"How did you get this? What the hell is going on?"

"I want you to clear me and my family from your Luke Ellison investigation."

"You—" He starts to say something, but I stop him.

"Talking to the murdered man's wife before his death doesn't look good for you. That, along with all of this—" I swipe my hand across the papers. "You made plans to meet on the night of the murder just before they say it happened."

"You think I…? You…" He stares at the messages with parted lips, then he sighs deeply.

"All this so your affair with Luke isn't outed?" he asks, of course not having any idea that if they keep digging, they'll find a lot more than an affair.

"Yes." I start to snatch up all my evidence and stuff it into my bag, keeping it away from him.

"You said you and Collin had an arrangement. Why would you do all this to—"

"I lied. I said that so you wouldn't question me sleeping with you or be suspicious of it. It worked. Finding out about an affair would kill him, and it would destroy my kids' lives, and you just can't let it go."

"That's what the other night was about? Are you kidding me?"

"Listen. You need to clear us from the investigation. Rule it a suicide. They said foul play was suspected. Not confirmed. You're the lead investigator. There was alcohol in his system, and he fell straight down, not as if he were pushed, and there is no weapon. I saw that all on the news already. So *you* can clear me and my family from any association with him, and in a week or two, you can close the case and rule suicide, can't you?"

"For fuck's sake. I don't think you killed anyone. You are taking this way too far."

"It's not about that," I lie. "My life will be over if Collin finds out about Luke, and if you don't shut it down and take my name out of it, and make sure your little partner Davis is on board, it won't be my affair that makes headlines. You'll be the one on the front pages of all the newspapers, unemployed and a registered sex offender. Fucking try me."

He doesn't move for a few minutes. The room is soundless except for our ragged breathing. I stare at his back and he goes to the bed and puts on his belt. I don't know what he's going to do next. I hold up the video on my phone again, the sound of his slap and grunting playing to his back.

"Or, I could just upload this to Instagram right now and let the chips fall as they may."

"I can't believe you're this fucking crazy. I didn't do SHIT TO YOU!" He smashes in the TV mounted to the wall with his hands and rips it violently until it hits the floor with a crash. He comes up within inches of my face, nostrils flaring. He pushes me, hard, against the wall. I can't cower. I don't know what he'll do, but I look directly in his eyes.

"There's nothing you can do. I'll keep your name off of it, if you do the same for me. Send me the report once it's done, proving I'm cleared, then that the investigation is dropped. No foul play."

"If you leak all of this after I do that, you're dead. That's a promise."

"I won't. Why would I rock the boat? I want this over."

He pushes off the wall, away from me, and grabs his keys off the table. Just before he opens the motel door to leave he screams, "You're a fucking sociopath!" Then he pulls the door open so hard it cracks the drywall when it hits the inside wall with a violent impact.

"All of this really happened. You really did all of this. It's just that you did it to someone else. So I'd say you're getting off pretty lucky. Oh, and if you go after Lacy, the deal's off. I'll ruin your life."

He slams the door behind him, and I lock it before collapsing on the floor in front of it, trembling violently. It's done.

33

As someone who has always thought my life as a suburban wife would never amount to anything anyone would want to read about, now I have a story, and it's a story that I can never tell anyone. Even if the writing group does start back up when Jonathan is back on his feet, I have a story I can never write down.

A week after my meeting with Joe, he sent me a copy of the report that says Luke Ellison's death has been ruled a suicide. I didn't tell Collin once I got the report. He can't wonder how I knew before it was public, so I wait, and a few days later, the tight-faced local reporter announces the news on channel five.

I'm still going to have to see Joe Brooks around town, and the thought makes me feel nauseous. But he can't tell my secret without implicating himself, especially now that he's rigged the investigation. So we're in an uneasy, unspoken truce.

I watch Collin absorb the life-altering declaration from a casual disclosure on TV. I am chopping cucumbers for a salad and sneaking crumbles of cheese down to Ralph on the floor below me when I see him get the news. His hand flutters to his mouth and every muscle in his back releases.

"Dad, what's wrong?" Ben stops his coloring to ask from his seated place on the floor near the coffee table. Claire makes a sound from her wheelchair, and Collin sees her reaching for her cup of water and kneels to help her.

"Nothin', bud." Collin turns to look at me with a well of tears filling his eyes.

I close my eyes and sigh, a gesture of solidarity, all we can manage in front of the kids. My phone vibrates across the kitchen island, and I wipe my hands on a tea towel and push Decline, seeing that it's my mother, whom I have no interest in talking to in this moment, but something familiar flashes in Collin's eyes as he sees me dismiss a call and slide my phone in my apron pocket. Suspicion?

But he only smiles at me, and I cock my head and smile back but with a question in my look, as if to ask, *What is it?* He just turns back to the television.

We look at each other over steak and peas at dinner, exchanging glances mixed with hope, tenderness and something else. Some foreign expression—a mutual knowledge that we are forever trapped under the weight of the secrets we keep, along with a fear that some faraway day, some cold case investigator might reopen the case. It may never entirely go away. We can't be certain.

Collin mentions a vacation to Panama to the kids without asking me first, but I know it's a chance to ask around about work and look at bungalows. "Just a week on the beach. I think we've earned it," he says, as they cheer in delight. Then I suggest an outing for ice cream and we all pile into the car.

We don't look at one another as we make our way to the Dairy Queen a few miles away, the kids chattering, happy, blissfully unaware of how deeply we have fractured their lives. We quietly drive into the slim stripe of purple horizon, which bleeds like ribbons of wet paint into the crimson clouds, burning low behind the setting sun.

ACKNOWLEDGEMENTS

Thank you so much to my parents, Dianna Nova and Julie Loehrer, who are always unconditionally supportive. A special thanks to my incredible husband, Mark Glass, who has had nothing but faith in me throughout my writing journey and always has a kind and encouraging word whenever I second-guess myself.

Thank you so much to my sister, Tamarind Knutson, and brother-in-law, Mark Knutson, for their support and to all my dear friends back home in Minneapolis. Even though we have been long-distance friends for years, their excitement and support for my first book was humbling and definitely noticed.

A special thanks to those who went out of their way to support me, Theresa Ford, Shelly Domke and Justin Kirkeberg.

Thank you so very much to my absolute dream agent, Sharon Bowers, who has always guided me in the right direction while helping me learn the ropes. Thank you to my magnificent editor, Brittany Lavery, who always takes the time for me and makes my work the best it can be.

I'm so grateful to Anne Healy and Kim LaFontaine, who have been friends and mentors to me and have allowed me to work remotely in order to pursue my publishing career. Thank you to all my colleagues at the University of Texas at Arlington, as well.

I can't leave out my Boston terrier, Spaghetti, as he surely makes the long days working alone from my home office... eventful.

Seraphina Nova Glass is a professor and Playwright-in-Residence at the University of Texas, Arlington, where she teaches Film Studies and Playwriting. She holds an MFA in playwriting from Smith College, and has optioned multiple screenplays to Hallmark and Lifetime.

@SeraphinaNova

For more fantastic fiction, author events,
exclusive excerpts, competitions, limited editions and more

VISIT OUR WEBSITE
titanbooks.com

LIKE US ON FACEBOOK
facebook.com/titanbooks

FOLLOW US ON TWITTER AND INSTAGRAM
@TitanBooks

EMAIL US
readerfeedback@titanemail.com